The Legend of Kwi Coast

~

A Tale from Beneath the Waves

by

Nicholas Checker

The Legend of Kwi Coast

Cover Art by *Jennifer Greeff*

The Wild Rose Press, Inc.
PO Box 708
Adams Basin, NY 14410-0708
Visit us at www.thewildrosepress.com

Publishing History
First Edition, 2022
Trade Paperback ISBN 978-1-5092-4342-6
Digital ISBN 978-1-5092-4343-3

Published in the United States of America

Piper continued echoing out signals for signs of similar life, when suddenly she received the "broadcast" of another creature. It was *immense*—lengthier even than the Basker! A great feeling of disquiet seeped through her as she sent out another band of echo-waves in the direction of the monster. The echoes that bounded off the distant giant and reflected back etched out an image that chilled her spine nearly into ice. She had homed in on the unmistakable, lateral tail-beat which characterized all Snag-Tooth; for there was the familiar outline of the high dorsal fin, the ridged points covering its skin like chipped stones, and the curved mouth filled with rows of glistening teeth.

Piper trembled. In her confused state she felt the creep of panic bidding for control. *The beast was after her.* It was quietly tracing her through the nocturnal sea. This was what her frantic calls for companionship had drawn—a Giant of the Deep that would have made even the Commodore tremble.

Praise for Nicholas Checker

"This was a marvelous story! Every bit of it was a pleasing and satisfying experience I won't soon forget. …Fantastic novel! I truly enjoyed this book!"

> ~*Colleen Donnelly, author at The Wild Rose Press*

~*~

Test readers for *THE LEGEND OF KWI COAST* included those with a marine science background who loved and praised the adventure and the accuracy of the science involved. Test readers also caught and embraced the story's vivid allegorical aspects.

~*~

"*THE SAGA OF MARATHON* is a beautifully written piece of historical fiction. Nicholas Checker's characters are rich, dynamic and wrought with complications. His battle scenes are crafted so viscerally you feel as though you're a part of the action. And the fantasy element he brings to the novel delivers the right touch of mischievousness. A very fun read."

> ~*Jason Filardi, Hollywood screenwriter*

~

"*THE SAGA OF MARATHON* by Nick Checker showcases his tremendous knowledge of the first Persian invasion of Greece. Battles are epic and democracy hangs on the strength of one young runner. A wonderful read."

> ~*Peter Filardi, Hollywood screenwriter*

Note: Both Peter and Jason Filardi (brothers) are accomplished screenwriters, who have co-written, amongst other things, the hit TV miniseries adaptation of Stephen King's *Chapelwaite*.

Dedication

The Legend of Kwi Coast is dedicated to the memory of Sassy—a dolphin I came to know well while researching this project at the Mystic Aquarium years ago. Dolphins are no longer a part of that aquarium—an organization now dedicated fully to public education, research, and rescue—but a sculpture of Sassy, by the gifted artist Kit Johnstone, graces the grounds there.

I will always cherish the time I spent interacting with Sassy and her fellow bottlenose dolphins—Kimo, Max, and Daphne. It was a correct move to no longer keep dolphins in captivity because they belong in the sea (though they were always treated there with kindness and love), and I must add that without getting to know them as well as I did, I could not have created my main character, Piper, as authentically and vividly, for her personality is modeled after Sassy herself.

~*~

Acknowledgements

The Legend of Kwi Coast actually began many years ago and under a different title, *The Saga of the Whistling Folk,* but then was set aside. Recently I resurrected it, and I'm glad I did. My daring young dolphin is no longer lost at sea, but swimming into the hearts and minds of readers. I am especially grateful to my editor, Nan Swanson, for the suggestion that this book "should be assigned reading in every grade, right on up through high school."

My gratitude goes also to Stephanie Lurie, who believed in this tale from the onset and perceived its value as a work for younger minds more than I had.

Though written for everyone—adults and school-age readers—its worth is apparent for encouraging youth that their actions can indeed change our world for the better. So, thank you, Steph!

With the research on the subject of cetaceans (dolphins in particular), sharks, the ocean and its multitude of inhabitants, I now feel like a marine sciences major. Sources consulted include (but are not limited to) the works of Jacques Cousteau; Edward R. Ricciuti's *Killers of the Seas*; *Whale Watch* by Ada and Frank Graham; the *Blue Planet* TV series; and a rising new pioneer of the seas, bravely exploring and protecting all forms of sea life, Susan Casey. Her book, *Voices in the Ocean*, is a must for anyone who cares about life on our planet.

Much benefit came from multiple visits to the Mystic Aquarium, then and now, and from its onetime trainer years ago, a gracious gentleman named Kurt Butkiewicz, who insisted, "Well, if you're going to write about dolphins, you should get to know one." That's how I met Sassy, to whom this tale is dedicated.

Thanks to loyal test readers Steve Loyd and Tim Valliere, with their valuable perspectives; to Lieutenant JG Cecelia Hosley, Executive Officer, United States Coast Guard Angela MCSHAN (WPC 1135)—an environmental enforcement vessel; to teenage marine science student Jolie Isenburg for loving Piper's adventure; and to the Aquarium's Sarah Wilkinson.

And my eternal gratitude to the gifted Wild Rose Press artist, Jennifer Greeff, who found this story's very soul and reflected it in the form of a cover image that mesmerizes everyone. And of course, THANK YOU to The Wild Rose Press for believing in my work.

PART I
KWI COAST

Chapter One
Piper

Inside a bed of giant kelp, the school of small black fish huddled together, afraid. Nearby, the silent flapping of a great tail had just caused a disturbance in the water. Something was wrong. Kwi Coast normally slept during the early morning hours, making it safe for smaller creatures to scuttle about and feed in the watery jungle. But now the quiet tremors that swept the coastal sea sent danger signals out to all its tiny residents. Something large and powerful was on the prowl.

Suddenly a blur of gray and white smashed through the tangle of tall seaweed. Two narrow jaws sprang open and snapped shut with the precision of a steel mouse trap as a mouthful of spiny teeth closed onto something soft. Before the startled band of mackerel had time to react, one of them was spinning round in the bottle-shaped jaws of the sleek invader.

The young dolphin cocked her head arrogantly, twisting the trapped fish in her mouth so she could gulp it down head first, the way the WhistlingFin prefer to swallow their prey. She paid no heed to the abrupt panic of her captive's fleeing mates.

Piper was a crack hunter, among the best in the Kwi Coast Pod, despite her youth and her size. Though barely six feet long and only a little over two hundred pounds—small for the bottlenosed WhistlingFin—she was lightning quick and could outswim and outmaneuver even the burly bulls of the Fury Squad. Piper took pride in that.

She lived in a clan that boasted of its strength and its fighting prowess, but she shunned those passions in favor of her own. Piper loved to hunt in the dawning sea. She enjoyed bolting through the foggy morning that belonged then to her. But once the Pod stirred from its nightly slumber, she had to share her favorite haunts and the glee of the private chase ended. Piper was a loner, unusual for a Whistler…and that caused others of the clan to regard her with suspicion. She had grown used to it, though, and rarely allowed it to bother her, yet it would cost her dearly in time.

She finished her morsel, forcing the feebly resisting mackerel down her gullet and, with one thrash of her muscled tail, launched herself surface-ward where she would take in a generous supply of air. The small blowhole atop her forehead was clamped shut now. Once she broke the surface, she would allow it to pop open so she could breathe. That was necessary every seven minutes. Unlike the GillFins, Whistlers and others of their cetacean kind could not breathe beneath the waves.

Piper spiraled up through the long brown strands of kelp, through a swarm of tiny, plantlike plankton creatures. She was careful to avoid bumping any of the half-conscious Whistlers who drifted by aimlessly in their slumbering state. Near the surface, she flapped harder with her flukes and broke through the rippling surf again, spinning over and over in midair with the grace of an acrobat.

Against the pink seaward dawn, the young female

dolphin careening in the gentle California sea seemed a symbol of a world at peace with itself. But inside, Piper was uneasy with the violence she knew to be rumbling quietly in the brooding world below.

Soon the Pod would waken, and it would be time for the hunt. Then the drills would begin. Piper felt her stomach heave. Drill Time often spoiled her outlook on a new day. She hated the brutal practice. The Fury Squad was insane and could only lead to a bad end. She'd always felt that. The Snag-Tooth were ill-tempered and dangerous, best avoided and left to their mysterious ways.

But Piper knew it was futile to bicker over such things. She had already tried. She was a "mere stripling" of but six seasons (three years) questioning the vast wisdom of Commodore RamStrong and the rest of the High Clan. Her cheeky remarks had landed her in trouble more than once. And if her late night spying antics were known to the Commodore, she would have found herself in even worse favor.

Yet Piper felt sure that RamStrong's dreary forecasts bore ill tidings for the Pod. Something terrible was going to happen before long if they kept on the way they were going, *something evil*. But she did not know what it might be or how to stop it from happening.

Depressed by her glum thoughts, Piper looked past the forthcoming drill session and to the warm afternoon, when she would sneak off and frolic in the waves of the Land Dwellers' Floaters. That recharged her spirits a bit, and she allowed a shrill whistle of glee to escape her blowhole.

The young Whistler submerged to join the waking

pod for the morning hunt. The joy of the afternoon always helped her in tolerating the ordeal of Drill Time.

Chapter Two
Commodore RamStrong

"Move in now...Drive! Drive! No! No! Not there...Go for the *gills*—or go beneath and strike!" bellowed the old dolphin.

Piper felt foolish. She always did when they played this ridiculous game of pretending one of the Pod to be a Snag-Tooth, while two others took mock swipes at it. She wasn't very good at it, either. So far she had fumbled up on every tactic that was supposed to render a full-grown shark helpless.

"The gills...the underbelly...that is where you must strike if you are to do these foul beasts any harm!" scolded Commodore RamStrong, his big glossy eyes wide with scorn. He hefted his twelve-foot-long, nine-hundred-pound frame out in front of the squad. He jerked his beak sideways, signaling Piper and her two young partners to rejoin the ranks.

RamStrong looked impressive as he paraded himself before his young gray charges. He was a grand specimen of an old-time breed of Whistlers. The Clan admired him as the luminary he truly was, for he had proven his valor many times in boundary skirmishes with prowling Snag-Tooth. Though most of the time such tussles were only with the Browners and the Sanders that were not of vast bulk, those Snag-Tooth were still just as fierce and spirited as the larger breeds.

And one time the Commodore had fought and slain one of the sleek Blues—a beast that stretched a good fifteen feet long—when it was in the throes of the vile Furies. Few creatures in the sea cared to battle a Snag-Tooth that had the feeding madness upon it, but Commodore RamStrong had fought the crazed shark and had won! A renowned warrior with a megillah of fearsome exploits that he proudly shared with them all, time and again, he was leery only of the much larger predators of the Open Sea.

Not even the cocky young bulls of the Fury Squad cared to test old RamStrong's strength. At thirty-six seasons (or more, though he would never admit to that), the Commodore was a legend at Kwi Coast. His word was revered throughout the Clan.

Now he lectured the row of forty silky-skinned dolphins, all of them either burly males or fierce, unmated females. Few were over fifteen seasons of age. It was the duty of the young to protect the Pod.

The squad was alert as the Commodore spoke. They pumped their strong-tailed flukes up and down, suspending themselves in place in the pale morning sea.

"Once you have struck its gills, the evil creature cannot breathe. Even if you fail to strike hard enough, his gills can still rip, and he will be too weak to move. The Snag-Tooth are not like normal GillFins. These evil killers must move if they are to even breathe. If not, they drown."

The squad dolphins all "clicked" in unison, making the strange sound that came from inside their high foreheads. It was the customary response paid any of the High Clan during formal gatherings. The odd noise filled the pale green waters with a sound that was like a heavy fishing line being reeled in. RamStrong lifted his weathered face, pleased with their etiquette.

"The underbelly is just as good a mark, for the Snag-Tooth's vitals are afloat inside there…loose. One good hit and those vitals are crushed!"

More clicking.

"But you cannot afford a miss at either of those targets! The cunning killers guard them well—they are aware of their own weakness. If you miss, you have placed yourself in a vulnerable position for their vicious jaws." The Commodore's husky voice darkened as the last words rose from his blowhole, and it seemed that the water darkened, too. "They are very quick—these silent ones—and in the mere instant your strong beak is twisted aside, a Snag-Tooth can spin under you and tear out your soft belly."

The squad clicked nervously, the long, snouted faces of the youngsters—and even some of the veterans—going pale as they envisioned those gleaming jaws chewing away at their stomachs. No one doubted what the Commodore had said. He knew more about the Snag-Tooth than any Whistler at Kwi Coast. Only the Commodore had ever seen the Snag-Tooth at their worst.

****

It was in his early life that young RamStrong had witnessed the savage destruction of his first pod—a small band of twelve Whistlers who had one day found themselves trapped in the Open Sea amidst hordes of crazed sharks. "The Furies," the shaken young dolphin had called their madness—when the Snag-Tooth indulged in a grotesque feeding ritual—slashing, tearing, and sawing at everything near them until the water became a bloody froth. RamStrong believed the Snag-Tooth worked themselves deliberately into such a madness so every living thing in the sea—even the WhistlingFins' much larger cousins, the fierce HunterKin, slinked away in fear.

Somehow young RamStrong had been ignored by the frenzied horde that day, and he had watched helplessly as his family died a violent death, their pitiful whimpers haunting him as he fled. And he had sworn he would never again let it happen to a Pod of his; nor would he forget the debt he owed those silent killers of the Deep. For he had never spoken openly of the guilt that tormented him whenever he recalled his impotence at the time of his first Pod's doom. "Strength through herding and drilling" became his mantra. And once he had proven himself to a new Pod at Kwi Coast, nearly thirty seasons past, he rose steadily in their ranks to the High Clan. Gradually, he swayed them to his own brand of wisdom, convincing the Clan Thane and Pod Elders that it was safer to dwell in the sanctuary of reclusive coastal waters, where the terrible dangers of the Open Sea like the larger Snag-Tooth did not exist, where a clever Pod might then prepare, undisturbed, for the Great Invasion—when all the Snag-Tooth would band together in one mass fury to plague the seas. "For the Snag-Tooth are a ruthless breed who will stop at nothing till every living creature in the sea trembles before them!"

RamStrong had promised that Kwi Coast would be ready for that day…as would the wiser Whistlers everywhere else in the sea.

****

Now the Commodore scanned his gray ranks. It

was time to close the morning session with a mock combat. His eyes fell on a large, well-muscled dark gray dolphin, and he nodded his beak in quiet approval. It was QuickFin, one of the squadron leaders, and RamStrong's prime protégé. Like most of the younger squad members, QuickFin had not yet seen actual combat with a Snag-Tooth, but when the day came to venture into the outer zones and engage one of that dreaded breed, the Commodore felt sure his young protégé would not fail him. The young squadron leader was a fast learner and eager to please. RamStrong was proud of him above all others.

Just how it had come to pass that QuickFin was of the same bloodline as the shiftless Piper had always mystified the old Whistler. It bothered him just thinking about it. He let his gaze slide over to the tail end of the ranks, and a cloud appeared to pass over his rumpled face. It was because of her kinship with QuickFin that the Thane had insisted (one of the rare times SilverFlukes insisted on anything) that RamStrong admit Piper into the Fury Squad.

"She is too small!" the Commodore had argued. He'd always wondered if Piper was really a "crossbreed"—and a distant Kin to the foolish "Jumping Whistlers" who sometimes swept by the cove on their seaward journeys and consorted with the local Kwi Coast Pod until the Commodore scooted them off. RamStrong had no use for the spinner dolphins and their flighty ways. They were not as orderly and somber as his own bottlenose breed. And whenever word came that a playful spinner pod was on its way, the surly old Whistler was always leery of whatever mischief they might cause. Piper's light markings and her careless antics in the waves were highly characteristic of their ilk. Somewhere, he often mused, those mischievous Jumpers had entered their bloodline into the Kwi Coast Clan…and Piper was it. *One was enough*, RamStrong thought.

From the start, Piper had done nothing but grate on the old dolphin's nerves. She didn't want to be in his Fury Squad, and the Commodore had made it obvious he did not want her there. But neither was going to change the Thane's mind. Yet even RamStrong had to admit that if the little scamp had been willing to use her marvelous speed for better things than careless romps in the waves and private hunting games, she might have made a decent Fury Fighter.

Still, it was hard for anyone to ignore what an attractive Whistler she was. Piper's rare excess of light, patchy colors and her foam-white flippers and fins made her a temptation. Even the two light cross marks over her brow, which gave her the coy look of a Jumper, added to her appeal. RamStrong felt he might have persuaded her through courtship—were he a younger bull—though that had already been tried by some of the squad youngsters. He wondered often if she might ever finally change. RamStrong glanced at her again and noted the faraway look in Piper's eye. With a quiet grunt he continued his survey of the squad.

He turned his gaze to the higher ranks. Next to QuickFin was another handsome young Whistler nearly the same size. Though not quite the full eight feet that QuickFin had already grown to in but nine seasons, Buffer, just a shade less in strength, was a staunch young battler. He even bore the same rugged look the Commodore had once flaunted in *his* youth—the bulky chest, the steel gray all over the dorsal side (though the years had faded the Commodore's). Yet RamStrong was not that pleased with Buffer, for he saw that the cocky youth seemed far too impressed with himself— unlike QuickFin, a tried devotee to the squad. Buffer's loyalty and devotion to the squad appeared hazy. It seemed the Fury Squad only gave him an excuse to brawl or to show off...for Piper, RamStrong thought. And it was obvious Buffer resented the constant praise heaped on the gallant QuickFin. Buffer might bear watching, he felt.

He put the cocky youngster from his thoughts and scanned the rest of the squad: SlickFin, the speedy scout who could echo onto a school of tasty GillFin fluttering over a mile away, and then predict exactly when those fish would cross over the Kwi Coast boundaries where they could be taken by the Pod; RipFin, who could command a squadron of Fury Fighters through maneuvers that would leave a band of prowling Snag-Tooth battered, bleeding, and fleeing; Snapper, who had learned to use his jaws in battle as though he were a Snag-Tooth himself. On and on it went. RamStrong knew the strategies and weaknesses of every one of his charges, all of them worthy of his praise in some way...all but one.

He turned his gaze on Piper, thought for a moment, then signaled a break for air. As one vast body, the squad soared for the surface. The training zone waters bordered the outer zones—where roving sharks sometimes lurked and spied on the mysterious pod of dolphins. That in itself pleased the Commodore, for he wanted the Snag-Tooth to know of the Kwi Coast Pod's fighting prowess.

RamStrong took his time returning, letting the squad wait for him, as was his custom. A round of courtesy *clicks* greeted him as he took up his place before them again. Then another spirited chorus of clicks sounded within the ranks as a beautiful, silver-colored dolphin came gliding out from around the edge of the kelp jungle. It was Thane SilverFlukes, the Royal Lord of the High Clan and descendant of a long chain of the Kwi Coast Pod's heralded rulers. At twenty seasons, SilverFlukes was the youngest to ever head the Clan. He was nearly as large as the Commodore, but unlike RamStrong, whose skin was dull and marred by the years, the Thane's shone like a sunlit surf.

Piper felt that Thane SilverFlukes was the only member of the High Clan that had any real sense. And though the Thane's word was final on all Pod Matters, he rarely resorted to it. SilverFlukes had been reared under the regime of Commodore RamStrong and the Pod Elders, and so he usually honored Clan traditions, bowing often to the whims of those deemed older and wiser. Piper had always wished Thane SilverFlukes would simply do as *he* saw fit, but she knew it was not his way. Except for rare instances, the Thane hardly ever asserted his bloodline authority.

RamStrong always made a point of pushing his squad to its fullest whenever the Thane was about. SilverFlukes greatly respected the Commodore's renowned military savvy, and the grizzled elder wanted to keep it that way.

"We shall examine the Initial Thrust tactics and how best to maneuver the enemy into vulnerability!" barked the Commodore in his most authoritative tone. Briskly the squad snapped into its fighting pose, their bullet-like heads lowered to protect the softer whites of their chests. They all looked formidable and menacing, with even Piper poised reluctantly at the tail end. She felt foolish.

RamStrong gave the impression of scanning the ranks for a pair of volunteers. It was a great honor to be selected for a display of might before the Thane himself. But RamStrong had already made up his mind that it was going to be QuickFin and Buffer. Displeased as the Commodore was with Buffer's attitude, he knew the burly young bull was a crack fighter. Maybe this display was what he needed.

"QuickFin...Buffer!" bellowed the Commodore. "Assume the attack posture...I shall play victim. Pay attention now, and we may learn something here of survival."

The dual-attack game was a favorite of the squad, for it was a novelty to watch the Commodore mimicking so perfectly the silent, stealthy movements of the Snag-Tooth—while two Whistlers charged at him. Even Piper, who could not stand the game, was amused by it. Though she often debated the sensibility of it all with her brother, she still enjoyed watching QuickFin flaunting his craft. And she was secretly pleased that the Commodore had given Buffer a chance to prove himself. Even if she did think Buffer a bit overbearing at times, Piper always felt sorry for him when the Commodore ignored him.

QuickFin and Buffer were an excellent team, despite the obvious dislike they held for one another. Their skills in "worrying down" and batting away a hungry Snag-Tooth rivaled those of the seasoned veterans. "Surpassed them," Buffer would insist. Soon they would do this for real.

The Commodore hefted his own bulk into a low fighting pose, brushing back and forth in slow, sweeping motions. It was an eerie sight, this giant of a dolphin imitating so well the sinister, slinking crouch of a prowling shark. Meanwhile, QuickFin spun his own rippling mass of muscle overhead while Buffer moved in haughtily from the rear. The Commodore barked out a number of commands for different maneuvers—calling sometimes for one attacker to act as a decoy, while the other launched a mock ramming of the "gills" or the belly, turning aside at the last moment. RamStrong would then score it a hit or a miss. The two young bulls feinted, retreated, and darted in and out of the quasi Snag-Tooth's range, and the Commodore reared his head and bared his teeth, giving a picturesque display of the malevolent grace of an attacking shark.

Both youngsters took turns scoring impressive hits—and the silent loathing they held for one another faded in the wake of their exceptional teamwork. Twice everyone had to break for air, QuickFin and Buffer effectively mixing their own breaths with the combat exercise. There was little doubt in the minds of the rest that the two could dispose of a real Snag-Tooth in a true skirmish. But the Commodore knew only time would tell for sure.

Thane SilverFlukes was pleased with the exercise and echoed his pleasure before departing.

After reassembling his legion, RamStrong warmly congratulated QuickFin and then commended Buffer for his "timely and refreshing display." Piper felt sure that the young Whistler had been stung by the Commodore's obvious reluctance to offer the morsel of praise.

"And fear not…little Piper," the Commodore added before dismissing them all, "I shan't ever embarrass the squad by displaying one as listless as you before the Thane."

Some of the squad snickered, while Piper seethed quietly. She knew Commodore RamStrong would forever try goading her into cooperating. *Never! Let the old fossil rant and rave all he wants.*

As the session broke up, Buffer slid by Piper and quipped, "Little chance you'll impress the Thane."

Piper sometimes wondered why she ever felt sorry for Buffer.

Chapter Three
Lofin

The Kwi Coast Pod dwelled in a restricted little sea zone north of the San Francisco Bay. It was a quiet, watery world filled with towering gray crags and forests of tall kelp plants. Scores of tiny fish and other dwellers of the continental shelf spent their entire lives in that weedy forest…just as the local pod of dolphins spent its entire existence within the rigid boundaries of the coast.

From a large cove that was nearly a mile long, out to the deeper coastal waters—where depths ranged anywhere from fifty to two hundred feet—life flourished. The perpetual feeding chain of the sea went on in earnest there, with the Kwi Coast WhistlingFin at its top.

The coastal floor of muddy gravel and broken shells was ruled by the Crawlers and the Clingers—the clams and crabs and lobsters. Sometimes those bottom dwellers climbed their way surface-ward, clinging to the fernlike kelp as they scuttled up its stalks in search of their microscopic prey. The Crawlers and Clingers, in turn, became delicacies for the prowling GillFin, and the fish, upon venturing too close to the outskirts of the seaweed forest, fell victim to hungry Whistlers.

The hidden cove of marine life was about a half-mile wide. Once outside it, the Pod was permitted to roam five miles north or south along the coast.

Whenever Pod members ventured west, they swam out roughly another five miles as far as the two-hundred-foot depths, the Boundaries, which they marked by echo-ranging the deep, using the sonar inside their high foreheads and lower beaks to home in on the jutting sea caverns below. There, the mysterious Slithering Ones dwelled. The realm of the dark cave eels marked the farthest point to which a Pod member could roam. For, beyond those Boundaries were the Outer Zones, where even the Commodore needed approval to patrol. Violent border skirmishes took place in the outer zones to protect the Pod from Snag-Tooth that had ventured too close.

Beyond the Outer Zone was the Open Sea—and *no one* was permitted there.

****

It was afternoon, and the sun hung high in the sky, a gleaming yellow ball that sent streams of gold speeding down to the sea below. A small, creamy gray dolphin played merrily in the churning waves of a great freighter. Piper had pushed away the sting of her morning drills and was now absorbed in leaping and twirling in the bow-spurt of a huge Floater.

Such spry behavior was common of most Whistlers, for, by nature, dolphins were curious and playful. But long ago, Commodore RamStrong had scorned such antics, deeming them wasteful, "A distraction from more urgent matters." Piper hadn't listened, as usual, but she did make a definite point of not indulging in her merry games whenever the surly old Whistler was about. Lately she had been leery of rankling RamStrong and the other Elders. She had argued often with her brother about her habit of scoffing at Clan Traditions, and it was obvious that QuickFin did not approve. Even though her games with the Floaters did not violate the Clan Code, they annoyed the Commodore. QuickFin's constant lectures had finally convinced Piper to play in such ways only when RamStrong and the Elders were not around. She would be careful, she always promised.

It was difficult for most to stay mad at Piper. She was a gentle creature, and her beauty was reflected in her stunning features. It was no secret that the young beauty was the most sought after she-Whistler in the Clan. Even the rugged Fury Squad veterans often gathered together and spoke longingly of her, though at six seasons she was considered a mere youngling. And it was also said that, on occasion, when the sleek young female glided by, one might detect a glimmer of lust even in old RamStrong's eye—causing wonder about what sort of talk went on within the circle of male Elders.

Piper never took notice of any of it, though—if she even realized it at all—and so she spurned the company of male suitors in favor of her private scamps in the waves.

"What would you do if you were threatened by a hungry Snag-Tooth?" complained a belligerent Buffer one day.

"Probably I'd swim away from him with my *great speed*. After all, I am the swiftest member of the squad, you know," she had replied coyly, knowing well that it annoyed Buffer to hear that.

"But not the bravest," snapped Buffer, puffing the thick of his heavy chest out, as though it were proof of his prowess.

"It's not always brave to fight when there are wiser ways out," she had answered.

"We shall see," Buffer had grumbled as he paddled off, disgruntled and adding a few extra-strong thrashes of his tail for effect. But Piper hadn't noticed his angry burst of speed. She had already spun off for another jaunt in the waves. Still, she liked Buffer. She never failed to notice what a handsome Whistler he was, and she often wondered if he was really as gruff as he acted.

One thing was certain though: Buffer's sentiments were shared by the rest of the Commodore's young charges. Every one of them was frustrated by repeated attempts for Piper's attention. But none cared to push too far, lest it meant risking a row with QuickFin. Even Buffer was unsure of his chances in an all-out brawl with the Commodore's young protégé.

Piper and QuickFin were all that was left of a family that had disappeared mysteriously over five seasons past. RamStrong had blamed it on the Snag-Tooth, insisting such tragedies would never happen if Whistlers avoided hunting at night and stopped wandering too close to the Boundaries where the nightly Snag-Tooth prowled. Stricter laws would have been enforced if RamStrong had had his way.

The Pod had accepted the Commodore's explanation of the family's disappearance, and everyone had mourned the loss. But Piper had never been completely convinced by it and wondered if there were more to it than had been explained. She promised herself a day would come when she would learn more.

****

It was a typical day of frolic for Piper, dashing in and out of the foaming bow-spurt of passing freighters and trawlers and hitching "rides" as far as the Boundaries. Checking the depths with her scanners to be sure she had not gone too far, she would then leap out again before the Floater trudged away into the *forbidden outer zone*. The fine spray of waves over her silky skin pleased her and made her recall how accidentally brushing against Buffer had sometimes excited her, though she had never given hint of it or understood why.

All was normal and pleasant until—while springing out of a large black freighter's surge—she suddenly echoed onto the presence of another being. Barely ten yards away a tiny dorsal fin broke the rolling surf. Then a stout black-and-white form wriggled up from the rippling blue. It was no more than five feet in length. Piper checked herself with several strong beats of her tail. She lifted herself up onto her flukes and suspended her body upright, giving the impression she was "walking on the waves" until free of the trawler's sucking force, then dropped back into the natural prone posture of a sea creature.

Piper recognized the intruder instantly. The Pod called them Harbor Waifs, but most sea creatures knew porpoises as Rovers. They were a carefree lot, these small cetacean cousins to the WhistlingFin. Despite their diminutive size and stubby look, they might have been mistaken for undersized dolphins. RamStrong loathed them. He and the Clan Elders, and even Thane SilverFlukes, had forbidden anyone at Kwi Coast to bother with the merry Rovers. Long ago, porpoises had been branded "reckless scavengers who fed on scraps thrown from the Floaters of the Humunz," who were Land Dwellers. It was said that the Harbor Waifs' speech was corrupt and that the mischievous wanderers were filled with foolish tales of their frequent romps out into the Open Sea...and that given the chance, they would lead the young of the Pod astray with their cunning lies. To be seen with a Harbor Waif tempted a hearing before the High Clan!

Piper had never been this close to a Waif. The creature was certainly not very impressive to behold. It was smaller than she was, its body chunky and round, its blunt-shaped mouth filled with spaded teeth unlike the conical teeth of the WhistlingFin, and the Waif's dorsal fin and its flukes looked ridiculously tiny for its plump body. It was that chubbiness that made Piper think of her Pod's disdain for the Harbor Waifs' gross feeding habits. Still, she could not help noticing the definite resemblance there was to a Whistler: the muscular tail and the small airway atop the creature's head. Spurters, as those of the sea knew the WhistlingFin and all their Kin...and though this homely creature sent a bristle of disquiet through Piper, she could not deny that it was a Spurter and, therefore, one like herself.

She felt she had already seen enough of their carefree Kin and so made to leave. Perhaps, thought Piper, the Commodore was right this time. A shrill call stopped her.

"Foolish...very foolish to play so close to the Land Dwellers!"

The Waif's voice had a screechy lilt to it, and it made Piper uneasy. And this one, a female, had spoken in a queer manner, not the sort of gibber the young dolphin had expected. Piper ruffled nervously, eying the chunky creature curiously. The porpoise paddled cautiously toward her, knowing the slightest hint of mischief might prove costly, for the Whistlers of Kwi Coast were renowned fighters.

"'Tis not wise to frolic with the Humunz, lovely Whistler, for they are a most sneaky lot, oh, yes." The porpoise drew closer.

"*You* talk of foolishness…Waif?" said Piper. "Who is it that grows fat and slow off their scraps!"

Piper knew it would have pleased the Commodore to hear her say that. She was learning already to dislike this little scavenger. But the Waif kept her poise, and her cocky manner baffled the young Whistler. A tiny voice whimpered inside Piper. What if she were caught here doing this?

"We Rovers keep our distance when we take their scraps, good Whistler. We never let the Humunz near enough to pull their tricks on us," the Waif replied sweetly. "Not like you WhistlingFin do."

Piper's dorsal fin tightened.

" 'Tricks'? You speak in riddles, Waif. The Humunz have never acted sneaky with us," said Piper, perplexed by the creature's words. "Why, they have even led us to some very fine hunting. And…and they hunt the Snag-Tooth sometimes," rambled Piper, not sure why she felt she had to add that.

"The HunterKin hunt the Snag-Tooth. Does that make them your friends too?" quipped the porpoise.

Piper shuddered at the mention of their larger cousins, the fierce killer whales, the orcas. She could not believe how loosely this Waif spoke of them. Truly, these mischievous creatures were as reckless as the Commodore had said. She grew more nervous. They were in full view and in clear sound range of any who might happen by. Their voices were high, especially the Waif's. The sensitive echo-locale of other Pod members might easily pick up this forbidden discourse if any were nearby and on the alert.

"Where do you think those missing from your Clan have gone?" the Waif said suddenly, as though making a final stab for Piper's attention. "Surely you don't believe the Snag-Tooth responsible for everything."

Piper was shocked, puzzled how this pudgy creature knew so much about her Pod and what she herself was thinking. A chilly thought crept up in the back of her mind. She suppressed it.

"Who are you, Waif?" demanded Piper. She was more used to the straightforward talk of her own kind. This creature's constant riddles annoyed her.

"I am called LoFin," the porpoise replied congenially, sensing the young dolphin's growing impatience. "I am one of nine…my Clan…my family," she continued, trying to soften in her tone. "We stay sometimes in the harbors of the Land Dwellers, that is, when we are not romping in the Open Sea. But we never come as close to those sly Humunz as you do. Oh, we take their food, yes, but at a good safe distance. And when we know they are on the hunt, we leave! We have no wish to be seized by them. Ah…and when we leave, and where we go…our journeys are most fascinating!"

Piper grew even more suspicious. Her curiosity had been piqued, but her inbred mistrust of these "lesser kin" to the WhistlingFin held her back. What of the Commodore's many cautions?

It seemed that the porpoise actually heard her thoughts, for she gave a coy flutter of her fins. Piper paused a moment. She glanced up at the cloudless sky that was filled with swarms of elegant seagulls scouring the surf for potential prey, then turned back to face LoFin.

"I dare not speak with you...LoFin. If I am caught with the likes of you, my problems with the Clan will be even worse."

LoFin nodded her beak, letting the insult pass. She was accustomed to it.

"It is forbidden for us to speak with Waifs, you know," said Piper when the porpoise did not reply. Her ashy eyes betrayed a growing fear of what she was doing. This was not a mere jaunt in the waves. For that the Commodore might only scold her. But this...this would earn her the wrath of the entire High Clan!

"Ah yes, my pretty white-fin," cooed LoFin softly, beating the water with her flukes. " 'You must avoid those wretched scavengers, for their foul words will corrupt you, indeed,' " she snickered in an almost perfect mimic of the Commodore's gruff manner. "Come Piper!" the Waif's mud-brown eyes flashed with an air of mischief. "We've heard of one so bold that she challenges the ways of her Clan. We know of you, brave Piper. Follow me to the BreakWaters. Your Pod never goes there. No one will see—and the waves are too noisy for any others to hear. Come, and I will tell you such a tale!"

Piper quivered in nervous excitement. She knew this was a grave violation of the Code...and that this LoFin might be nothing more than a diabolical liar. But the Waif had touched something in her, perhaps unknowingly. And the sting of the morning drills still lingered. Why shouldn't she go?

She knew if RamStrong ever found out, she might even be banished: *The Hundred Dawns. Exile. The Black Waters!* Piper had been reared on the horrors of Exile. They all had. Her eyes clouded with confusion and fear.

LoFin sensed it and was taken aback. She knew something of the Kwi Coast Pod's beliefs, and their superstitions too. It made little sense to her, but she was amazed at the strength of its power over them.

Finally Piper spoke. "All I know of the world beyond Kwi Coast is what the High Clan tells us. You, LoFin, have been places I have known only through old tales. There…there are many things I would ask you."

"Then let us go," said the porpoise urgently, for she began to realize just how long they had been out in the open together. "We tarry here too long, my lovely Whistler. I do not wish to bring down the wrath of your warlike Clan upon my own little family."

"Be warned, though, 'friend' LoFin," barked Piper in a tone of uncharacteristic menace, "we of Kwi Coast know how to defend ourselves should you lead me to more than talk." And at that moment, Piper was grateful for what little Fury Squad training she had picked up, and for some reason, she felt good in knowing it might have pleased old RamStrong.

"Of that, I am sure, good Whistler," uttered the porpoise gravely.

And with that they swam off for the dangerous BreakWaters.

Chapter Four
At the BreakWaters

Piper poked her head up through the surf and watched the speeding roll of spraying white breakers racing inland. The roar was deafening. If she'd had worries that their talk might be detected, those were now quelled. Still, she was uneasy. The BreakWaters was a dangerous zone with its fierce currents. And though it was not forbidden to go there, it was deemed foolhardy. One who roamed too close to the choppy waters invited the possibility of being dashed to death upon the jagged rocks that sprang up from the ocean floor. The Clan Elders would not have been pleased with her recklessness.

LoFin propelled herself about in the churning surf, obviously quite accustomed to it. She seemed amused by the flailing of her companion.

"Are we comfortable?" the porpoise asked.

Piper looked anything but comfortable, but nodded her beak just the same. Both of them thrashed hard with their flukes, LoFin having the rhythm down to a smooth, easy beat. Their heads were high above the shifting water level so their voices would fade into the thunderous surf. Rovers were not able to remain underwater as long as the WhistlingFin, so much of their talk would remain above the waves.

"Sometimes," began LoFin, "the Humunz draw the

WhistlingFin into choppy waters like these where the Floaters make the waves even higher. The silly Whistlers think the Land Dwellers are playing with them, or leading them to a feast of tasty GillFins. And it is right when the Whistlers are close enough that the Humunz pull in the nets they had dropped into the water earlier—and then the GillFin and Whistlers are all pulled up onto the Floater. *No one ever sees those Whistlers again.*"

"Where do they take them?" asked Piper, not entirely certain if the Waif was being serious.

"That, I am not sure of, though I have heard very queer tales. But I do know it's true. Why, I've even had the terrible misfortune of seeing it happen, and not far from here!" The porpoise paused abruptly in her story, for she saw that Piper had gone pale. The dolphin looked suddenly sick, as if she had just swallowed one of the poisonous Stingers—the ugly jellyfish creatures—that drifted around in the kelp jungles.

"My parents," said Piper in a muffled squeak. "They disappeared in the first season of my life. You said...you've seen Whistlers taken by Humunz near here?"

For the first time, LoFin was at a loss. She sensed what the young Whistler feared. "Yes, friend Piper, but one cannot say for certain that is what happened to your parents," said the porpoise gently.

"Shouldn't the others be warned?" asked Piper, aghast at the thought of such capture. She felt sure that horrible things were done to the Whistlers. Why else would Humunz trap them so? It sounded as frightening as legends of their cruel HunterKin cousins who chased down other Spurters and *ate them.*

"And what will you tell them, sweet Piper?" retorted the chubby porpoise. "That you heard such a yarn from a scavenging Harbor Waif? No, it is best to say nothing, for it will only earn you more grief from your rather strange Pod. So perhaps I should not alarm you any further with these dreadful stories."

LoFin slipped back under the rolling surf and then popped her head back up a second later. She paused and listened to the sizzling hiss of the waves. "I mean only to caution you...you who have shown me some tolerance at least. I have yet to meet any other from Kwi Coast like you. And I mean only to caution you, not frighten you with silly tales of horror like those told by your boorish Commodore."

"You tell me this terrible tale but still take the food the Humunz toss from their Floaters," said Piper.

LoFin gave a shake of her pectoral fins. "Ah, you Whistlers...always a quick answer rather than listening to what you've been told. Yes, we do take bits of dead GillFins and Crawlers and 'scraps' that are cast back into the sea by Humunz...but not before knowing for certain it is all safe to eat!"

Piper bristled in discomfort, the tiny crossmarks on her brow knitting. "I do not understand."

"Of course you don't, sweet Whistler. Your kind never understands until too late."

"Then please help me understand...oh, wise Waif."

The chunky porpoise wagged her beak in a tiny circle. "I shall try, dear Piper...for I do like you. You see, from our many journeys into the Open Sea, we learn much. And some of it has been seeing how Humunz have—shall we say—*stained* our cherished waters with a filth none of us can understand. Among

28

the worst of it is the Food-That-Is-Not-Food…and how dangerous it is to eat!"

Piper peered curiously through her ashy eyes at the Waif, lost in her odd talk. "But how do you…"

"Best hope you never must know," LoFin said grimly. "But if ever you come across what looks and even feels like food from the sea itself, yet seems it may not be so…pay heed and *taste first* to be sure."

Piper shivered at that and nodded her beak in solemn agreement, though still puzzled by all of it.

LoFin submerged again. She was growing restless. Rovers did not like staying put for long. She beckoned with her diminutive flippers for Piper to follow her into the churning blue.

The two Spurters fluttered through the booming surf, leaping and plunging with irregularity as LoFin continued in her screechy voice. "Be warned that it would be foolish to try to caution others of your mad Pod, for they will not listen to your warnings any more than they would listen to mine. For all their seeming intelligence," groaned LoFin, "the WhistlingFin never seem to use it where there are lessons to be learned. Beware for yourself is all I can tell you."

They pushed on through the whitened BreakWaters. Piper forced the chilly theory of her parents' disappearance into a remote corner of her mind, not wanting to consider it any longer. There was nothing she could really do about it now, other than paying heed to what the Waif had told her—if the tale were even true. Then she remembered another reason she had been willing to follow this strange Spurter into the BreakWaters. Why not ask? LoFin claimed to have traveled far and seemed to know much about the Open

Seas.

"LoFin…what of the Snag-Tooth? What do you know about them?"

The porpoise stopped, suspending herself above the roll of the waves with deft strokes of her stubby tail. She surveyed the graying sky as she spoke. "They, my friend, are a dangerous lot," she said gravely. Then she added immediately, "But not nearly as bad as your Commodore would have you believe."

"You don't think they are so evil that they want to conquer the entire sea?" Piper did not realize how fearfully serious she had sounded and was therefore taken aback by LoFin's reaction.

The porpoise squealed hysterically, making no effort to control the shrill peeps that blew out from her blowhole as she twirled round and round in tiny circles. Piper was embarrassed, hurt by the Waif's reaction. She had never really believed in that prophecy herself, but her Pod did. She turned her beak to one side. Was the Waif simply making fun of them? Was this little spin in the BreakWaters the sort of mischief the Commodore had always warned them of? Piper's thin face twittered; she was confused.

"I didn't mean to be so humorous…*Waif*," said Piper acidly.

"Oh, I am sorry, friend Piper, truly I am," squeaked LoFin, nearly gasping now from her outburst. "But surely you cannot possibly believe those mindless garbage eaters capable of such a scheme! Why, my dear new friend, they would wind up quarreling so much that before long they would tear each other apart like they do when the Mad-Eating is upon them," said LoFin darkly, all humor gone from her tone now. "It strikes the Snag-Tooth when they sniff out blood—for that is one thing they can do which we cannot: the Snag-Tooth can *smell* their prey, and it gives them a great advantage. The mere scent of blood drives them wild. I warn you—if ever you are in pain, *do not struggle too much*...for the Snag-Tooth also have crafty sensors inside their toothy hides, like tiny ears—something like our scanners—that can hear almost anything from the greatest distance. I don't really understand how they do it, but I know they can find you as soon as you start to flutter too wildly."

LoFin paused, eying the wide-eyed young Whistler closely, then continued. "Then the worst things happen when they find their prey, for that is when the Snag-Tooth go into their Mad-Eating. Oh, it is a horror to behold, even from a safe distance. They rip and chew at everything—even themselves—and they make the most frightening growling sounds. Why this happens no one really knows."

"Our Commodore calls the Snag-Tooth's madness the Furies."

"Yes, I know," answered LoFin, "and that is a good name for it."

"But don't they cast this madness over themselves on purpose before they attack?" asked Piper anxiously. For so long she had wanted to know the truth about this. Did LoFin know?

LoFin studied the young Whistler carefully, stifling the laugh that started to well up inside. The Rover suddenly realized Piper was serious in her fears, whether the youngster doubted her Pod's fears or not. LoFin saw that as strong-willed as Piper was, she had still been touched by the Kwi Coast Clan's mad beliefs.

And why not—when day after day it was drilled into them. What a dreadful band of WhistlingFin, with their Snag-Tooth invasions, odd living habits, and hostility toward their own kind. So unlike the merry ones she'd met when romping the Open Seas. And so ignorant and trusting of the sly Humunz. But then, weren't most of the WhistlingFin too trusting? Surely this mad Pod is doomed, mused LoFin grimly. But this fine young Whistler here should be saved. That much she would try to do.

"Listen, friend Piper," began LoFin, "the Snag-Tooth are a queer breed and have many strange ways. They are superior hunters too…but they are not very smart. Now, it is possible that they resent us Spurters because they sense we are smarter than they are, and are able to breathe the way Humunz do. Some even say the Snag-Tooth believe we are not really of the sea. They sometimes call us 'FalseFins' because of old legends that long ago our kind lived on land."

Piper had never heard that before, and again recalled Clan warnings of the Harbor Waifs' sly talk.

"But even if we are smarter," LoFin continued, "it has not allowed us to survive any better than the Snag-Tooth. Why, they outnumber all the Whistlers, Rovers, HunterKin, and BigFin all put together! That surely says something for the Snag-Tooth's might. Dear Piper, if they were all going to gather together and attack us, they would have done so by now."

"Do you think they ever will?" Piper asked darkly.

"Only if they knew how to band together under some great leader. But that will never happen. They are far too quarrelsome. And, as for these 'Furies' your Commodore is so concerned about, the Snag-Tooth have no choice in that. They certainly do not 'cast it over themselves.' The Mad-Eating is just a sickness that passes over them. They have no control over it. What nonsense! They may go off into foul moods and snap at a Whistler or a Rover now and then because they are short-tempered and despise our merry ways…but these creatures are also very lazy. Massing together for some great purpose is not something the Snag-Tooth would even consider, let alone *plan*. HunterKin might do something like that, but not Snag-Tooth."

Piper wrinkled her narrow snout in consternation. What she was hearing was so different from all she had ever been taught.

"But one thing your Commodore says that is true," LoFin continued, "is that all in the sea do flee when the Furies come over the Snag-Tooth. For then, those silent killers know no fear and no pain! And they swarm together in numbers so great it is impossible to even count them. They don't stop slashing with their jaws until everything around them is eaten or destroyed. Some go so mad they chew out their own stomachs and don't even feel the bites! Ah, yes, even our fearless cousins, the HunterKin, will not bait the Mad Snag-Tooth. Your Commodore is a fool if he thinks he can train his Fury Squad to battle such killers. You will all pay dearly for such folly."

The porpoise paused, noting the terror welling up in the eyes of the young dolphin. She softened.

"No," she continued more gently, "leave the Snag-Tooth to their peculiar ways. Stay together, and you never need fear them. Remember, they are just simple hunters who will usually avoid a strong group. They would much rather strike at easier prey. I know this because I have seen many Snag-Tooth in my time in the Open Seas. And it is only when the Mad-Eating comes over them that you need flee…Do *not* bait them then. All you can do then is flee!"

"Are all Snag-Tooth taken with this Madness?" Piper asked with a shudder.

LoFin paused and shook her stubby black-patched head.

"No, not at all," she said. "There are those whose teeth are so tiny that all they can eat are the little plant creatures, as our cousins the BigFins of the Open Seas do. And, like our giant Kin, these Snag-Tooth are very large and gentle. We call them 'Baskers.' You see, all Snag-Tooth are not to be feared. Now, your Commodore isn't all wrong about them, but in other ways he is very mistaken. He has stayed far too long hiding here, just like the rest of you. You must understand, my pretty white-fin, that the Snag-Tooth are no more your mortal enemy than you are to the tiny GillFin you Whistlers prey on. It is truly all the same. Why, I could tell you such a tale about the…"

"Perhaps another time, friend LoFin," interrupted Piper, who saw that the chatty porpoise could go on forever. The Commodore was right about that much, at least—Rovers were definitely impressed with their own ability to ramble on and on. But now the tiny nerves inside Piper's lower beak began to twitter, amplifying the faintly echoing flutter of dolphin sonar vibrating through the waterways. Somewhere, not far off, was a Boundary Patrol; and though it was still not possible for it to detect the conversation taking place here in the choppy BreakWaters, Piper did not want to be found there, with or without LoFin. It was getting late in the afternoon, and if she tarried any longer, she knew she would be late for the evening hunt. That would arouse suspicion.

"I am very confused by all this, LoFin, but I will think about it," said Piper. "I...I no longer see you the way our Commodore does."

LoFin appeared very pleased with the young dolphin's kind words.

"In the ten short seasons of my life, I have travelled a fair distance, good Piper," said LoFin with quiet arrogance. "Leave that mad Pod and see for yourself that what I have said is true. And say *nothing* of our meeting—or you will find yourself in greater peril with your crazed Commodore than you might ever imagine." With that, the chatty porpoise turned and sped off.

Piper watched the Waif's stubby flukes haul her off into the distant, darkening blue. And when she rejoined her Pod later, the afternoon's escapade was still heavy in her thoughts, making it difficult to concentrate on the task of the hunt.

More would change due to this afternoon's odd jaunt than she could ever have suspected.

Chapter Five
The Wrath of the Fury Squad

Piper did not sleep well that night—or in the nights that followed. Dolphins, in fact, do not actually sleep as other creatures do. They fall off into a semi-conscious slumber so they can maintain a steady surfacing pattern and thereby avoid an accidental drowning. Part of a dolphin's brain *must* remain awake to remind itself of the need to breathe while slumbering. Yet, even in that drowsy state, Piper was still haunted by the lingering images of all that LoFin had said that strange afternoon.

It was early morning, a week later, when Piper heard the call. It came to her, shrill and sharp, piercing through the thick fog that had encased her sleepy brain. Instantly she was alert. She recognized the unmistakable clicking and whistling they had all rehearsed so diligently. A final jolt of alarm sounded from deep inside. She shook off the last bits of haze and woke fully.

Dolphins whizzed by in hissing gray blurs, churning the early gloom of the dawn waters into foaming white bubbles. Mothers called frantically for their young, and above all the din, husky voices could be heard bellowing commands. It was impossible to see clearly, for the frantic beating of the water by the mass of thrashing flukes obscured her vision, while the constant static hampered her audial powers as well. The cove was one vast cloud of gloom. But through the din, her sonic impulses zeroed in on Commodore RamStrong's gruff commands. The message he coughed out came back clearly: *Snag-Tooth Invasion!*

Piper could not believe it. Never in the history of Kwi Coast had any of the Snag-Tooth dared venture so close to the Boundaries as RamStrong's clicks and whirs now signaled. She picked out the tactical commands the Commodore was issuing rapidly to the seasoned veterans and to the fledglings. If all that he called out were true…

LoFin. Had the Waif lied to her? Everything she had said had made so much sense. Or was it simply because she had wanted to believe it all because it had fit so conveniently with her own feelings? Piper was terribly confused. Up to now, all this talk of Snag-Tooth threats and invasions had all been one gory fantasy: a grizzled old Whistler's Mad Prophecy. But now suddenly it was real! Something of great cunning had stolen upon the sleeping Pod. And if indeed it was a horde of maddened Snag-Tooth, could the small Clan of Kwi Coast hope to withstand them? Piper recalled LoFin's grim account of the Mad-Eating and conjured a picture of the Snag-Tooth's cold, empty eyes…and the gleaming jaws of death!

At that moment the young dolphin felt suddenly secure with the thought of being near the stouthearted Commodore. For all his pomp, RamStrong was yet capable of filling even the meekest of heart with his brimming confidence. And Piper now envied the likes of QuickFin and Buffer. Their heartiness in training had given them the nerve to confront almost anything. It made her resent the queasy feeling welling up inside which made her two-hundred-pound frame quiver violently. She did not want to be a coward here. From somewhere, she would muster the nerve.

So she sped through the steaming murk, zipping in and out of the tangle of plant stalks and the swarm of scurrying dolphins. Schools of jellyfish and plankton were batted in a hundred directions by the charging Whistlers, all soaring on to the Commodore's call.

Then she came upon a sight that sent chills up her cetacean spine and down her flukes.

The waters near the Western Boundary had cleared a bit, revealing a row of over thirty dolphins lined across in perfect battle formation. RamStrong's sturdy bulk passed casually along the gathering banks of Fury Fighters. Piper marveled at his poise. And, as expected—it was reassuring. Though the entire Squad (even the hardened veterans) seemed nervous, the eerie glint of battle that shone in the Commodore's baleful eyes was reflected in every one of them.

Piper slipped into the ranks beside her brother, knowing she should have been at the tail end. But she needed to know that QuickFin was beside her. Deep in a tizzy, he barely noticed his sister there. The mood was one of an impending storm. A tremor of disquiet swept through her as she beheld her fellow Clanists, in all their battle zeal, frighteningly similar to LoFin's description of Mad-Eating Snag-Tooth.

Then it appeared.

Not a charging pack; no horde of ravenous hunters. Just one. But one unlike any they had ever seen. Even the Commodore was shaken by this sight. He wished now that they had scanned it earlier. For, less than a hundred feet away, an enormous dark gray Snag-

Tooth—well over twice the length of any Whistler in the Pod—was drifting quietly by the Boundaries, giving hardly a passing glance at the pack of thirty blood-eyed dolphins.

There was a stunned silence as the entire battle squad of strapping bulls and fiery-eyed females all watched the lone giant paddling by. The beast was fully aware of the dolphins, for his acute nervous system was attuned to the slightest vibrations for a lengthy distance. He had detected the presence of this pod earlier, but was not alarmed. Most of the Snag-Tooth regarded the WhistlingFin as potentially dangerous, but only when threatened. And this giant of the seas had seen many Whistlers in its time. In the depths of its tiny primitive brain, the giant Snag-Tooth knew of certain laws in the sea that were automatically obeyed. The creature understood the mutual Boundaries that were not to be crossed. So it paid these Whistlers no heed, knowing they, in turn, would do the same.

There was not a single member of the Clan who had imagined a Snag-Tooth so huge. All any of them had ever seen—including the Commodore—were the sleek Blues, or the stocky Browners and Bullers, or the speedy Sanders...but never anything the size of this black monster.

It was larger than any of the HunterKin!

Some quivered at its dark shade, wondering if it might even be one of the fell servants of the evil Cold Lord: *Arkitu*. The image of the Evil One always sent a wave of fear through the Pod. It opened up hidden pores where their deepest terrors lurked. Had Arkitu, Lord of the Black Waters—Ruler of the Midnight Depths—had He sent this *thing* to claim one of the Kwi

Coast Pod as a prize to be brought back to his Dark Lair?

Were the Snag-Tooth secret minions of the Cold Lord?

RamStrong had not expected such a monster. Nor the effect it would have on his superstitious Pod. He had heard, in his youth, legends of mighty White Giants that grew among the Snag-Tooth but had never seen any for himself. And he had never heard anything of a creature like this!

The monster did not appear to threaten them at the moment, but still, it was a Snag-Tooth, and it was on the Boundaries of Kwi Coast. And it had come closer than any had dared venture before. The dark giant had had a telling effect on the Commodore's proud Fury Squad. There was but one choice.

"We shall attack!" barked the Commodore to the amazement of all. His scarred face was cold, and the thunder in his voice jolted them from their collective trance and back into battle poise. "This may well be one of their great leaders," he announced hoarsely. "It is probably scouting our strength to see if we are afraid. When we destroy it, the word will pass back to the others that even the mightiest of the Snag-Tooth will fall before us!"

The Squad clicked in unison, much of it by rote and some of it as a means of mustering courage.

The Commodore nodded his beak again in approval, then added, "And if it be of the Black Waters, then even Lord Arkitu will know that Evil may not enter Kwi Coast! From here on we shall be safe from all peril!"

A feverish clicking filled the gloomy water in

response to the bold commands. Surely he is mad, thought Piper, to openly bait the terrible Cold Lord of the Black Waters. But it was her sudden glance at QuickFin that made her innards tremble all the more—for she saw in him, and in the eyes of all the others, the same madness.

Something was very wrong here. This giant creature from the Open Sea was fearsome to behold, yes, but so far it had done nothing more than pass by and glance at them. And as soon as the clamor began, it seemed that the Snag-Tooth had begun moving away faster—as if in fear?

Then came the command.

"Squadrons Sea-Flash and Storm-Shot, take to maneuvers…Circle-and plunge!" barked RamStrong.

Piper froze. Her stomach turned to sponge. Sea-Flash was *her* squadron.

Now it was no longer the fear of the unknown, but a growing dread that there was something very foul in what they were about to do. The black giant was not hurting any of them. In fact, she thought it might even be trying to flee. Despite its massive bulk, the creature did not appear to be a fighter.

Piper tried thinking back on something LoFin had told her about such monsters of the Snag-Tooth, but the Sea-Flash squadron of five had already begun its circling maneuver, and the Storm-Shot followed suit on the other side of the attack. The Fury Squad was using its "Crawler Formation"—attacking in the shape of a giant lobster. The outer squadrons acted as the long, hooked claws, which cut off the victim's escape, while the main body of seasoned fighters bore straight on, acting as the tearing beak.

Piper wanted desperately to protest, but one look at the smoldering fires of her comrades' eyes, and at Commodore RamStrong gathering his hefty bulk into fighting pose, warned her against it. This pack of gray fiends was not the familiar Clan she had always known, nor was their manner simply the swagger of cocksure braggarts. *This horde she did not know.* Killing would be no object to them. She wished Thane SliverFlukes were here to stop the senseless attack, but she knew that he and the Elders were all stationed back in the cove, massing the rest of the Clan for one last defense should the outer perimeter of Fury Fighters fail. For all his pomp, RamStrong was pragmatic. He knew it was possible for his Squad to come up short, for the lesson of long past had not faded from his memory.

The Squad sped straight on, driving their torpedo-like bodies ahead, slicing through the chilly dawn waters with powerful flaps of their tails. It was frightening—QuickFin at the fore of the Sea-Flash squadron, Buffer off to the left heading the Storm-Shot unit, and the main body of battle-scarred veterans roaring down at the center of the formation with RamStrong's burly frame surging along in front. The grim commander was certainly not lacking in courage. He would be first to make head-on contact with the dark intruder.

It took barely a split second for the primitive giant to detect the mad battle lust in the frenzied pack that sizzled at him through the gloom. For an instant, the creature had a vague imprint in its mind of the deadly HunterKin packs that prowled the Open Seas.

But these were Whistlers.

There was no time, though, to reflect on the

paradox of WhistlingFin behaving like their predatory kin. *Escape* flashed through its tiny brain. The big fish thrashed frantically through the wisps of broken kelp stalks, disrupting a colony of small garibaldi fish that had been preying on the shrimp and crabs stuck to the drifting plants. The force of the giant shark's impact sent the garibaldis and their prey spraying in a score of directions.

Piper sensed the panic in the fleeing monster. And then it came back to her, what LoFin had said: *Harmless giants, those whose teeth were so tiny they fed only on the little plant-creatures. Baskers.*

Then there was no need to kill this grand giant! It meant no harm. She must somehow try to save the gentle creature from her crazed Pod.

With several strong beats of her flukes, Piper was out in front of QuickFin. Two more beats propelled her well ahead of the entire lobster formation. Her sudden maneuver had not gone unnoticed by the Commodore, who, even in his fervor, nodded his beak in approval. He hadn't expected such abrupt heartiness from her in battle. Perhaps this was what she had needed all along, he thought. Finally the true Whistler had been flushed out of the little scamp. RamStrong felt his heart swell with pride at the sight of Piper bearing down on the giant beast, the Squad zooming in behind her. It did not matter that she had broken ranks. She had become a *fighter*.

The Basker knew it could not outswim this speedy pod. He was frightened, for he was not a fighter like his own savage Kin, but now he would have found their fearful company a welcome sight. Only his great size could aid him in gaining precious time for escape. One of the Whistlers, a small white-finned one, was well ahead of the charging pack. He would take the foolish pest out with one swipe of his massive tail, and perhaps that might discourage the rest.

The Basker swirled around with a mighty twist of his gargantuan frame. A small school of mackerel scuttled away in panic at the sight of the grisly chase advancing on them. The pursuit had gone well into the OutZone and now approached the dark spectrum of the Open Sea.

In her haste to save the huge basking shark, Piper nearly lost her life! She zoomed in too close and barely missed being struck by the roaring black tail. She cried out at the dark giant, scanning its massive shape with her sonar, amazed at how closely the creature resembled its more savage cousins: the sturdy, streamlined body, the low underslung jaw…and for that instant she thought she might be mistaken. What if this beast *was* dangerous?

Then the two caught each other's eye. Piper saw fear in that ebon stare, not the usual cold glare that was typical of the silent killers. This Snag-Tooth was more like images she had had of the stately gray GhostFins— the gray whales of the Open Seas, of which she'd heard many legends. So she whistled and cried and clicked at the Basker again, hoping it would know enough to turn and flee. There would be no reasoning with the shrieking horde she barely recognized as her own Pod. For this beast to stay and fight would be folly. The odds were too great. And the Basker knew nothing of the Kwi Coast Pod's prowess. Piper saw there was but one chance for it to escape.

She tried sending an image to the big fish that she

would try diverting the attack by intercepting the first of the Fury Fighters to home in on it—even if it meant trying to obstruct the bullish assault of Commodore RamStrong himself! She was dreadfully frightened, but to allow her Pod to slaughter this innocent creature would be a terrible disgrace. If she could distract them, perhaps it might escape in all the confusion.

It was to no avail. The shark merely stared at her almost stupidly, puzzled by the babbling dolphin which, instead of attacking, held its distance and seemed to be scolding him. The shark lowered its jaw—as if to speak?—and Piper stared hard at it. Its teeth were so tiny they would not have been able to grasp hold of anything stronger than a Stinger. This Basker was indeed *harmless*.

If the shark had truly been making an attempt to communicate with Piper, it was now too late. It had waited too long. QuickFin was the first to strike, slamming heavily into the huge gill slits! The Basker moaned in agony. It glanced over at Piper accusingly, betrayal in its witless stare. The shark wailed in horror as Buffer made contact on the other side.

"No!" shrieked Piper. And she drove straight on at the cocky Buffer, bumping the burly youngster off course before he could land another telling blow. But by then, QuickFin had spun underneath and had driven his hard snout into the basking shark's underbelly, tearing a horrible hole in its stomach. Piper tried intercepting her brother's next assault, but now the Commodore and the rest were upon the giant.

RamStrong drove head-on and then swerved in for the gills, while the rest of the Squad swarmed all over the hapless creature like a nest of yellowjackets whose ground lair had just been trampled on. Blow upon blow was rained upon the helpless shark. There would be no counterattack from the Basker. The giant shark had been out of balance from the moment of QuickFin's first hit.

And as the pack of frenzied cetaceans swarmed all over the defenseless fish—letting forth from their blowholes frightful howls and cries like some swarm of underwater banshees—Piper zipped in and out, trying futilely to block any attack she could intercept.

"But it's harmless! Look at its *teeth*! No…this is wrong!" she cried.

The Squad, though, was deaf to her shrieking and oblivious to her actions. The slaughter continued long after the Basker had died. Even after the creature had broken up into bloody hunks and shreds, they continued ramming the pieces about with their beaks.

Piper felt sick, guilty that she had inadvertently set the beast up for such an easy kill. If only she had let it be, it might at least have had a fighting chance. For the first time in her life, Piper wished she had never known the disgrace of being born of the WhistlingFin.

Chapter Six
In the Wake of Death

It was over. Long after the Basker had drowned in the wake of the first blows that had shattered its tender gills, the frenzied dolphins still batted about the torn chunks of flesh that drifted in the red-stained water. Finally the fervor subsided, and RamStrong gathered his victorious ranks above the carnage, which sank slowly to the sandy bottom. Not a Whistler had been lost. The kill had been swift and clean. Kwi Coast was safe. RamStrong had begun congratulating each of his charges when the eruption came.

"Cowards!" hissed the cold whistle of the only one to remain outside the grisly circle of death. Piper paddled back into the midst of the primping Whistlers. Her ashy eyes were ablaze with fury, her white pectoral fins curled up in a gesture of rage. The young Whistler's shrill voice bit into the pack like a cold knife searing through tender raw flesh.

"If I did not think you slightly mad, Piper, I would punish you myself for such impertinence," growled the Commodore, his thick face pulsing with anger. "Now fall into the ranks and cease with this senseless babble! It is bad enough you will have to face unpleasant consequences…"

"Perhaps a good thrashing is in order now, my Commodore," clicked Buffer, puffing up his dull white chest. "It was my attack she first bumped."

"Perhaps you'd like to try—you chattering heap of Waif scrap!" retorted Piper, lowering her head in battle gesture, to the amazement of all.

Buffer was stunned. He had not expected such a return from the little female. It annoyed him. One light thump with the side of his beak would teach her. But he'd barely thrust off when he felt himself banged heavily in the side, careening him off course. Buffer spun round sharply and found himself staring at a glowering QuickFin.

"And now *I* have bumped your attack, 'bold Buffer,' " sneered QuickFin arrogantly.

Buffer eyed him back savagely. "You won't always be so eager to do so...'favored one,' " he retorted, though not sure this was the time for a head-on spat with QuickFin.

"That will be enough!" roared the Commodore. For it had all taken place in a matter of seconds, and he wanted an immediate halt to it. They were all still under the feverish spell of the kill, and the slightest rift could easily wind them up again. "You, Buffer, should be more annoyed with this insolent youngster's slurs on her own Clan than with your wounded pride!" snapped RamStrong. "And you, QuickFin, should know better than to quarrel openly like that," he added, his voice dropping a bit.

He turned back to face the entire Fury Squad. "Now, reassemble—everyone!"

The Commodore's husky voice echoed throughout the murky underwater world, sending shock waves out at all the lesser creatures around them. The Squad was subdued instantly with the resounding boom of

RamStrong's voice. None wanted to tempt the old Whistler's wrath. Buffer sulked under his Commodore's scolding, noting that the favored QuickFin had not been rebuked as strongly.

"QuickFin…take charge of your reckless sister!" barked RamStrong. "See to it that she is quiet and orderly. She is in enough trouble as it is."

QuickFin clicked obediently, then turned to Piper, giving a half-pleading wave of his flippers, to which she yielded reluctantly. She did not wish to put her brother through the embarrassment of an even more unpleasant task. She fell in with the rest of the Squad.

Still flustered by the young she-Whistler's outburst—having never before been challenged by any of his own legions—RamStrong gathered himself together. "The defense of these waters was a successful one!" he proclaimed grandly. "Kwi Coast is once more safe from attack, for one of the more dangerous of them—a fierce leader for certain—has been vanquished! Let all the sea know that the might of Kwi Coast lies in the strength of its Fury Squad!"

The Squad promptly clicked its agreement. QuickFin nudged Piper…who appeared on the verge of retorting but refrained from doing so.

"And as for this matter of dissension," RamStrong added, shooting Piper an ugly stare, "that will be settled before the High Clan."

A hush fell over the gray ranks. None of them had ever been before the High Clan's Council of Justice. Piper might well face Exile unless she repented. Even then…

"Judgment and consequence shall be decided there," said the Commodore in finality. The Squad responded again with the prescribed clicks and then broke formation.

Piper swam back toward the cove with QuickFin, benumbed…her mind in a fog. She did not notice the cold glare of nearly every member of the Squad, or the quiet grumbling of Buffer, who felt his own brand of justice would have sufficed. But even he shuddered at mention of the dreadful Council of Justice—and what that meant.

Commodore RamStrong remained behind, grimly contemplating the fate of the impertinent youngster. He swam off, paddling casually through a patch of floating plankton that had been spit up by the Basker when it had first been hit.

The dead plantlike creatures drifted aimlessly in the red-stained murk.

Chapter Seven
The Clan and the Code

A cold gray morning crept over the sea the day of Piper's trial. Many a season had passed since the High Clan had assembled the Council of Justice. The threat of Exile was enough to keep dissenters under control, for there is nothing a Whistler dreads more than solitude.

The WhistlingFin were an emotional lot, always in dire need of comradeship. Without it they were lost, stranded on a desolate sea. And though solitude was a cruel punishment, it was also understood that a violator of the Code threatened the Pod's unity...its very means of survival. Codes varied from clan to clan, and freedom within a pod also varied, but the belief that such laws must be revered was strong within every one of them.

At Kwi Coast, a violator found guilty was faced with the "Exile of the Hundred Dawns"—from which none had ever returned. The Hundred Dawns meant banishment to the Open Sea, where one was at the mercy of Snag-Tooth hordes and marauding HunterKin packs. And it meant the threat of the Black Waters, an ancient evil that every Whistler at Kwi Coast had been raised to fear. For in the faraway ocean depths dwelled the Cold Lord, Arkitu, who commanded terrible dark things that sometimes rose from the gloom to snatch away lone sea creatures—captives the Evil One's minions brought back to their cruel master's lair. There, the Cold Lord gobbled up those hapless captives, feasting on them voraciously. And once his greedy hunger was satiated, he fed the scraps to his groveling minions, so they might remain strong enough to seek out and bring him more victims from the bright world above.

Some said there was even a foul breed of Snag-Tooth that served Arkitu, for it was noticed that fearsome-looking black ones were seen stealing into the dark caverns below, where the silent Slithering Ones dwelled. Only creatures of evil would dare mingle with so depraved a lot and stay so long in their shadowy dwellings. For weren't there Snag-Tooth who sometimes lurked in the ooze of the sea's floors...and others whose young ate one another while still inside their mothers' wombs? Were the caves of the Slithering Ones a place where the evilest of the Snag-Tooth plotted secretly with Arkitu's minions?

And when the sea pitched and heaved, it was believed that Lord Arkitu had caused it to happen so his legion of dark fiends could fly to the surface in search of more prize catches...for he was ever hungry. There was nary a Kwi Coast Whistler who did not fear being cast out to such a fate.

So they all paid heed to their Code.

****

Now Piper faced them: The Five. Settled back on their flukes, the council dolphins rested against a craggy cliff that sprouted a huge lip-shaped section at its base. And from that cliff, Thane SilverFlukes, Commodore RamStrong, and the three Elders addressed the Clan on formal matters.

The cliff rose high from a sandy bed of gravel, its mighty walls strangled in the growth of the tall, brown kelp-weed. Globs of jellyfish floated everywhere, while the usual clutter of lobsters and crabs scuttled all over the floor of tiny stones and shells. They were one mile out from their Home Cove, and a vast forest of kelp surrounded them on almost every side. The chilly morning waters were a sallow green, making the world beneath the waves gloomy and foreboding.

For Piper it harbored an air of menace. Her usual swagger had faded under the weight of the pending trial. She now wondered if she ever should have interfered with the attack. Nothing she could have done would have saved the Basker anyway. If she had only let things be in the first place, the giant beast may have had a better chance of surviving the assault. Everything had taken its toll on her—the trial, the Pod's disturbing talk of Exile, and dreadful murmurings of the Black Waters... And it pained her to know how her own Clan now spoke of her as "a deviant and an evil influence on the young." Piper had lived in scorn for some time, but this was different. Her own Pod *hated* her...and inside she cried, for she had loved them and had only done what she thought was right. And she knew she would do it again if she thought it might save some harmless creature of peace.

The Pod was gathered in a large semicircle round the Council Cliff. They brushed the floating wisps of broken seaweed aside with their beaks as they waited patiently for Piper's trial to begin, holding their prone postures with steady flaps of their flukes. Only the High Clan was permitted to "sit" during a formal gathering.

Thane SilverFlukes sat at the middle of the moss-covered cliff's lip, the Commodore immediately to his right. An Elder, the only female of the High Clan, sat beside RamStrong, and the other two flanked the Thane on the other side. Piper could never remember the names of the three Elders. All she knew was that they were very old (easily over forty seasons) and not very attractive to look at. Their faces were wrinkled—and always the trio of aged Whistlers acted very solemn, as though they were ready to scold some younger Clan member just for breathing wrong. Their skin was mottled and stale gray, and Piper used to think if they swam too fast they might accidentally swim right out of it. She could not help wondering what kept such timeless fossils alive. She used to joke about them to QuickFin, but he had never found it funny.

Now they did not appear so comical. The three Elders looked very austere…very cold, their long, beaked faces hardened by the forthcoming task. Piper wondered if they had already made up their minds. A glance over at RamStrong gave her cause to believe he had certainly done so. Her stomach turned at the notion of her trial being nothing more than a mere formality—punishment soon to follow. Even her brother bore a frosty air about him, and Piper wondered if he too had already passed judgment.

Once more she questioned the good sense of her own actions. And so much of it due to the clever words of a chattering Harbor Waif. Had she been duped? *Could* the Basker have been dangerous? She had been so sure of herself at the time, but now nothing made sense to her. Perhaps the High Clan would think her mad. A Mad Whistler could not be banished; Piper knew that. But she had never felt so frightened. Why did they all have to look at her so hatefully? And, oh, how Buffer must be enjoying all this!

"The Offender will now address the High Clan!" proclaimed RamStrong, sounding like some rusty old bell tolling the final hour of judgment. Piper ceased in her ruminating and fluttered over to the cliff lip nervously. She steadied herself a few yards from the semicircle of the High Clan. She felt tiny and insignificant before them—while behind her, the great circle of Pod members looked like the mouth of a giant clam ready to swallow her up on command.

"I am the Offender..." she squeaked, barely audible.

There was a pause, and then one of the male Elders began. "Are we to understand that this upstart here, barely beyond her weaning period, has not only defied the Clan Code but has even gone as far as condemning the efforts of our longtime Commodore?" The grizzled Elder waved his scarred snout in disgust, and it seemed for a moment that the rictus of his mouth—which gives all dolphins that semblance of a smile—actually reversed and turned downward into a scowl. He followed up piously, "Why, our gallant Commodore has saved at least six or seven good Whistlers from a gruesome death. But for his quick response to danger, any one of us might have found ourselves crushed between the jaws of a ferocious giant of a Snag-Tooth!"

The Clan clicked in agreement as if on command. Piper suppressed a strong urge to protest regarding the "jaws" of the giant. She did not want to mar her chances of explaining herself. She needed time to gather her composure so she could think clearly...and rationally.

"What is it, if I might be so presumptuous to ask," continued the Elder Whistler in his raspy voice, "that provides one whose flukes barely yet flutter with such insight into the ways of our mortal Enemy that she may shun the foresight and judgment of our Clan's strongest defender and even scorn our very customs? Where does your vast knowledge come from—Offender?"

RamStrong suppressed a nod, hiding his approval behind a stony glare that marked his bullish face. He was satisfied with these opening proceedings, and he was not displeased with the Elder dolphin's flattering remarks.

Piper remained silent, her motion stilled, her ashen eyes solemn and quiet. She felt depressed and irritated by this gibber she was hearing from Elders she had been raised to respect. The queasy feeling inside her had now subsided under the barrage of jibes. Was this the way the WhistlingFin acted in times of serious matters? And did Thane SilverFlukes approve? She stared sullenly at the grim half-circle of Clan Rulers. In the sallow green of the morning murk, they looked more like pallid ghosts of yore...brought back to pass sentence upon the cocky upstart who had violated their sacred ways.

Her silence appeared to rankle the Elders.

"Perhaps," interjected the she-Elder, a rather rumpled old dolphin, "perhaps our young rebel here feels that she owes no explanation."

"Or perhaps she prefers the Snag-Tooth to her own Kin," quipped RamStrong.

"Yes, let her frolic with *them*," snickered the other male Elder, who had yet to put in an opinion. His crusty chest puffed out as he spoke, displaying a network of wrinkles and scars. "Why, she might even find a mate among them. There must be some reason our little beauty snubs the males of her own Clan."

"That's not true!" chimed Piper, unable to hold back any longer. These Elders were being ridiculous, and it aggravated her. But it was RamStrong's slur that had angered her most. A williwaw of chatter erupted within the Pod. There were few males in the Clan who had not made a play for Piper and been spurned. The Elder had voiced the frustration of every one of them, and Piper was sure he had done it on purpose. The old fossil was probably voicing his own frustrations as well, she mused.

Above the clamor, Piper thought she heard her brother's smooth voice rising in an angry pitch as if he were arguing with some other young bull. It comforted her in spite of everything else. And she would have been surprised indeed to also see the angry eye Buffer had shot at the Elder who had made that banal remark about her. But now she was furious and no longer cared what she said—or what would happen to her. They had made their minds up already anyway. What point was there to a trial when decisions were made before it ever began? Piper did not flinch in the least as she spoke.

"The Basker was harmless, it was peaceful—and you knew it!" she fairly hissed. A stream of bubbles roared out from her blowhole and into the fog above. "You didn't have to kill it...but you wanted to!"

RamStrong's face darkened. His eyes flashed, and the scars on his blunt snout pulsated. He was about to rebut when Thane SilverFlukes interrupted. "Let us break for air," the Thane commanded, and the fervor subsided. Whenever he gave an order, it came from a long line of regal Whistlers whose memories were sacred. None, not even the brash Commodore, was foolish enough to question it.

"The Offender shall be granted a chance to explain her actions," SilverFlukes said smoothly. "Let us not forget that this is *Kwi Coast*. All may speak their piece when they choose."

The Thane's cut-off was timely, for Piper knew she had nearly let loose with a barrage that would have sealed her fate. Had she been allowed to retort then and there, she'd have suffered badly for her impertinence. Was the Thane simply preserving the rights of the Offender…or was it possible he thought there might be more to her actions than treachery?

The Pod rose to the surface, Piper swimming between two of the Elite Fury Guard. She knew that when it came to a decision, the Thane's vote counted as two. If he made his feelings known, he might even sway an Elder, maybe more than one. And if the vote were a tie, then it would be SilverFlukes who broke it. She would be careful, from here on, in how she presented herself.

Tension was high when the Pod returned. The dolphins arranged themselves once more in trial fashion and awaited Piper's defense. SilverFlukes seemed relieved when he saw the youngster taking her time before resuming. She chose to picture the Basker for them—using elaborate sonic projections to illustrate the image of the giant peaceful beast. Then she conjured the same images LoFin had told her of—how these tiny-toothed sharks fed on plankton and krill, the very plant-creatures that the great gray whales feasted on.

Finally, she conveyed to them a vivid impression of their attack on the basking shark.

The Pod was attentive. There had been no interruptions except for several quick breaths of air, which they had all done in complete silence. They seemed fascinated by the image of this unusual giant of the seas, an apparent freak of the Snag-Tooth hordes. But at Piper's mention of the near useless teeth, and the glimpse of fear she had detected in the creature's eye, RamStrong broke the spell.

Piper had been doing too well. Danger signals were rumbling inside the old Whistler. The young upstart had etched a most convincing picture of a harmless herbivore, and before she could go any further, the Commodore's voice broke in like a boom of thunder blasting away the tranquility of a sunny afternoon.

"This is utter nonsense!" he bellowed. The picture suddenly shattered, and the mood vanished. "From somewhere inside her infantile mind, this brash deviant has dared insult our intelligence. We are the WhistlingFin—the most intelligent creatures in all the sea! How dare you try making fools of us?"

Piper was taken aback by his outburst. She wanted to respond, but felt suddenly lost in the wake of the Commodore's fire. RamStrong wasted no time in following up his advantage. He had their audience back again and had to strike before Thane SilverFlukes stopped him.

"We all know how the Snag-Tooth were named!" he boomed, hefting himself out from his seated position so that he rose several feet higher than the other Council members. "Have we all forgotten how their teeth become *snagged* in the flesh of their victims—and how some fall out, only to grow back later? Do we forget our basic lessons in Snag-Tooth lore?" There was a click of agreement from somewhere in the throng of gray bodies circling the Council Cliff, and RamStrong pressed on. "This vile monster we slew had likely just killed and had yet to grow in its next full layer," he explained, as though lecturing a group of youngsters for the very first time. "Our cunning rebel here merely saw in that monster Snag-Tooth's jaws the result *after* it had shredded its last meal."

The Commodore seated himself again at the close of his statement, smug in the assurance he had won back the Pod to his side. A glance toward them all, and then to the High Clan, told him he had every reason to gloat. He'd won. Every Whistler there looked embarrassed at having even considered the Offender's fantastic tale, which now they felt sure had been a mere trick to make fools of them all. A storm of angry squeals and grunts erupted amongst them.

SilverFlukes signaled another break. He was confused. Piper's story had not sounded so farfetched to him, but much of what the Commodore had said also made sense. RamStrong's feelings went along with everything they had ever known about the Snag-Tooth. The Thane wanted more time to think about it, but now all was chaos.

The clicking and whirring of over fifty cetacean voices filled the water as they surfaced for air. "Of course the Commodore is right!" could be heard. "There are no peaceful Snag-Tooth...they have always sought to rule the seas!" Even the Elders were bickering and hollering on the way up and back down again. Nothing like this had ever happened at Kwi Coast before.

When they had reassembled, SilverFlukes decided he would delay the rest of the Hearing till he had ample time to think about everything—and then to confer with the High Clan privately. And had Piper known that, or simply waited as she had before, she might not have made so terrible a mistake.

"You are all so blind!" she cried in a voice that startled even the Commodore. "The Rover was right! You refuse to think. You are all doomed!"

Piper's mention of the lowly Harbor Waifs—especially her using their true name—brought a grim hush over the entire gathering. *This scamp has had frequent meetings with the scavenging Waifs. And they have corrupted her with their sly speech.* Even SilverFlukes was appalled by it. Here was one of the most serious violations of the Kwi Coast Code! There could be no delaying the trial now...nor even a judgment of Madness. It was suddenly clear to them all where Piper had gone every day to frolic.

"So it is from the Harbor Waifs you have learned such blasphemies," snorted RamStrong. "And is it they who taught you to scoff at the danger that has always threatened us?"

Piper knew it had been a mistake to let that slip, but the frustration of the Commodore ruining her one chance to explain herself had been too much. They hadn't even let her finish! What kind of freedom was that? Oh, but it would have been different if she had been saying what the Commodore had wanted to hear!

"No danger threatens us as you would have us believe—you bitter old tyrant!" cried Piper in a boil of anger. Her ash-black eyes flashed like brilliant ebon

61

fires, her sleek gray-and-white body twisting and contorting as she spoke. She was no longer the timid little scamp they had always known. Not anymore. "That Basker never lost any teeth. It couldn't bite anything bigger than a Crawler. And your Furies are nothing more than a sickness of creatures too simple to even form a hunting party of their own. You all just want an excuse to kill Snag-Tooth and…and someday the Land Dwellers will come in their big Floaters and take you and the Snag-Tooth away…and then where will you be?"

Piper was terribly confused. Too many thoughts flew at her in the welter of rage she was feeling. She knew what she'd just said had been so jumbled that it probably hadn't made sense to any of them. But the anger had passed through her quickly. She was drained now and sorry for her rash words. She hadn't meant to hurt anyone by what she said, not even the Commodore. But the damage was done.

"Hear this upstart!" roared RamStrong. "She violates the Clan Code, endangers her own Pod, and then mocks her own leaders and her Clan's most precious beliefs!"

The three Elders were already nodding their beaks in a rapid, hushed anger. SilverFlukes, startled by it all, dropped into a glum silence. The chatter of the Pod died as quickly as it had begun. All was still. Thane SliverFlukes lifted his silvery body above the mossy cliff and pronounced the sentence he had been dreading. He knew he had to enforce the Code of the Clan. There was no other choice.

"The Offender, Piper, leaves us no choice but to enforce the Exile of the Hundred Dawns," he proclaimed quietly and solemnly. "Survive, and you are free to return and live once more under the laws of Kwi Coast. This is the judgment of the High Clan."

There had been no need for a vote. Piper had openly admitted her own guilt. She felt the Thane's grief, knowing he had never wanted to pass the dread sentence of Exile. She eyed him sadly, then turned her gaze toward the gray ranks of her Clan. She could not find QuickFin in the swirl of bodies, but did catch the cold faces of all the rest and the frosty gaze leveled by many of them back at her.

Then Piper spotted Buffer and thought she might be mistaken, for it looked to her as if he had dipped his beak in a gesture of sorrow.

Finally she spoke. "You are my Pod—and I will always love you."

Chapter Eight
Outcast

Buffer didn't like any of it. The whole trial had left him feeling disgruntled and hollow. Piper hadn't really done any serious harm to the Pod. He couldn't see why she had to be cast to the mercy of the sea's darkest terrors. He shuddered at the thought of her trying to cope with hungry Snag-Tooth and HunterKin—and the other dangers of the Deep. Surely a good scuffing with a hard beak was all she had earned. His anger at her had faded the more he thought back on that "battle" with the Basker. So she had ruined his chance at impressing the Commodore. Buffer never could stay angry with Piper for very long, even when she spurned him. And impressing the Commodore now seemed very unimportant.

What truly baffled the brash young Fury Fighter was that the big beast *had never even fought back*. What sort of victory was that? He had expected much more of a fight, considering all the time they'd spent training for it. Was this the powerful enemy they had dreaded for so long? By the way everyone had been gloating, it was as if they'd routed a hundred Furied Snag-Tooth—not one timid giant that seemingly couldn't even flick its tail in anger. Something was very wrong with all this talk of heroics and pride in fulfilling Commodore RamStrong's "great cause."

****

Piper was startled when she received a visit from Buffer. Shortly after the verdict, she had been escorted by two of RamStrong's Elite Fury Guard to the OutZone, where she would await Thane SilverFlukes' formal command of Exile. So she was baffled by the familiar swagger of fins and flukes as the burly young battler paddled out to her. Piper had been puzzled by Buffer's behavior, particularly his seeming melancholy during the Hearing. She had not understood it at all, but she was glad to see him now.

"Well, you little scamp, you've got yourself into a nice tidy fix here, haven't you," he quipped with a soft cetacean laugh.

Piper had never known Buffer to joke.

"You…don't hate me, Buffer?" she asked.

"Hardly," he answered. "It was about time you showed you were willing to fight. At least I won't have to worry about you out there, I can see."

Underneath his light tone, Piper could see he was dreadfully worried. It moved her.

"The Waifs have all gone, you know," Buffer said suddenly, first making sure the two guards were spread far enough away to allow them privacy.

"How do you know that?" she asked in surprise. They surfaced for a breath under the watchful eye of the nearby sentries.

"Because I went looking for them," said Buffer with a toss of his beak. "Your tale made me curious." He blew out a stream of vapor, pleased with himself, satisfied that his recklessness may have impressed Piper.

"Buffer—that's dangerous," she uttered quietly,

not wanting their voices to carry. "You could have been caught!"

"I suppose so," he said matter-of-factly. "Oh, but certainly not as dangerous as whacking away at ferocious Snag-Tooth giants, eh?" he snickered.

Piper was stunned. Of all the Whistlers in the Pod, Buffer was among the last she had expected to start thinking for himself. Now she realized there was so much more to him.

They stayed above the waves for a few more moments, feeling the afternoon sun's bright warmth. The morning fog had broken, and the sky had become a cloudless blue. The sea was shiny and calm.

"I think it best that I return now," said Buffer, "before my visit here causes problems. Do be careful out there," he said, sounding almost tender. "And if you come back with anymore farfetched notions, you'll feel the side of my beak," he cooed softly, waving a flipper. Piper didn't want him to go.

"Perhaps then we can be friends, Buffer," said Piper.

"Perhaps," he answered. Then he was gone.

Her encounter with her brother did not go as well.

"What matters, Piper, is that the Clan be protected at all costs," QuickFin had pressed. "We all have to make sacrifices, sometimes even the things we believe in most."

Piper had been through this so many times with her brother. He was so much like the rest of the Pod. All of QuickFin's beliefs were colored by whatever he'd been told by the Elders, and especially by Commodore RamStrong. She knew it was pointless to argue with him.

"Brother, I love you dearly, and I appreciate what you're trying to do for me, but I can't do as you ask," said Piper.

"But it might save you from being banished!" he cried, wagging his long handsome face. He looked so much as Thane SilverFlukes must have in younger seasons, she thought. She wondered if this was what the Thane was like in those times: sincere, gallant... gullible.

"Even if it did, QuickFin, it would make everything I've said sound foolish," she said gently, trying to make him understand why she could not recant her actions and beg forgiveness.

"But that's *why* you have to!" chimed QuickFin, beating his strong flippers against the smooth current. "Then the others will all be sure you were wrong...and you'll at least be here, safe."

"I wasn't wrong!" she snapped, annoyed with his rationale.

"Of course you were. Why else would they have banished you? Commodore RamStrong knows a lot more about the Snag-Tooth than you do. And if he says you were making it dangerous for the rest of us, you can be sure it's true."

They streaked to the surface for a quick gulp of air. On the way up, Piper tried once more to make her brother understand, in spite of the rigid dogma that had long dominated her Clan's thinking.

"QuickFin, haven't you always been one to point out here at Kwi Coast we have the right to see our own way about things; that we may speak what we feel at Clan meetings? Even if it's different from what others think? And haven't we been told that if the Snag-

Tooth ruled, this would no longer be so?"

QuickFin looked puzzled as they popped above the surface and rolled through the gentle swells. He hated these little exchanges with his sister. She always brought up strange ideas that confused him. He didn't have answers for all these clever questions she probably spent all sorts of time thinking up. It frustrated him. Piper shouldn't have to think so much when the answer to everything was right here at Kwi Coast. The High Clan was the place for thinking. They were the ones who had to make the laws.

"Piper," he began in a tone she sourly recognized, "there is a point where you must be careful in what you say and do, because it might influence others."

"What a dreadful thought, dear brother," said Piper in mock distress. "It might even change Kwi Coast for the better."

QuickFin paled, not believing what his sister had just said. It troubled him to hear her talk so.

"Don't you realize, sister, that because of what we did to that monster yesterday, Whistlers like you are free and able to go around saying things like that!" he scolded as they dove under.

More slogans, she thought.

"The Commodore is very strong within you, brother," she answered softly.

QuickFin was not sure whether he had been complimented or chided.

When they returned, the sounds of a small procession of Whistlers informed them that the Thane was on his way for the formal decree of Exile. QuickFin did not want to be present for that; he could not bear it. He knew his sister was not going to renounce her actions. Their argument above the waves was forgotten in an instant. And if a dolphin could shed actual tears…that is what QuickFin did. His love for Piper was unyielding and his respect for her courage, immense—even if he did disagree with her. He never had understood Piper's ways.

"Do remember the little hints I gave you on using your speed in a scrap," he said in a voice that shook like weeds in a storm. "Use your speed and use your wits…and never let an enemy know you're afraid. Sometimes a good bluff will give you all the edge you'll need," he said. "Goodbye, my sister."

They touched beaks. Piper told him again that she loved him. No matter how they argued, QuickFin would always cherish her, and she would always feel that way about him. Her brother might even have tried going with her, but a harsh Clan law said that such a willing traitor would be cast out forever. Otherwise, desertion might have posed yet another threat to the Clan.

Piper wondered if the same conflict she had seen in Buffer would ever go on inside her brother too.

****

Over fifteen of RamStrong's finest Fury Fighters had come along as the Thane's formal escort. SilverFlukes, as always, was a magnificent sight to behold against the backdrop of the dark kelp jungle and towering gray crags. His smooth skin glowed in the pale light of the afternoon, and his turquoise eyes sparkled like a pair of oyster pearls. Strangely, RamStrong and his procession were commanded to remain behind, while SilverFlukes surprised everyone by swimming into the OutZone alone.

Piper was baffled by the Thane's actions. The ritual

called for a brief decree of sentence before the Commodore and an Elite Guard…and nothing more. A personal escort into the Deep by the Thane himself was completely unexpected.

Away from the others the two swam—almost into the Open Sea where, until the attack on the Basker, Piper had never been in her life. Then SilverFlukes stopped and regarded the younger Whistler thoughtfully. For one of the very few times in her life, Piper was speechless. She waited, puzzled by the strange behavior of the Clan's leader, with whom she had never been alone. Finally he spoke.

"I was taught the ways of the Clan, like every other Whistler, by Commodore RamStrong," he began. Several air bubbles rose over the melon of his forehead. He paused, as though not sure how to express his next thoughts. "I was but an eager youngster then, thrilled to be a part of the Fury Squad, boldly batting away any prowling Snag-Tooth and crying out the words that made the Commodore and my father both proud. I never once said anything or did anything that might displease either of them."

Piper waited, unsure what SliverFlukes was leading up to. Why didn't he just banish her and be done with it?

The Thane continued. "In all my seasons at Kwi Coast, I have never known of a single Whistler who dared oppose the Code so boldly." Then he added quickly, "But the Clan cannot permit such recklessness…*It threatens our survival*." His tone had changed abruptly to one of formality, as though remembering his role as Thane. But then his eyes softened in spite of his words. "Still, I cannot help admiring your choosing to do so—knowing full well what your punishment would be."

Piper nearly choked as she heard Thane SilverFlukes speak in such a way—while nearly all the rest of the Clan now scorned her.

"I do not think you *mad*, nor do I believe you to be a traitor," he declared, utterly surprising her. "But what you have done has violated every principle of our Code. And for that, I must banish you."

Piper and SilverFlukes regarded each other a long moment.

"I understand," she finally said meekly. What the Thane had said to her here meant more than any of the slurs she had endured from so many of her fellow clanists...more than the dread of the unknown fate awaiting her. And before realizing what she was doing, she paddled over and gently touched his beak with her own.

"I shall think on all you have told us, Piper," he said quietly, his pearly eyes glimmering in the sea's azure light. "With all my heart I hope we will see you again, Goodbye, my brave Whistler."

And with that, the great silver-and-white form of the Kwi Coast Clan's Thane turned and swam back to his Pod.

'Thank you, dear friend,' Piper beamed quietly to herself. Then she cast a final glance at the only world she had ever known and, after a long, sorrowful moment, turned away and thrashed her small white flukes in a grateful plunge into the great unknown.

PART II
EXILE

Nicholas Checker

Chapter Nine
Into the Unknown

The Open Sea was very different from the kelp-infested Kwi Coast. It was a vast stretch of sloping grassy plains sprouting up from a muddy bottom that went on forever. Schools of small red fish swarmed near the surface, but scuttled away in panic at the sight of the oncoming dolphin. On several occasions, Piper saw the rare sea otters that lived in the outer kelp forests and preyed upon spiny sea urchins and starfish. Sights like these were novelties and helped her in coping with her sorrow.

As the day wore on and Piper flapped farther away from Kwi Coast, the remains of the great coastal kelp beds were replaced by thicker patches of sea grass: endless clumps of tall weeds that swayed gently in the lower currents. And she passed over sandy slopes, which at times bore the skeletal remains of dead animals. The bony rubble made Piper uneasy, causing sonic images of hungry HunterKin and Snag-Tooth to creep up into her mind. So she pressed on faster with lightning-quick beats of her flukes.

The realm of the Open Sea also fascinated her. Sometimes the brilliance of this teeming outer world—from which she had long been isolated—caused her to forget her plight and forced the darker incidents of the past few days into some remote corner of her mind. Her life at Kwi Coast now seemed but a wisp of a dream as she experienced the world of undersea hillocks and plains. She swam gracefully over the slopes and valleys that were populated by schools of ugly groupers and hefty bluefish...and always the billowing clouds of misshapen jellyfish. Food would be no problem in the Open Sea, for her favorites, the black mackerel and tasty lantern fish, were everywhere.

One thing Piper discovered, to her delight, was that there were currents in the Open Sea which she could "ride," allowing her to save energy and providing her also with little bursts of pleasure. Not since infancy—when she had squirted out from her mother, tail-first—had the young dolphin experienced so many thrills of discovery. It was not until late afternoon of that first day, when the clear sunlit waters turned gray, and everywhere the descending gloom began to close in on her, that Piper became fully aware of her plight. All of a sudden, the bubbling, energetic world around her seemed more like an alien dungeon. She thought it might help if she zoomed in a sonic picture of the endearing sea of earlier. Her sonar would guide her through the dark, and with her echo-ranging she could easily home back in on her elegant surroundings. But the sight of the darkening, fogging sea was a grim reminder—a reality she could not escape. *She was alone*. There would be no company for Piper this night.

The water seemed unnaturally cool as she paddled on. The thriving swarms of sea life had mysteriously vanished with the gradual descent of night, and Piper found herself sorely in need of companionship. Though she had spent a good deal of time alone at Kwi Coast, those were during periods of play...and she had known that QuickFin was always about somewhere if she had needed him. There is only so much solitude a Whistler can endure. They love to chat, play, nag, gossip, and joust. And without that company of one another, they soon suffer an unbearable emptiness. Even a Fury Squad session would have been welcome at this point.

Piper was desperate. She echoed for some sign of familiar life, but all that came back was the grinding of crabs and the distant groans of a few prowling groupers, none of which made for suitable Whistler company. Aside from her own Kin and the Harbor Waif, LoFin, Piper had never even met another Spurter. She knew of no other creatures in the sea that chatted in so similar an idiom.

For six hours she had streamed through the dimming waters. But every time she echoed, it was the same familiar sea sounds. And most disturbing was the grim picture of a dwindling watery wilderness, growing skimpier as she travelled farther out into the Deep. The grassy slopes and teeming valleys below faded off into rotting stalks and blackened mud. And with that, the population also faded. The nocturnal waters were much quieter, and the Snag-Tooth's keen sensors beneath their rough outer skin could detect prey much more easily then.

Piper did not think of that as she whistled and squeaked and clicked over and over, hoping she might draw the attention of some passing pod of Whistlers— or even a band of Rovers. Perhaps LoFin had heard of what happened at the Hearing, and she and her family were waiting out here, a good safe distance from Kwi Coast. The Rovers had been wise to leave as soon as they'd heard about the Basker incident. If RamStrong had had any chance of linking it to them, the Clan would have dealt most harshly with the porpoise pod. How stupid that would have been, thought Piper, for they were close Kin who should have been helping one another.

She continued echoing out signals for signs of similar life, when suddenly she received the "broadcast" of another creature. It was *immense*— lengthier even than the Basker! A great feeling of disquiet seeped through her as she sent out another band of echo-waves in the direction of the monster. The echoes that bounded off the distant giant and reflected back etched out an image that chilled her spine nearly into ice. She had homed in on the unmistakable, lateral tail-beat which characterized all Snag-Tooth; for there was the familiar outline of the high dorsal fin, the ridged points covering its skin like chipped stones, and the curved mouth filled with rows of glistening teeth.

Piper trembled. In her confused state she felt the creep of panic bidding for control. *The beast was after her.* It was quietly tracing her through the nocturnal sea. This was what her frantic calls for companionship had drawn—a Giant of the Deep that would have made even the Commodore tremble.

And then a more frightening thought came to her. Didn't Arkitu's Legions emerge from the depths of the Black Waters when night fell upon the Open Sea? And weren't some of the Snag-Tooth thought to be minions of the Cold Lord? How else could a Snag-Tooth grow to such a size?

Piper pictured the haunting image of scores of ugly fiends swimming just below her in the inky depths, waiting for the command from their Master to seize her and drag her down to his lair. She thought of the gruesome feeding ritual: Lord Arkitu squatting in the center of all his minions as they fed him their catch of hapless Whistlers and Rovers and other tormented wayfarers of the sea. And how the "Lord of Gluttony" accepted the prizes in his spindly arms and gnawed at them with his horny beak.

Piper could no longer bear the grisly scene in her mind. She panicked! She fled wildly through the black fog, which by now had engulfed everything in the sea. The terrified young Whistler sent out frantic directional impulses as she sizzled through the dark waters at a blistering pace, surpassing any speed she had ever reached in the past. Blind, unreasoning fear pushed her on.

****

Long after the probing great white shark had given up, knowing the futility of pursuing a speeding dolphin that was leagues away, Piper was still rocketing through the ebon sea. Now and then she spiraled to the surface and bolted above the swells that rolled on endlessly under a starless sky, her mind wrought with the horror of an unbearable loneliness and the ever-lurking terrors of the Deep. And it would go on and on, day after day, night after night.

Piper felt it might be better just to die as she raced on through the nightly sea.

Chapter Ten
Dangerous Kin

For days Piper drifted on, neither knowing nor caring where she was headed. The strange new world around her changed constantly. Often she beheld wonders the Whistlers of her own Clan would have marveled at in disbelief. That was the problem: disbelief. How foolish it had been of her to have even thought of convincing the Pod of its own folly. Now she wished she had never tried.

She thought of QuickFin—how naïve and trusting, yet how his valiant pride in what he believed had made him so lovable, regardless what it was. Despite their differences, his loyalty to his sister had remained unyielding to the end. Piper felt saddened as she recalled how her brother had tried to convince her to repent, just so she might spare herself a miserable fate. And she could not help thinking of Buffer, who had startled her with his silent sneering at the Pod's ways. Then again, Buffer had always seemed more concerned with touting his own swagger than rallying round the Commodore's "Great Cause." It should have come as no surprise to her.

Piper could not forget how impressive Buffer had looked when she had last seen him—or how excited she had felt those times when they had accidentally brushed against each other. She had always kept that to herself, but if she were to see Buffer this very instant, she knew that would change. Still, she wondered how much of Buffer's doubting the Pod had to do with what she had said at her hearing, and how much had to do more with his jealousy of QuickFin. How wonderful it would have been if Buffer and her brother could have been friends, for they had much to offer each other.

These thoughts, though comforting at times, only made her sorrow greater, for they were a constant reminder of her loneliness. Piper was dismayed that she had not come across signs of other Whistlers or Rovers with whom she might share some company. Now and then she had tuned in on the distant images of what may have been small bands of either, but they were always too far away. She did not want to take the chance of alerting a pack of hungry Snag-Tooth to her presence. The memory of the silent giant that had pursued her days earlier was still fresh in her mind, and that was a terror far greater than the eerie solitude she currently endured. And those times when she did detect signs of prowling sharks, she would break into her wild bursts of speed, which always discouraged them. LoFin had been right when she'd said they were a lazy lot.

It seemed, though, that the Snag-Tooth were everywhere in the sea. From the images Piper could etch—based on their movements—she also saw that LoFin had been right in calling them mindless hunters interested only in gorging themselves on whatever was convenient. They did not seem conniving or sly at all. And the images she zoomed in of their feeding habits made her doubt the Commodore's sanity all the more. For the Snag-Tooth were as brutal in their feeding as they were in their hunting tactics. She was glad to be a safe distance from them. Nothing about the Snag-Tooth seemed sensible or sane, and she agreed they were best avoided at all times.

The nights had been most difficult to endure, for the darkened sea always brought on the dreadful premise of the Black Waters, which made every pore of her creamy skin tingle in horror. Even during the day—which she had tried spending closer to the bright surface—when she gazed down and beheld the darker blues dimming to a pitch black below, she shuddered at the dread of what might be lurking there. For, though the higher levels of the ocean teemed with colorful little fish and drifting fragments of broken weedy plants—all of which reassured Piper that she was still in the great blue sea into which she had been born—the night brought on the blackened waters, when strange flickering lights (which she had never seen back at Kwi Coast) appeared far below. And she could not help wondering then if Arkitu's minions were passing on signals to one another…calling for the Cold Lord himself to rise up from his lair and snatch away the frightened lonely Whistler.

Once a storm sprang up, tossing Piper above the waves, where she was horrified by the chilling sight of thundering mountains of foaming water rising and crashing down at her, threatening to batter her to bits. And during that fearful time, strange misshapen chunks and bits of debris spewed up from beneath the waves too—her first glimpse ever of human waste and filth dumped into the oceans—and the mere touch of it sent tremors of discomfort through her. So she dove deep to escape all of it—recalling tales of how Arkitu could make the seas churn and heave thus, driving all the panicky surface creatures into a blind flight and right into his many waiting arms.

****

It was a moderately calm day, nearly a month since her exile had begun. Piper paddled on, listless and slow, when suddenly she perceived a faint chorus of shrill squeaks and cries. The sounds had not fully registered at first, coming to her through the haze of half-sleep. The young dolphin had resigned herself to her fate. She knew she could not continue trying to outlast the overwhelming power of the sea. If the Snag-Tooth were to find her, or the evil hunters of the Black Waters were to come snatch her away, or she were to starve to death, she no longer cared.

Suddenly she was alert!

She recognized the familiar clicks and whirs of cetacean sonar, the shrill cries she had known and heard her entire life. *Whistlers*! Or maybe a band of Rovers! In her groggy state she could not tell for sure, but it did not matter, either. They were *Kin*. Perhaps even LoFin and her little band? She would be so happy to see that chatty little Waif again. What tales Piper had for her! She felt alive once more. Friends with whom she might frolic through the sea and hunt! She could show them all her great speed and how it would help them. Piper knew she would be a good Pod member for them, and she'd obey all the laws of their Clan. If only to chat and gossip and to hear such merry voices and just to see the look of her own kind again!

So the young Whistler hurried off on a quick hunt and to refresh herself with a brisk jaunt in the waves. She zeroed in on a small school of herring and feasted on several, reviving herself a bit, then sent out waves of sonic impulses from the melon of her forehead, hoping to home in on her new friends. A lifetime in the confines of Kwi Coast had conditioned the young bottlenosed dolphin into associating but two breeds of creatures in the sea with those squeaking sounds. And as she soared westward like a pale speeding bullet, she finally zoomed in on the source of the clicks and cries she had first heard.

Something was wrong.

The echoes that returned and registered in her head were of five creatures—very much like Whistlers—but frighteningly larger. One seemed nearly as large as the massive Basker her own Pod had attacked and slain. But now she detected the presence of yet another being, one of tremendous bulk and larger than anything Piper had ever imagined. The five huge Whistler-like creatures were swarming all over the massive beast…which dwarfed them all. *The giant creature was their quarry!*

And when Piper finally came upon the ghastly scene, a hundred feet below the surface of a foreign sea, she had a sudden flashback to that horrid day at Kwi Coast and the harmless basking shark. For she had just burst upon the sight of the HunterKin—*orcas*—the fierce killer whales that preyed on the WhistlingFin and other Spurters, earnestly at work ravaging one of the legendary GhostFins.

Chapter Eleven
Heroics

It was a terrible sight to behold. The killer whales were ferocious hunters. Their quarry fought back gallantly, but the toothless gray whales—though sometimes as long as fifty feet and over thirty tons—despite their bulk, were not fighters. Orcas were.

The GhostFins were known to those in the sea as a wise and ancient breed, and too few now to be slaughtered. But the HunterKin were brazen in their ways, boasting there were none in the sea they feared—not even the largest of the Snag-Tooth—and that they were bound to no codes other than their own. They grew to over twenty-five feet in length and most creatures fled at the slightest hint of the burly black-and-white Hunters approaching their waters.

Piper saw clearly that the reputation of the Whistlers' larger, more ferocious Kin was well-earned. The savagery of their attack was brutal yet masterful. Two of the orcas ripped at the GhostFin's underbelly while another nipped at its flukes—gracefully avoiding the huge thrashing tail of the gray giant, which, with one swipe, might have battered the largest of its assailants senseless. A fourth one pecked at the GhostFin's eyes. The last of the attacking pack, a massive bull of at least several tons, barked out commands to the rest, even as it chewed at their victim's eyes. And once that huge maw finally opened (out of sheer pain), the leader would then snap through the snarls of weed-like baleen and tear out the tongue with a single bite of its strong conical teeth. It was a ruthless system, but it guaranteed success. For all creatures in the sea had to feed in order to survive…and this was the way of the orcas.

If the attack on the Basker at Kwi Coast had shaken Piper's pride as a Whistler, this display by her larger cousins sickened her all the more. These HunterKin resembled Whistlers…but in a dreadfully fiercer sort of way. And for all she had been told of Snag-Tooth cruelty, she wondered what could possibly be more vicious than these shrieking marauders. What she did next—and from where she mustered the nerve—she would never know. But Thane SilverFlukes had been right when he'd said there was more of a Whistler in Piper than many had realized. She recalled suddenly the parting words of her brother, QuickFin: "Use your speed and use your wits…and never let an enemy know you're afraid. Sometimes a good bluff will give you all the edge you'll need." Piper nodded her beak as though her brother was right there beside her at that telling moment.

"Ho there, my cowardly Kin!" she piped in a whistle so shrill that a geyser of bubbles spewed up from her blowhole. The sound was so sharp that it rose above the high-pitched squeals of the orcas. "Are the HunterKin such feeble hunters that it takes five of you to bring down one tired old GhostFin?" The barnacles and scars that covered the gray whale's mottled skin showed he was indeed an old one.

Piper maneuvered her sleek light frame into an

upright pose, steadying herself with several thrusts of her tail. Her movements were deliberately static and loose, the rictus of her mouth looking like an actual wide smile of mischief. A round of chirping Whistler's laughter poured out from her blowhole as she chided the marauding killer whales.

"Why, not one of you overgrown Harbor Waifs is a match for a good Whistler. I am truly disappointed… oh, brave 'Kin!' " That last jibe dribbled forth like a stale carcass sinking to the ocean floor. Piper knew she'd have to move quickly.

The orcas, at first, were stunned. *Never* had any Whistler dared defy them. The only sounds that ever passed between the two breeds were the Whistlers' cries when the HunterKin dined on their smaller cousins. But this one, this little white-skinned snip, *baited* them—challenged them!

The bull leader knew he could not ignore such insolence. He signaled one of his band to silence the pesky scamp. Three of them were large she-Hunters, fierce and proud, the other a smaller male, too small and too young to yet pose an authentic threat to the bull's authority.

Piper anticipated the attack. She was confident that her tremendous speed could carry her safely away from them and hopefully draw them off the GhostFin. If not, she might just as well die. Her exile had made her reckless…carefree. Better to die in such a proud way than whimpering away in the night.

Only a single one of the fierce HunterKin pack left the GhostFin to dispense with the meddling Whistler. The other four continued ravaging the gray giant, who had not failed to perceive Piper's antics. The old whale was not sure, but it appeared that the chattering little dolphin was *risking its life for him*. Or had it simply been touched by some madness of the sea? But the whale had no time to ponder this, as four of the orcas resumed their attack. So he fought on with renewed effort.

It was one of the females that attacked Piper, plunging straight at her, jaws agape. Piper thrashed her flukes and, with one strong, horizontal wave of her body, inverted herself and spiraled down under the onrushing killer whale. The huge black-and-white Hunter shrieked, not expecting so coy a maneuver, and dove down after the young Whistler. But the clever speedster of Kwi Coast surprised her attacker again. She twirled round and spun back up, only inches from the plummeting she-orca's dorsal fin.

Piper's attacker saw the ruse too late to check her own speed and continued on a downward plunge as the young dolphin flew safely toward the surface. Piper broke through the waves in a plume of blue-and-white spray, gasped heartily for air as she careened nearly ten feet above the water, and plunged straight back down— *toward the climbing predatory killer whale*.

The maneuver shocked the orca. Here was a Whistler actually charging! More for leverage than concern for the Whistler's strong beak thrust, the killer whale shifted away to get a better angle for a quick bite. But at that instant, Piper veered away, squealing in mock victory.

"Oooh, but the HunterKin are indeed brave—so brave that they turn aside for the WhistlingFin! Who are masters of the seas now, my clumsy *cousins*?" And with that, Piper spiraled into the midst of the thundering battle with the GhostFin, the fuming female orca hot in pursuit.

Piper flew past the young killer bull as it flirted with the torn, bleeding tail of the GhostFin. The old whale's plodding swipes had been ineffective against the lightning thrusts of the much swifter orcas. The GhostFin's barnacle-crusted body was shredded from countless bites, but he fought on valiantly. He saw the brave little dolphin swim in, and it looked as though the sleek creature was trying to draw off the one attacker that still gnawed at his tail. The gray giant echoed in the distance between the prowling female killer whale and the brave young dolphin. He detected the younger bull disengaging to lash out at the fleeing Whistler, whose uncanny speed made the old whale marvel in quiet amazement.

Through the pain of the ceaseless biting at his torn stomach and jaws, and through the sting in his eyes, the half-blinded gray whale homed in and measured the distance between the she-Hunter and the Whistler. He thrashed twice with his massive flukes.

The young bull orca saw the tail too late to completely avoid it. He went sprawling from the force of the mighty swipe which had merely grazed him. The female Hunter did not fare as well. She had been too obsessed with seizing the chattering Whistler that had embarrassed her and never knew what struck her. She had paid no heed to the giant cetacean's second swipe, which, with all the momentum gained from the first, slammed into her body with the impact of a cannon shot. There was a ghastly squeal as the she-orca's insides exploded under the thundering force of tons of flailing gray fury.

A limp black-and-white carcass sank to the depths.

The gray behemoth then turned on his three remaining assailants. Now all was different. Though their quarry was severely cut and bleeding, there were but three left to continue the attack. The older bull knew the GhostFins were more dangerous when wounded.

The gray giant charged, its oversized underjaw clamped tight to its bleeding upper lip. The vast mountain of gray blubber and hide churned toward the remaining three HunterKin like a speeding express train. They parted barely in time as he ploughed by. The force of his charge stirred up fierce undercurrents which threw his trio of smaller foes spinning over in a swirl of flukes and fins.

By now the young bull had regained his senses enough to paddle erratically over to where his companions had been flung by the fury of the gray whale's charge. A circle of scavenging blue sharks had gathered nearby, awaiting the battle's outcome. Below, some of them had followed the sinking carcass of the she-orca to the depths, where a grotesque feeding ritual had already begun. The smaller Snag-Tooth party had yielded the sinking carcass to the others for the moment. Now they were attracted by the younger bull's erratic paddling.

The four orcas huddled together, eying their giant adversary and its diminutive rescuer. The black slits that were their eyes flashed like angry storm clouds as they surveyed the two.

It was over.

The lead bull's large white teeth glowed in the murk of the gray-blue sea. The round mouth opened in what seemed a wide leer. Piper shuddered at the sight of the great white circle of teeth, realizing that one snap of those powerful jaws could end her life. She scuttled closer to the gray hulk of the GhostFin.

"We shall remember you—brash little Whistler!" roared the older bull, his jaws raised up so hideously that it almost seemed to Piper that the sound came right from the orca's mouth and not from his blowhole. Then he eyed the wispy forms of the circling Snag-Tooth.

The rapidly massing sharks had sensed the fierce orca poise ebbing and were drawing closer.

"You will regret your bold taunts, oh, light-skinned one. For the misery you have caused us here, I myself will tear out your tongue and feed it to our younglings. Then we shall see how you dare mock the HunterKin!" With that, the pack of four vanished, for the swarming Snag-Tooth were growing in numbers and closing in— while the GhostFin had begun mounting another charge. The disoriented killer whales were not willing to risk yet another untimely death.

Piper remained where she was, shaken by the grim promise of the orca pack leader. She was unsure what to do next as she found herself alone in the company of a mysterious sea giant, a creature she had known only in the lore of legend...while below lurked an ever-gathering horde of hungry Snag-Tooth.

Chapter Twelve
SlugFlukes

Even in its battered state the beast bore an air of majesty, the likes of which Piper had never beheld in any living creature. Over fifty feet in length, its vast gray bulk reminded her of the Floaters she used to play with in the Kwi Coast surf and, for some foolish reason, the young Whistler pictured herself cruising along the surface in a "bow-spurt" created by the GhostFin's powerful thrashings.

Still, she was nervous. She had saved the creature's life, but in its shaken state it may yet harbor hostility toward anything that dared approach it. So Piper held her distance and waited in the foaming murk. The GhostFin absolutely fascinated her. Its face, grizzled and aged, bore the same rumpled look as old RamStrong. Yet there was also an air of gentleness about this behemoth of the open waters. She felt sure of that. But she had just witnessed the gray giant sending a twenty-foot-long Hunter splattering to its death with but a single swipe of its flukes. She was loath to draw closer.

Then Piper felt a wave of impulses beaming softly into her head: *a visual image of her valiant rescue.* She saw once more how cleverly she had duped the killer whale pack…how she had outsmarted the big she-Hunter and drawn it into a coy trap. The sound waves echoing toward her were quiet and gentle. A sense of warmth swept through the young dolphin now. She felt proud. She wished QuickFin could have witnessed her actions here, for he would have seen that his advice had not gone unheeded. And what other Whistler of Kwi Coast—even old RamStrong himself—would have dared defy those yawning jaws of death? Even the mighty Snag-Tooth were leery of challenging the powerful HunterKin. And reminded suddenly of another danger, Piper glanced around and behind, but a quick scan showed that the Snag-Tooth scavengers had followed after the small group of Hunters, staying just far enough behind to be safe should the fierce orcas suddenly turn on them. Likely the Snag-Tooth were waiting for the wounded young bull to falter.

Though the GhostFin bled profusely and was spent from the deadly attack by the orcas, he was still far too formidable a target for these sharks, the largest of them twelve-foot lemons and blues. The great bulk of the gray giant and the might it still wielded in its huge flukes posed more danger than they cared to risk, despite their own numbers. The wounded orca swimming erratically behind the small group of its own HunterKin seemed a more pragmatic victim. So they followed, waiting for the young bull to fall farther behind.

Piper now saw that it was through guile and cunning that one survived in the Open Sea—much more than through brute strength, or even speed. The blind fears which had previously plagued her throughout her exile had faded, and she felt herself filling with a sense of pride as she relived the rescue of the GhostFin. She had never realized she possessed such courage.

Then the young Whistler heard a gravelly voice that rumbled like the roll of distant thunder.

"Come, little friend, there is nothing to fear in me."

It was the first friendly sound Piper had heard since she'd been cast out from Kwi Coast. So she forsook all sense of caution, trusting to the giant's gentle tone, and fluttered in closer, trilling quietly in delight. The massive head of the GhostFin appeared to her like a craggy sea cliff, a shining orb peering out wistfully from either side. The gray whale waited patiently for a response.

"I…I am called Piper," she squeaked softly, awed by the huge angular face that studied her with interest. Such intelligence she had never sensed in the presence of another living being. How could the HunterKin even think of slaying—worst of all—*feeding* on such a stately creature? For were not the BigFins and HunterKin and WhistlingFin all *Spurters*…all of the same lot? True, all those who dwelled in the sea must feed, but…

"You are different from the SongFins I have known in these waters," rumbled the gray giant as a parade of huge bubbles burst out from his wide blowhole. "You've come far, for I have seen your breed only in the Eastern Seas."

Piper was charmed by that name: "SongFins." Was that what the WhistlingFin were called here? It pleased her. But the GhostFin spoke of her home as the *Eastern Seas*. Had she truly traveled so far that her own LongBeaked breed was rare in these waters? Piper had no sense of how far across the mighty Pacific she had gone. It was more than her young mind could conceive at the moment. But it mattered not. She had found a friend—one whose mighty presence overwhelmed her. She was especially taken with the GhostFin's immense lower jaw, so much out of proportion with the upper half. And the whale's stern snout fairly amused her, for it looked more like the rough prow of a large Floater. Piper felt sure that, in a rage, this BigFin, whose lower jaw alone dwarfed the largest of Whistlers, was capable of smashing a Floater to bits! He would make a terrible enemy.

She spoke again, cautiously and with all the courtesy she could muster. "How do you feel now...after your terrible fight with those HunterKin?"

The answer, of course, was quite obvious, for the deep gashes along his eyes and mouth bled freely, causing streams of discolored dark green blood to mix with the gray waters around him. His movements were erratic, due to his fins and flukes having been ravaged. But the GhostFin remained poised.

"Oh, I am much better now than earlier," he said in a booming, humorous voice. "And make no mistake, little SongFin, eh...Piper—if not for your courage and wit..." He did not finish the thought.

Piper ruffled her flukes in pleasure, mildly embarrassed by his praise.

"I am curious how you have come to be here, this far from your Eastern Seas—and all alone," the whale continued. "But as your need for air is greater than mine, we might best find our way above the waves first, mmm?"

Piper was relieved, for her lungs felt as if they might burst at any moment. So, together, whale and dolphin soared for the surface. Piper broke the waves in her usual flamboyance, careening high into the air

while tossing herself over in an elegant back flip.
Meanwhile, the old whale smashed through the rolling
swells, causing a mountainous waterfall of foaming
blue. He blew a gusty spray of vapor and water out
from his blowhole, which rose at least ten feet into the
afternoon air. He watched Piper silently, thinking that
she was indeed a coastal SongFin, though that seemed
unusual for her LongBeak breed. She seemed to bear
many of the traits and antics of the Jumping SongFins
who roamed the Open Seas and often frequented these
very western waters.

Above the surface, the two cetacean cousins
resumed their thoughts together.

"My name is SlugFlukes, aptly so for my slowness.
That is why the HunterKin find me such tempting prey.
We GhostFins keep a lagging pace, at best. And as you
saw, our skills as fighters are limited to lucky swipes
with our tails...or a good head-on ramming. It is not
often we are fortunate enough to strike as I did, with
your help. But when we do, it reminds those killing
brutes of our might...and for a brief while they lose
their stomach for the fight."

SlugFlukes spoke as slowly as he moved; his
grinding voice sounded like a great freighter cranking
up in port, every word being uttered from his blowhole
with a meticulous deliberation. "There are few of my
kind left in the sea. Quite possibly, I may even be the
last of them still here in these waters. And if not for
your courage, little SongFin...Well, in time, I shall
repay that kindness."

Piper wagged her white-lined forehead back and
forth, the two cross-marks on her brow fairly twitching
as she spoke. "There is nothing to repay,

eh…SlugFlukes. Any SongFin would have—"

"No, my little white-finned beauty," said SlugFlukes, regarding her with quiet admiration. "I have long roamed these Western Seas, and have visited the Eastern Seas too. The SongFins of the East are a brasher breed than the more timid ones here—but make no mistake: not *any* of your kind would have acted so boldly. And though you might say you did so merely for the sake of companionship, what old SlugFlukes feels is truly in your heart cannot be hid."

Piper was amazed how much this magnificent giant could perceive. How could the HunterKin—with all their supposed intelligence—fail to recognize the wonder of such a creature? This huge Spurter might easily have taken her help for granted and abandoned her to the mercy of the enraged pack. But he had stayed to protect her, knowing well that his tormentors might have resumed their attack, or signaled help from others of their own not far off. Theirs was a breed renowned for its fierce pride and rarely did the HunterKin depart without their quarry. For like any other creatures of the sea, they too needed to eat. Piper felt certain they'd have taken it out on her for foiling their hunt, had the GhostFin not remained.

And now this SlugFlukes, as he called himself, wanted to befriend her. For the first time since her exile from Kwi Coast, the young Whistler felt comforted. She welcomed the gray whale's friendship—and his protection. She had not forgotten that last threat from the large orca bull. And she felt sure such fierce creatures did not bluff.

"How is it you have strayed so far from your Pod…Piper?" asked SlugFlukes, interrupting her thoughts. "SongFins, as I know them, rarely travel alone...especially so far."

The GhostFin's eyes sparked with a glow of wisdom gathered over many seasons. Piper felt certain he was older than Commodore RamStrong or the other Pod Elders. She wanted to tell SlugFlukes everything— her loves, her hopes, her fears...there was nothing she wanted to hide, for she could learn much from him. So she nodded, and together they dove beneath the waves, making a bizarre pair indeed.

And Piper told her tale.

She spoke to him of Kwi Coast, and of Commodore RamStrong, and of her Pod's strange Code. And as she explained the dark fears the Clan held of the Snag-Tooth—and what LoFin the Rover had told her of those fearful scavengers that plagued the weak and the wounded—the lumbering old whale, still bleeding from his many cuts, wished the SongFin would hurry on to another part of her story. He knew the porpoise was accurate in its knowledge of the toothy predators...and that it was only his great size and strained efforts to bear the pain by swimming casually, that kept a distant trailing dozen of the silent killers from soaring in and having at them.

The GhostFin had scanned their almost magical emergence earlier and had tried not to give off any telltale distress signals, absorbing himself, instead, more fully in Piper's remarkable story. He listened with great interest as she spoke of her brother, QuickFin. Her obvious love for him made the old whale sad as he guessed how much she dearly missed him. And it was with amusement that SlugFlukes listened to her go on about Buffer and the mixed opinions she had voiced of the swaggering young bull's odd courtship. It made him think back to well over forty seasons…when he had courted a young she-gray in the topsy-turvy way in which only youth can blunder so gracefully. This, too, made SlugFlukes sad. For he also recalled the fate of that young gray, and how he still mourned her.

They paddled on over towering oceanic mountain ranges and cloven valleys and long undersea meadows. Sometimes they rolled to the surface to breathe, and Piper noticed SlugFlukes did not need to do that as often as she did. But most of the time they stayed beneath the waves and enjoyed the dazzling frontier of the sea. And as they passed through a colored fog of drifting seaweed and floating algae, Piper quietly mentioned the dreadful Black Waters—and the terrible Cold Lord, Arkitu, who "ruled the sea's abysmal depths."

For the first time since she had begun her tale, SlugFlukes reacted, giving a strong shake of his big flippers. He seemed about to interrupt, but then thought better of it. Piper took it as a sign that it might be best not to discuss the Cold Lord too much, especially here in the midst of the Great Sea with nightfall not far off. So she moved on to the tragic attack on the Basker and how she had come to be banished for her "treachery against the Pod."

SlugFlukes grew especially somber during this part of the tale. The account of the Basker fascinated him more than anything else. Never in his lifetime had he heard of such a Clan of SongFins. What cruel reasoning, he thought, could warrant casting a young innocent like this gentle creature to the mercy of unknown terrors? Why, this barely half-grown SongFin knew almost nothing of a world in which she should have been romping freely her entire young life. Who would ever believe that a band of intelligent SongFins could be foolish enough to isolate themselves—and near a *cove*, of all places. And to entertain such mad superstitions…that was not at all like their breed.

"Well I must say, Piper, this pod of yours is quite, eh…rare," rumbled the old whale as they rose above the surf and glimpsed a flock of frigate seabirds soaring toward the red of the setting sun.

"Was LoFin right, SlugFlukes?" asked Piper eagerly. "Was she right about the Snag-Tooth? Are they really just mindless scrap eaters?"

"Well, eh…hmph! Not really. That is, not entirely," said SlugFlukes.

Piper felt dejected. Wasn't there anyone who knew the truth about them?

"That is," continued SlugFlukes, "your friend the Rover is not entirely wrong, either. It's just that the Snag-Tooth are indeed rather crafty hunters. They have roamed these seas even longer than my kind—or any other Spurter, for that matter."

Piper remembered LoFin mentioning something of that sort, but the Rover had not seemed particularly clear on it. The porpoise had told her of things she had *heard;* the old gray whale, who had seen so much more, spoke of what he *knew*.

"Why, once the Snag-Tooth were masters of the seas!" boomed SlugFlukes.

Piper was shocked to hear that.

"There were even some that grew to be as large as me—even bigger!" he emphasized huskily, flaunting his massive fifty-foot frame.

And with that, Piper thought back to the giant of a Snag-Tooth that had stalked her weeks earlier. She shuddered. What had SlugFlukes just said? That the Snag-Tooth were once masters of the seas? Wasn't that what old RamStrong had always feared? Now she was truly confused. Did the Snag-Tooth want their "rule" back? And was it the Spurters that had overthrown the Snag-Tooth so long ago? Did the Snag-Tooth now want revenge?

"But that was all long ago, before the time of even my eldest ancestors," said SlugFlukes, aware he may have frightened the youngster terribly—for he caught the look of horror on her thin face. So he felt it best not to tell her that he had *seen* the White Giants of the Snag-Tooth race, some as large as the HunterKin—some even larger. Large enough so he himself would have fled them.

And Piper, in her eagerness to befriend the GhostFin, had left out certain parts of her odyssey…including the monster that had followed her. Such things, like her terror of the dreadful Black Waters, were too frightening for her to yet speak of completely. Despite her resistance to the ways of Kwi Coast, Piper had still succumbed to the strength of many dark fears that had been implanted in her since birth.

SlugFlukes widened his mouth like a yawning sea cavern. Streams of filmy baleen draped down from his upper jaw while he took in a generous heap of drifting little *krill* creatures, the first of many batches he would feed on. It was necessary for so large a beast to feed often, for it took massive portions of his miniature prey to nourish his forty-ton frame.

He continued his tale after he strained the gobs of tiny delicacies from between the filters of his fiber-like baleen strands, then spewed out the water. "It is likely that the early Snag-Tooth resented the coming of the first Spurters, for it brought to the seas a greater cunning. Now there was *more* to survival than natural hunting skills, for the Spurters had an edge over all the GillFins—including the Snag-Tooth. Many of the sea resented the early Spurters. They thought of our kind as freaks that belonged back on the land, since we have to rise to the surface to breathe…so it is to this very day. 'HalfGills' they called us. Intruders! And when the Snag-Tooth saw that these 'intruders' nearly matched them in size—for the Snag-Tooth back then grew far larger than those of today—they felt threatened. Even some that roam the seas now are thought to feel that way about us. And it is no lie about those silent killers being a cruel and ruthless lot who bask in their power over weaker beings. Just look at their harsh hunting ways."

SlugFlukes paused a moment, as though he was reconsidering his next thoughts. And while he did, Piper marveled at how much of what he had said so closely paralleled the very words of LoFin. Her respect for the chatty Rover increased. And though the porpoise clearly was not as versed on the lore of the sea as SlugFlukes, she still knew more about it than all the supposed learned minds of Kwi Coast. Never again would Piper doubt LoFin's wisdom.

"What about the Great Invasion, SlugFlukes?" asked Piper.

"Oh, I don't foresee any sort of war the Snag-Tooth might be planning. No, your roving friend was right about that—the Snag-Tooth would only wind up quarrelling so much among one another they would probably chew each other to bits in one of their Mad-Eating crazes. And that, my fine SongFin, is nothing to scoff at. It is one of the few times you will actually see them band together. It is a fiendish lust for blood that draws them, along with the frantic sounds of those expected to bleed. That is what lures them into those terrible 'Fury Packs,' as your Commodore calls them... not revenge or any desire to rule the sea. The Snag-Tooth cannot control their madness any more than they would be able to settle down long enough to organize themselves."

SlugFlukes' scarred face grew very dark and his gray eyes flashed coldly again. "But I caution you, Piper...*Do not underestimate their cunning*! Whether it's a lone Snag-Tooth or a small band that has even accidentally grouped together, all are as sly and dangerous as a pack of HunterKin. They may be wild and unruly, even simple, but they are not stupid!"

Piper trembled as SlugFlukes pounded in that last point. "Then there really is no cause to quarrel with them, is there?" She snared a small herring as she spoke, twisting it deftly in her long mouth, then swallowed it in a twinkling.

"Of course not," grumbled SlugFlukes. "Nor was there cause for your brute of a Commodore to order your Pod to slay the Basker you told me of. That creature was no more menace to you than I am. Your clan was behaving more like HunterKin, not SongFins!" rumbled SlugFlukes. And as he spoke the last few words, his gentle old features seemed almost to twist into a scowl. The gray whale's barnacle-crusted face flushed with a dark wave of anger, and his fins tightened. "And as for your terrible Black Waters, I suspect where that folly has come from, too."

The young dolphin bristled uncomfortably at that. SlugFlukes noticed and softened his tone.

"All I can say, Piper, is that there are indeed many dreadful creatures and queer mysteries that lurk in the Cold Depths—where the SongFin should not venture anyway—but in my entire life, I have never known of a 'Lord Arkitu who rules them all.' "

Of all the GhostFin had reflected on, only the Black Waters maintained the same frightful effect on the superstitious youngster. And though it did her well to hear old SlugFlukes scoff at much of it, Piper knew that, by the dark of night, it would take more than their talk here to quell such inbred fears.

"SlugFlukes?" called Piper, as they surfaced again. She fluttered nervously, wondering if she were asking too many questions. She could see the old GhostFin was tired and that his wounds bothered him a good deal more than he let on. She had noticed him scanning the distance earlier, likely for signs of the band of roving Snag-Tooth that had picked up on his trail of blood. But the scavenging pack seemed to have gone on in search of smaller, easier prey. She sensed the old whale's pain as she scanned in directly on his movements.

"Is it the HunterKin, then, that we…SongFins need fear most? Are they our greatest threat? After all, they hunt and kill other Spurters and…nearly slew you, and…" Piper stumbled over her own words, not knowing quite how to say what she was thinking. "I mean, I'm sure the HunterKin have slain many GhostFins and SongFins and Rovers…"

SlugFlukes grew silent and pensive. He stopped. They were about twenty feet below the surface, directly beneath a swarm of globby jellyfish whose thousands of colors defied imagination. He gazed squarely at her with one of his great oval eyes and regarded her thoughtfully.

"No, my brave little SongFin," he said softly. "Our worst enemies are the Killer Imps. There is nothing in all the seas so foul and cruel as they." SlugFlukes paused, his broad, weathered face looking as if it were holding back a silent scream of rage. "They murdered my entire Pod."

Chapter Thirteen
Dark Mysteries

Piper remained with SlugFlukes, travelling with him day after day. The taciturn old whale shared with her much of the lore of the sea, and often she marveled at how sheltered she and the rest of her reclusive Clan had long been. In a mere fortnight, the two weeks she had spent with him, she realized how complex the sea truly was, so much more than any at Kwi Coast could have imagined. And she was filled with a swelling pride that she had survived what few of her Pod could have endured.

She had even grown less fearful of the night, for SlugFlukes' hulking presence was forever there. And though she had not forgotten her lore of the Black Waters, many of her other fears had been curbed as she became more familiar with the night sea. And now that she had seen the notorious HunterKin, she realized that even they were vulnerable.

Still, Piper would never be able to erase the memory of the absolute fury she had seen in the eye of the great Hunter bull when he'd uttered his ghastly oath to tear out her tongue. Truly, such creatures had to be the most wicked of all living things, for what other would kill their own Kin and eat them? Was it not the HunterKin who called themselves "Masters of the Seas?" And were *they* not the mortal enemy RamStrong should have feared instead of the Snag-Tooth?

It seemed only SlugFlukes could answer such questions—especially about this mysterious and terrible creature called Killer Imp. For, if these Imps were so wicked and dangerous, how was it she had never heard anything about them before...not even from LoFin? But SlugFlukes had grown loathe to discuss such matters any further, and he would speak only of the sea's beauty and the best ways to hunt and survive.

His wounds had healed considerably, though there were still ugly white gashes over his mouth, eyes, and flukes where the orcas had bitten deeply. He had gained back full control of his movements, though his swimming pattern was still erratic at times. But it was strong enough so it no longer sent out invitations to hungry Snag-Tooth. Before long, the old whale would be healthy and fit again. The remnants of cuts and sores would soon fade into the rest of the network of scars that smothered his hide.

It was during a cool morning when the air was very wet with the sea's moisture that Piper finally asked SlugFlukes something that had troubled her for so long. They were in the midst of scouting out the prime feeding regions for plankton and krill, and for the mackerel and herring which Piper fed on, when she raised the question.

"Is it because of the HunterKin that we've not yet seen any SongFins?" she asked, for she ached for even a glimpse of another Whistler and the sweet sound of their shrill calls. Fond as she had grown of the old GhostFin, Piper still missed her own kind. She was disturbed that she had not come across any since the beginning of her exile—though much of that had been due to the extreme caution she had exercised in journeying the sea.

"No," he answered quietly. "They too fell victim to the Killer Imps when those Evil Ones were here not long ago."

Piper was startled by the answer. Not so much by what he said, but that the taciturn old whale had once more brought up the subject. She pressed him to continue, but he stiffened. She trembled at the fearful way in which one such as SlugFlukes regarded creatures so seemingly mysterious and dangerous. How was it that the Commodore and Thane SilverFlukes knew all about the Black Waters and all the other terrors of the seas, but not these Killer Imps? SlugFlukes assured her that in good time she would have answers to all her questions.

****

Another week went by. Piper found that the Pacific waters of the Western Seas were more bright and colorful than those of her eastern home. And with each passing dawn she grew fonder of SlugFlukes. His bizarre feeding habits never ceased to amaze her. It was always a spectacle to behold the awesome sight of the gray whale's huge, cave-like mouth widening and gathering in the globs of minute brown-and-red krill creatures. Piper wondered how SlugFlukes ever found time to do anything else than feed, given the demands of his massive appetite. But how magnificent he was, she would think to herself, so gentle and wise. If only she could have brought him back to Kwi Coast; perhaps his wisdom could persuade her Pod to abandon its folly and maybe even come out from its little cove hideaway. And she wondered how Buffer would react to a creature like SlugFlukes, for he was always impressed with size and strength.

And what would Commodore RamStrong and the Elders have to say if they knew the truth about the Snag-Tooth? SlugFlukes would certainly give the High Clan something to think about. Perhaps, if she ever returned, she might convince Thane SilverFlukes of the beautiful world beyond Kwi Coast. Piper wondered if the Clan even believed her dead by now. It had been sixty dawns since she'd been cast out.

Such moments of sorrow did not go unnoticed by the insightful old whale. He sensed the young SongFin's growing need for her old ways and, from her talk of Kwi Coast, the two invented a game. SlugFlukes would cruise along the surface when the waters churned and heaved on stormy days, causing a funnel of swells in his own wake. Then Piper would leap and twirl in it, as she had in the wakes of Floaters back at Kwi Coast. And she shuddered when the old GhostFin actually cautioned her about such play with the Humunz' Floaters—for she had heard the very same from LoFin.

Times such as these were merry ones, and they allowed Piper to push her sorrow into the back of her mind, giving SlugFlukes a relief from her persistent queries about the ruthless Killer Imps. The time was coming, though, when she would finally see them—and he knew he would then have to restrain her from making the terrible mistake of answering the call of fellow SongFin that were doomed.

It came one day while SlugFlukes was teaching her to conserve air on deeper dives. They were well below the hundred-foot level that dolphins normally held to. SlugFlukes, of course, had the resources to remain under twice as long as dolphins and at much greater depths. Now he had taught Piper to do the same, restricting the amount of bubbles she blew out and only at intervals. It allowed her to go longer without having to surface as frequently. He knew it would benefit her in time.

The cry came, distant and sharp, during one of those long dives. *Whistlers*. There was no mistaking the sound, and Piper felt every fiber of her being quiver in nervous excitement. She grew unbearably restless. She wanted to be off with them, but SlugFlukes grew suddenly very cross with her, telling her she would be following them to her doom. Piper no longer cared for cautions and lessons, or further talk of the HunterKin and Snag-Tooth and Killer Imps. Now she wanted only to feel the gentle rubbing of the silky Whistler skin and to be among their chatty, gossipy antics once more. It made her recall when a small band of wanderlust Rovers had swept by once. She had wished they would stop to talk and romp a bit with her and the old GhostFin. But the porpoises had been in a hurry and scurried along, as if a matter of great urgency was upon them.

"They know these waters," SlugFlukes had said. "The Rovers are more cautious than our Western SongFins. They have witnessed the coming of the Killer Imps—and they do not wish to tarry where there is such peril."

Killer Imps…*perils*, thought Piper as she recalled the coming and going of the porpoise band. She had finally grown weary of it all. As much as she had come to love this gentle giant of the sea, she had begun to wonder if age had touched him. But she did not wish to aggravate him further, so she restrained herself and did her best to ignore the distant call of the Western Whistlers. There would be more of them, she felt sure.

As the days went on, Piper could not help feeling that SlugFlukes' obsession with the Killer Imps was not unlike the Commodore's dread of the Snag-Tooth. Hadn't the loss of their Pods driven them both into wild fears of other creatures? She began to understand the Commodore a bit more and wondered now if she should have scorned him so. She saw plainly, through SlugFlukes' misery, what the slaughter of loved ones might cause. Perhaps these Killer Imps were just simple hunters like the Snag-Tooth. It was hard to believe there could be anything so horrible in this wonder of a sea. She no longer wanted to dwell on these mysterious marauders that SlugFlukes spoke of with such dread.

A sandy shoreline was not far off, and it brought back familiar feelings. Piper was homesick. The looming sight of the nearing coastline was a comfort to her, and though there were sharks the size of dolphins roaming these coastal waters, it did not alarm her. The Snag-Tooth here seemed a natural part of this environment, paying little heed to anything else around them. There were dusky sharks and bull sharks, with their brown-and-gray markings, and even the sleek blues, whose sinister appearance yet bore an air of majesty and grace. Piper wondered if she ever might speak with one of these Snag-Tooth and perhaps learn from them something of their ways—rather than always being told everything by others. Whether the sharks were ignoring her due to SlugFlukes' intimidating presence or because they had already fed, she did not know. But they did fascinate her. It was the first time she had ever been able to observe the Snag-Tooth so openly, and without fear.

Throughout their approach into the shallow coastal zone, SlugFlukes had grown very somber—off somewhere in his own thoughts. He had been aware of Piper's growing fascination with the very different world of the West, and he was pleased by it. Even her probing queries about where they were going did not seem to bother him as much. He knew that a probing mind was an active one. The time he'd spent with the young SongFin made him understand what it would have been like had the chance to father a youngling been granted him. And he did not want to see this beautiful creature meet the same fate as his onetime Clan. But he also understood she was growing restless and that the time was near when she would learn one of the most horrid truths of the sea.

One day, as Piper tumbled and careened in the roaring breakers of SlugFlukes' wake, the gray giant homed in on the sounds of a small pod of spinner dolphins a few miles off the coast of Iki, Japan. From the direction of their movements, and the unmistakable traits of the fish they chased, he knew their destination—and their fate.

"Today, Piper," he said, halting suddenly and causing her to crash into the slow-rolling swells, "today, you will learn the lesson few have learned and lived to tell. What you will see this day you will pass on to your own younglings, and they shall pass it on to theirs," he added darkly. "Ask few questions and watch closely. And above all"—the gray whale's crusty face hardened—"*stay by me at all times* if you wish to see another dawn. Now come!"

Chapter Fourteen
The Killer Imps

Piper was shaken by her big friend's cryptic warning. Her curiosity of the Killer Imps had been piqued once more. With each passing day the GhostFin's manner had grown more sullen, and the sizzling caution he had just uttered was the most he had spoken since entering the dark, moody waters. So she followed without question, and SlugFlukes was not displeased by it.

Soon they cruised through a murky sea, stained by a slimy ooze that felt alien to the water itself. SlugFlukes appeared somewhat accustomed to it, though Piper wriggled in discomfort at its very touch...her first experience of swimming through waters streaked with oil. A recent storm had stirred the sand and mud up from the bottom and strewn it all about. The surface was chilly and unpleasant, and the entire coastal region was still under a grim cloudy sky. It was a day that bore ill tidings.

It was not long before they heard the shrill piping of the Western WhistlingFin. SlugFlukes, having once again anticipated the difficulty Piper would feel in resisting the strong urge to follow, grunted a warning for her to contain herself. When the dolphins were a mile away, Piper echoed onto them. There were twelve playful Jumpers, light and sleek and active, very much like herself, the sort RamStrong used to chase away from Kwi Coast. They careened in the choppy surf as they cruised along the shoreline, the way Piper always had in the past. She grew restless and anxious.

Farther on, Piper and SlugFlukes sallied through the hazy sea until finally they saw the small pod. Piper's first glimpse of the playful dolphins sent tremors of excitement through her. These were the first Whistlers she had caught sight of since she had watched Thane SilverFlukes paddling away from her the day her exile began. They were beautiful! She liked them instantly. A mad desire to follow swept through her; she wanted to swim with them, hunt, play—even drill if necessary—anything to be with her own kind again! What harm was there in what they were doing, where they were going? What doom? She could see nothing wrong here.

Once more the sage old gray whale anticipated Piper's reaction. He rumbled another of his bleak warnings for her to stay by his side.

"But they are in no danger," protested Piper testily. She beat her tail annoyingly at the loping swells that tussled them both about. "You must be mistaken, good SlugFlukes," she said, wagging her beak back and forth.

"FOOL!" roared the old gray whale. "You know nothing of the evil in these waters! Do you think I have brought you here just to let you play with a band of silly SongFins?" His craggy head shook as he spoke, and the dull gray of his eyes swirled like a brooding storm. "They are doomed—do you understand? Doomed!" He thrashed his enormous flukes emphatically, causing a flurry of whirling eddies to fly out from its wake. The force of it sent Piper spinning sideways several times. For that instant she was frightened by the fury of her giant companion; but a benign look from the whale assured her it was only a chiding—that his patience had but worn thin.

"This little band is going to be slaughtered. They will die in the ambush the Killer Imps have prepared for them," SlugFlukes said in a more subdued tone, for he saw that he truly had alarmed the youngster with his outburst.

"Why don't you warn them?" asked Piper meekly.

"Because they never listen. They think SlugFlukes is a *mad* old fool who tells such tales because his tired brain has gone on too long. Do you think so too?" he boomed.

Piper wagged her head no.

"Ah...there we are," said SlugFlukes. "You see that school of GillFin they are following?"

Piper looked and saw a swarm of brownish-red fish, all with bright yellow tails. She was puzzled. Were *these* the mighty Killer Imps the GhostFin spoke of with such awe? Why, they seemed hardly a match for the smaller GillFin she herself often hunted. *Was* the old GhostFin beyond his years? Had he gone mad, as she had thought of the old Commodore?

"What do the Killer Imps do to my kind?" Piper said quietly, not sure why she was asking.

"They slay them and eat them," SlugFlukes said bluntly. "And they do other dread things that none in the sea can truly understand." He thundered along, only some fifty yards from the streaking pod.

Piper trembled with growing perturbation, though not fully knowing why.

"There is much to learn here now," he said. "Ask no more questions, but watch!"

So Piper followed in silence, confused by the perplexities of this great GhostFin and his cryptic words. They were roughly a hundred yards from a rocky shoreline that was being bombarded by an onslaught of sizzling breakers. The Jumping Whistlers were making for a small dark cove. They were closing on the odd yellow-tailed fish—and the spinner dolphins' apparent lust for the meal reminded Piper of the Snag-Tooth horde that had descended upon the sinking orca carcass.

"The little yellow-tailed GillFin always swim into these shallows when the sea is angry," said SlugFlukes. "The Imps know this. They also know that the SongFins will follow the GillFins in there, for the Killer Imps and the Jumping SongFin both feed on them."

That explained the yellow-tails, thought Piper. But where were these deadly marauding Imps that SlugFlukes kept speaking of?

She did not have long to wait for the answer.

No sooner had the Jumpers zoomed into the shallows when suddenly the murky cove was swarming with *Humunz*—Land Dwellers who sprang out from behind the nearby rocks! Some of them swung large sticks and clubs that were thick and blunt; others wielded long, sharp poles.

Piper watched in horror at what she beheld next. The shrieking men scurried around in the shallows of the cove, jabbing their pointed sticks into the midst of the confused spinner dolphins, while those who bore the heavier sticks clubbed the helpless Whistlers over their heads. The pathetic cries of the trapped dolphins reached Piper as she huddled closer to SlugFlukes.

"I tried warning that very group," muttered SlugFlukes. "They laughed at me. They said the Land Dwellers were their friends because their Floaters always led them to the best feeding zones, because they had seen the local Humunz hunting and killing the Snag-Tooth. Now see their friends," he said gravely. "Do you believe the horror of the Killer Imps now, my little Eastern SongFin? Is old SlugFlukes so *mad*…eh? Or does he know the sea?"

Piper trembled. "Oh…SlugFlukes, I am so sorry for ever doubting you!" cried Piper. She could not bear the pitiful screams and whimpers of the tormented pod any longer—or the grisly howling of the predatory little fishermen. Her blood chilled, and for the first time in her life, Piper understood *hate*.

"Let us be gone," said SlugFlukes, "for I have long been sickened by this."

And the two turned and swam away from the Dark Cove.

Chapter Fifteen
Lore of the GhostFins

Piper swam listlessly through the Open Sea, trying to blot out the gruesome incident along the coast of Japan. It was nearing nightfall, and the blackening sea was a gloomy reminder of the day's evil. Since her departure from Kwi Coast over two months ago, nothing had filled her with as much horror as the ugly display by the brutal Killer Imps. And, after a seemingly endless stretch of quietly drifting through darkening, oil-stained waters, SlugFlukes finally broke the silence and began his full tale.

"Long ago, we GhostFins were many, and were then known as the GrayFins. We used to spend the warm seasons in these very waters here—which were a good deal cleaner and of greater comfort then—and other times we visited waters not far from where your own Pod dwells. When the cold seasons came, we always went south to the Eastern Seas where we bred in the comfort of the shallows...much like those we visited today. And we thrived throughout the seas, getting on well with the other BigFins—for there are others about that are much like us, but different, too— of whom I will tell you sometime."

SlugFlukes paused a moment, then added in a dry tone, "Oh, yes, the HunterKin still stalked us, but we learned to band together and drive them off so they

118

could only prey upon stragglers, or the weak and sick who had strayed away from the rest of us. You see, the HunterKin are not unlike the Snag-Tooth in that they kill only to survive...though my ancestors, like us, wished they ate something other than their kind when they hungered." The GhostFin paused solemnly. "Then the LandFolk came in their big Floaters—well over two hundred seasons past—tiny beings next to us...but Imps with a lust for killing."

Piper shuddered as she recalled again what LoFin the Harbor Waif had told her: "I wish only to caution you of your play with the Humunz...and to *stay clear of their Floaters.*" How many times had the Rover's warnings sounded in her head now? What tales she herself would have for LoFin if she ever saw that chubby Waif again.

The two surfaced, farther away from where oily streaks had infiltrated the water densely and sent sickly tremors through them both, the young dolphin especially. But once beyond that tainted space, Piper settled into a more comfortable roll through the nightly waves and listened intently. Neither paid heed to an unnatural chill that had seeped in gradually throughout the Coastal sea, for the temperatures both in the water and the air seemed to change in queer ways now and then. SlugFlukes continued...

"The Humunz' Floaters were so large they could spit out smaller ones that some of the spindly little Killers scrambled into. Then they paddled up slowly and quietly to where the tired BigFins were taking in breaths of air they would need for diving back under the water. And when the Imps were close enough, they cast sharp sticks out from their smaller Floaters and into the

BigFins' thick hides! The tired BigFins panicked and tried swimming away, but the sharp sticks were tied with long ropes to the shrieking Imps' Floaters. They could not escape and were too tired to even dive back under the waves."

SlugFlukes paused, studying Piper and considering how much the little SongFin had already been through this day.

"SlugFlukes, what happened after that?" she implored, her eyes holding the interest of a child watching her first horror movie—too mesmerized by the fear to turn away. So SlugFlukes went on.

"Very well," he said resolutely. He paused again, his rumbling voice restraining a telltale tremor. "Then one of the Imps in the smaller Floater drew out an even longer pointed stick...and jabbed it into one of the BigFin's skulls." He paused again. "That killed it because the point went straight to its brain."

SlugFlukes wondered how many times he had heard this very tale from Clan Elders—telling that the evil Land Dwellers had come and slaughtered the GrayFins and many other BigFins—how often it had played over and over in his mind. Most Spurters kept their Lore in the visual images they passed down through generations of their offspring. Yet even now he quaked as he told the grim old tale to this bewildered young SongFin. He was sure her ebon eyes showed the same anguish and confusion his own had shown so long ago.

"But why?" cried Piper. "Why did they do it? For the same reason the ones in that cove killed the Jumping Whistlers?"

"No, not really," said SlugFlukes. "It has been said

that the ancient Humunz sought something that is part of us...something of great value to them that they cherished." Neither the old gray whale nor any other of his species would ever understand human usage of cetacean innards that produced oil and other byproducts for the world marketplace.

"But what about the rest of the dead GrayFins?" asked Piper nervously. What did the Humunz do with that?"

SlugFlukes looked terribly uncomfortable now. He wished she had not asked that very question. He could see how such an inquisitive youngster would not be appreciated in a Clan as restrictive as hers.

"That which was left over—and with the GrayFins it was most of their bodies—was torn up and thrown to the Snag-Tooth."

Piper felt her innards heave. She paled, and SlugFlukes pushed himself into telling the rest.

"In time, though, these Killer Imps went too far," he continued. "Oh, it was a dark day indeed when they discovered our Breeding Waters. The pleasant shallows we cherished for rearing our young were soon to become a horror. And it was far uglier than what I have shown you today, Piper. Those butchers did not care whether it was elders or younglings they murdered. Ah...but they were to receive some surprises from our early Pods of valiant Grays."

Something akin to a smirk crossed the features of the old gray whale...if that were possible.

"It was the females of the Clan that first struck out at the Humunz—after a number of young Grays had been attacked and slain. First, one angry mother, then another and another, and soon the entire Pod took turns ramming the big Floaters that were finally battered to bits; the screaming Imps aboard them fell into the water and drowned—all caught in the grasp of the sinking wrecks sliding beneath the waves. Glorious it was said to be!"

Piper trembled as she imagined the thunderous might there must have been behind the charge of an entire Pod of enraged GhostFins. She was right in her earlier feelings of what a terrible foe one like SlugFlukes would have made. "That's why they call you the GhostFins now!" exclaimed Piper. "It must have seemed you had all died and returned."

"Yes," said SlugFlukes. "Not only that, but the whole slaughtering by Humunz nearly happened again a hundred seasons later. But the GhostFins fought back again and returned from the dead once more, this time to stay. And we shall survive these Killer Imps as well!" he rumbled defiantly. "Though I must say, they certainly seem to be the worst of all those my kind has had to face…hmph!"

SlugFlukes settled himself comfortably in the rolling swells. Despite the pain of relating the tragic history of his race, he was pleased when he thought back on the majesty they had shown in their grim struggle for survival.

"How did the Killer Imps destroy *your* Pod, SlugFlukes?" Piper asked cautiously. Though she could see that the old whale bore many deep wounds of flesh and spirit, she had also seen his pride swell with the tale of the GhostFins' struggles. Now was the time for answers to the mysteries that surrounded this gray giant.

SlugFlukes was not upset with the question. He had

expected it and meant to tell everything this day.

"They came upon us in the night," he began softly—a faint rumble of anger resounding with him—"while we slept and were unaware they were on the prowl. Their Floaters were not loud, for they had somehow made their usual roar into a *purr* that was too soft to rouse us from our slumber. It was, of course, foolish that we had no sentry that night—as with the Clan so long ago—but we were all spent. There were but twelve of us, and we'd been fleeing a distant herd of HunterKin that must have numbered a good hundred strong. And if it was the HunterKins' plan to wear us down so we'd be too tired to fight, it had been working well. Yet we managed to lose them by going into choppier seas where they could not hear us as easily because of the much noisier waves there.

"When finally we stopped, there was no sign of the HunterKin. We were exhausted, too weary to flee any longer…too tired to even put up a fight. We felt relieved to lose them in the rough seas and to finally be in calmer waters where we could detect their approach if they came near. You see, we were worried and fearful of HunterKin, not Humunz. And we'd had little trouble with the Land Dwellers in those days. Most of the Evil Lore of their kind was well in the past. Besides, we were in the Eastern Seas, where it was said to be safest from such perils. How wrong we were!" SlugFlukes' mottled face twisted in pain. "I was but six seasons and not wise in the ways of the sea."

Piper found herself unable to picture the grizzled old giant ever to be the same age as she now was.

"When we first heard the purring, we thought nothing of it. Often the Humunz hunted for GillFin there, sometimes even Snag-Tooth, so we paid it little heed. Then, as it loomed up out of the dark, the most terrible thing happened. This Floater was as big as two GhostFins together…and the Imps aboard it were pointing long sticks at us! But they did not slip out into any smaller Floaters—as the old tales had told—and did not throw their pointed sticks at us. Instead, something else came flying out at us…something that made a loud horrible noise and streaked through the water faster than a Snag-Tooth! It buried itself inside one of our Pod bulls, an older one who'd seen many seasons—PloughFin, a good old fellow." The old GhostFin shuddered, pausing before pressing on.

"As soon as this 'firestick' had passed through old PloughFin's tough hide, the poor fellow started writhing around like one of the Slithering Folk. He cried as I've never heard a living creature cry, over and over, about a cold heat inside of him that burned him so. And he twisted all about in great spasms. Then the Imps shot more of these firesticks into the water and every single one found its mark. Even now, I do not know how those vicious little beasts could be so true in their aim."

SlugFlukes was sickened by his retelling of the terror of the whalers' cold harpoons, something only human beings could devise as weapons for slaying other living creatures—creatures that posed them no threat at all, but simply lived as nature had decreed.

Piper wanted him to stop. She could not bear to hear any more. And if she had not witnessed the massacre of the Jumping Whistlers herself, she might yet have thought the old GhostFin a bit touched in the mind from age. But she knew different now and grimaced as he continued.

"Once they all stopped squirming and bellowing from the pain of 'the cold burning'…then the eager Humunz all jumped into their smaller Floaters to gather in the dead GhostFins and bring them back. That's when I saw the Killer Imps for the first time in my life. I will never forget it."

Again the GhostFin paused before pressing on, one baleful eye studying the young dolphin.

"I watched them go back to their huge leading Floater and"—the whale shuddered again as he forced himself to go on with the terrible saga—"soon I saw bits and chunks of my Pod family being cast into the water, where hungry Snag-Tooth all waited eagerly. Those horrid Humunz paid no attention to the pack of silent killers who chewed at the remains of my family and friends."

SlugFlukes' voice trembled, and he was forced to pause once more. "I was overlooked because I dove just in time to miss the first of the firesticks they shot at us. I swam away, far enough so they would not see me. Then, a safe distance away, I surfaced. I knew I was powerless to do anything against such fearsome weapons…but I forced myself to stay and watch, *so I would never forget*."

SlugFlukes stared hard at Piper. "So now, friend Piper, I roam these Western Seas, warning as many Spurters as I can of the Killer Imps. Many of the BigFins listen, for they are a somber breed…and the Rovers have never really cared for Land Dwellers, so they too have listened. Ah, but the playful SongFins— especially those like the silly Jumpers—they think the Humunz are their friends. Remember how I told you the

Jumper pod trusted them because Land Dwellers led them to rich hunting waters? And because they sometimes see Humunz hunting the Snag-Tooth?" The GhostFin shook his massive head woefully. "Too many of those SongFins foolishly think the sea is always safe for play. They never listen. They laugh and tease and say old SlugFlukes is full of silly tales he likes to make up because he is feebleminded. Yes...then they learn too late.

"You see, the Imps here are very thorough when they kill...and very cunning, too. They make sure none of those they attack ever live to tell about it. And they kill where it is not likely they will be seen or heard. Oh, and I have seen them slaying SongFins in the Open Sea...not just in choppy coves. There are many ways the sly Humunz do their foul deeds, sometimes even using the SongFins' own needs. For when they are far out at sea, the Imps lure your kind in closer to their Floaters by making sounds like those you hear from large schools of GillFin. I do not know how they do it, but I think it has to do with something they put into the water. I have heard it for myself—and it seems so much like large groups of swimming GillFin. Why, these Imps can even make sounds like SongFins and HunterKin! Yes, very sly they are...much more so than our own kind."

"But how do they catch Whistlers in the Open Sea?" Piper asked darkly. She was terribly confused by it all. Even if SlugFlukes had understood the whalers' techniques of recording and reproducing sea sounds by using underwater speakers and amplifiers, it would have been impossible to explain that to Piper...or to anyone else.

"This part is the saddest," said SlugFlukes. "Before they are ready to lure in the SongFins, the Imps spread their nets all around the area where they expect their victims to be. The meshing they use is very thin and very strong and very difficult to detect, even with keen scanners. And so the SongFins, in their rush to feed, all zoom in to where they hear large groups of GillFin swimming—or where they hear only the flapping sounds of GillFin—and then they wind up getting themselves tangled in the nets, trapped there. That is how the Killer Imps catch both!"

SlugFlukes paused again, then turned a baleful eye on her. "Have you ever been tangled in a net?"

She wagged her head sideways.

"Well, it's a terrible thing," said SlugFlukes. "SongFins of every kind panic when caught like that. Some freeze and are unable even to move." The whale closed his eyes momentarily, lost in thought once more. He lifted his crusty snout, then opened his eyes again, pondering all he had just told Piper. "But no!" he roared suddenly. "I am going to cheat those foul killers of as many victims as I can, for I owe that to my slain Pod. I will warn all the sea of this menace!"

SlugFlukes stopped and regarded Piper, calming himself. He knew how desperate his lone quest had been, and always would be. "Of course, I must say it has been most difficult thus far," he heaved quietly. "Unless one sees, one witnesses such things—as you have now done, dear little SongFin—it all sounds like some wild ramblings of a foolish old BigFin. But I will never stop trying." He took several deep breaths and submerged. The old GhostFin was through with his tale and felt drained from it. He did not like saying so much at one time, and it was with more than a little pain that he had recounted those old wounds and sworn, once more, his Oath of Justice. But it was the least he could do for this brave little creature from the east who had risked her life for him. At least now he could feel certain there would be no further doubt in her mind who her true enemies were.

Piper indeed had no doubts now. She was horrified at the chilling saga, yet fascinated by the romance of his sworn crusade against the Killer Imps. And then suddenly the most terrifying of thoughts struck her like a giant storm breaker crashing down hard.

"SlugFlukes," she asked, shaking all over as they cruised thirty feet below the surface, "how far did you say the Killer Imps travel on their hunting missions?"

"Over all the seas," he replied grimly, expecting the question. "I know what you are going to ask, and the answer is *yes*. Your fool of a Commodore is spending all his time massing for a Snag-Tooth attack that will never come…while a far greater menace may even now be stalking your Clan. And you, my little SongFin, are very fortunate to have been banished from there. That cove at Kwi Coast is as deadly a trap for your Pod as the southern cove was for the early GhostFins—and as the one where you watched those foolish Jumpers being slain."

"No!" cried Piper. A million thoughts raced through her head as she visualized QuickFin… Buffer… Thane SilverFlukes… All of them! Was it the Killer Imps that had taken her parents? "I must go back…I must warn them, SlugFlukes!" Her thin, whitish body shook like an eager puppy's tail.

"Hmph!" snorted the whale. "Do not be foolish,

Piper." His fins tightened, and the deep sorrow that had lingered after his tale instantly vanished. "They did not heed you before. What in the name of all the sea makes you think they'll believe anything like this? You yourself would not have believed it had you not seen so with your own eyes. No, I have told you this and shown you the Killer Imps only so you might save yourself from a gruesome death. You are one of the more decent creatures I spoke of earlier. But there is nothing decent about a Pod that casts one of its own out, *alone*, to the dangers of the sea! No, make your home here now, my brave little SongFin, and help me alert those who dwell in these waters of their grave peril. For this is where the Killer Imps prowl in vast numbers. Forget Kwi Coast. They cared little for you or for your life."

Piper regarded the great gray behemoth for a long moment. "Could you ever forget your own Pod, SlugFlukes?" she asked softly, her tiny voice chiming in the crystal blue-green water. "Wasn't there a QuickFin among those in your Clan...or one such as Thane SilverFlukes that you admired? Would you go to save old PloughFin if he were still alive?"

The angry, rumbling bull inside of SlugFlukes grew silent. He stared long and hard at Piper. She knew how much he had wanted to save them...and how he was still tormented by the guilt of his flight from the marauding Killer Imps.

"Very well, my foolish young friend," he rumbled quietly. But I do think you're going to risk a terrible death for creatures who will neither heed nor appreciate your tidings. Hmph! They are not worthy of one such as you." He paused a long time. "Old SlugFlukes will not forget you."

"And I will never forget you, my wise friend," said Piper, her tiny voice breaking.

Together they swam off through the nightly sea.

PART III
RETURN

Nicholas Checker

Chapter Sixteen
Old Acquaintances

Piper's farewell to SlugFlukes had not been easy. The grand old whale had been a warm friend when she had needed one most. SlugFlukes had guarded her and counseled her in the Ways of the Sea. And he had offered her companionship just when the darkness of solitude had nearly overwhelmed her. She owed him much, she felt, even though she had saved his life. Had he not saved hers as well?

No, it had been no easy matter bidding him farewell. But she knew it would have been worse to remain and forever be tormented by the specter of her own Pod being stalked and slaughtered as the Jumpers had been.

"Do not be hasty in your tale," SlugFlukes had cautioned her, "else you will find yourself in great trouble again." The GhostFin had been grumbling on all morning about how her Pod would react. "Expect their doubts. They have been isolated and ignorant for too long. I do not expect them to change their ways now."

Piper had made to protest that, but the whale hefted himself up onto his flukes, towering over her like a vast sea mount, and stared hard. It was clear that he intended it as another of those times she was to listen without interruption.

"They are not worthy of the risk you are taking for

them, but I do understand your devotion," he admitted with just a touch of pride in his tone. Piper had wriggled in embarrassment, pleased at any time when she had earned SlugFlukes' praise. "Goodbye, my little SongFin," he said. "Never forget the gratitude I will always feel for what you have done. And perhaps, when these Western Seas grow colder, I might stop and…eh, pay a little visit on my way to the southern waters, mmm?"

Piper was delighted to hear that. She swam over to him and nudged him gently with her beak.

"I will never forget you, SlugFlukes," she said. "Do come to us one day." And with that, Piper swam off, hoping she truly would someday see the majestic gray giant again. She realized, as she paddled once more through the lonely jade sea, how much she would miss him and all the marvelous times they had known together.

Piper had, at first, tried persuading SlugFlukes to return to Kwi Coast with her. It most certainly would have helped convince Thane SilverFlukes, at least, for the stately Clan leader had great respect for the wisdom of older creatures. But she realized SlugFlukes could not leave his home seas. He had much to do there—just as she had much to do in her home seas. Besides, she thought, he would have slowed her down terribly. Despite all his might, the aging GhostFin was a pathetically slow swimmer—especially when compared to a Whistler. No, she was on her own now. All she could hope was that they would listen to her.

****

The green coastal zone soon changed to a darkening blue as she moved farther out into the Open

Sea. She passed through a bog of tiny jellyfish and wriggled through them in discomfort. The feel of their clammy touch had always bothered Piper. She had never cared for the sticky little Stingers who sometimes pricked her when they clung to her smooth skin. And now the waters seemed especially filled with them...just as the sea itself seemed to harbor queer shifts in temperature at times, unsettling her.

Two hundred feet below, jutting up from the muddy bottom, the battered hulk of a once proud Floater returned the echoes she sent down. Scores of crabs and small gobi fish scuttled in and out of its cracks and fissures, while slimy wolf eels, fearsome in appearance, writhed and slithered over its broken hull. From the returning echoes she scanned a clear image of the wreck—a stricken old freighter that had lain entrenched in the ooze, probably even long before SlugFlukes' time—a sad victim of the beautiful but treacherous rocky world Piper now glided over so peacefully.

The ancient wreck caused Piper to think once more about the Killer Imps and their Floaters that prowled these very waters. She wondered what had sent this giant one to its doom, so that now it was just a mossy ruin for GillFins and Crawlers to swarm over. What sort of Humunz were once aboard it? Were they as cruel as those she had seen in that Dark Cove?

She passed over the last scattered patch of red-brown kelp, still pondering the mysteries of the vast Open Sea. Were there good Humunz...like there were harmless Snag-Tooth? And were all the ones that dwelled near shallow coves evil? She had never before seen Humunz behave like the vicious pack of them that had slaughtered all those Whistlers so savagely.

Absorbed in her thoughts, she did not notice the panicky flight of a school of tasty mullet fish as she flapped toward them. Her mind awhirl in the sea's unanswered mysteries, Piper passed dreamily over a craggy sea mount, oblivious to the shrill piping in the distance. Closer and closer it came, until finally it pierced the haze in which she had enshrouded herself. It was the sound of great thrashing flukes sending powerful impulses through the waterways.

Piper was suddenly alert to the peril she'd foolishly allowed to creep up on her. She did not pause to home in on them—they were too close. Their exact locale was not important now. *Escape* was. From the pressure of the waves, she knew they were moving at a blistering pace...and gaining. Something told Piper that the vengeful HunterKin had probably been tailing her ever since she'd left the protection of SlugFlukes. She shivered as she realized the small band of Hunters had likely monitored SlugFlukes and her all through the three weeks they'd been together—waiting with a sly patience for them to separate.

She fled in blind panic.

"Where is your courage now, brash Whistler?" she heard the high lilt of the lead bull orca's voice. It was frighteningly close. "There will be no GhostFin to save you this time—little whitefin!" taunted the younger bull. "Ah, but we will leave a tidy meal for the Snag-Tooth who follow!"

Piper felt the clammy grasp of terror seize her as she quickly scanned a distant, scavenging Snag-Tooth band, already alerted to the killer whales on the hunt. The sharks followed at a safe distance, anticipating the leftover feast. Then she saw the Hunter pack, zooming in from the left. They had built up such tremendous speed they were now only fifty yards away. The water was very clear, and Piper could see well enough ahead of her. But that meant even greater peril. Orca eyesight is superb. She scanned ahead desperately and detected the distant, irregular roll and beat of deep ocean swells. If she could make it out to those choppier waters and beyond the sight of her pursuers, she just might lose them in the noisy waves.

"We shall leave just enough of you for the Snag-Tooth to finish!" chimed one of the she-orcas loudly. And the screeching pack began to converge.

Piper knew she must contain her terror if she was to think clearly and elude them. The HunterKin were cunning and often frightened their victims into a blind flight marred with miscalculations. Most of the WhistlingFin were thus trapped in such ways, and the tactic appeared to be working here. It was merely a matter of time.

Piper thrashed her flukes, flapping her streamlined frame in one great roll, and was off! She changed her course and turned north, knowing the waters there were said to be unbearably chilly, but knowing also that the echoes of the booming surf came from that direction.

The orcas were puzzled by her maneuver, but they turned and followed. The young dolphin was unexpectedly swift—swifter than any they had ever come upon before. And she seemed to possess a cunning beyond what they had seen previously in a Whistler. But it mattered not. They would follow the meddling little pest from one dawn to another until finally they caught her.

Piper burst above the surf in a high swooping arc and expelled a blast of salty vapor and water. Several more leaps and she had time to refresh herself and take in a number of breaths. SlugFlukes had instructed her well; she was diving deeper than the pursuing Hunters had expected. She knew they were waiting for her to surface soon. If she could remain under for as long as SlugFlukes had taught her, she might fool them into waiting for her above the waves—allowing her more time to lengthen the distance between them. While swimming along the surface, their scanners could not home in on her movements. But it would take all she could muster to evade them. The HunterKin were frighteningly faster than she had imagined, and she was now doubting her ability to outrace them. They had a good deal more stamina than she. Eventually they might simply wear her down. Her life depended on craft now as well as speed.

The orcas knew the length of time a Whistler could remain submerged. Soon this little white one would be forced into rising—and close by, too. The small pack had seen her dive, and they sped along the swells to where they believed she would soon surface. The young bull had scanned the depth of her plunge. Clearly the Whistler had panicked, he thought. Her plunge was so deep she could not possibly put enough distance between herself and them. If they moved swiftly enough, and measured her rise for air correctly, they would be there when she breached.

A good five hundred feet below the surface, Piper slipped along in the cool murk of the lower sea. She was not yet wanting for air and was cautious of the number of bubbles she allowed to dribble up from her blowhole. The noisy slapping above informed her that the vengeful Hunters awaited her there. Had Piper been more alert, she might have realized that the small band of dusky sharks had disappeared.

Unlike cetaceans, sharks did not attempt to second-guess their victims. They instead tracked their prey as *instinct* directed them, always waiting a fair distance off before launching an attack. But this Whistler they now followed had behaved most strangely; so the leery Snag-Tooth had kept their distance. And when the dolphin sped on further, showing no signs of weariness or need for air, and then surfaced a good mile away, the sharks became discouraged and left.

Farther off to the south, the young bull orca broke the surface, confused as he bellowed out an angry report that he had echoed onto the sounds of a small Whistler breaching the waves—somewhere north.

Chapter Seventeen
The Lair

Unsure whether the Hunter pack still followed, Piper had not let up in her speedy flight. Though she had lost them, she knew they might still home in on her, even from so far a distance. So she veered toward the choppy seas she had scanned earlier, where the erratic crash of heavy surf would clog the orcas' sonar. Treacherous as such waters were, Piper knew her pursuers posed a far greater threat. And her course to the fiercely breaking Northern Sea would also bring on a chill she had never experienced.

Night fell upon the moonless water, and Piper relied entirely upon her sensitive sonar beams to guide her. The little nerves inside the melon of her forehead quivered often, alerting her to the presence of drifting objects and passing creatures. She avoided them easily and swam on, not bothering to identify them. She felt sure that by now she had lost the HunterKin, but still she was loath to take chances. Piper had not forgotten the terror she had suffered when she'd first heard the eerie cry of her larger cousins. There was no other sound in the sea as fearful or terrifying.

So she glided through the alien waters, careful to avoid overusing her scanners. Piper had no idea how far off her pursuers might be, for the boom of the surf had made it impossible to monitor their movements. Had she been less obsessed with them and paid more heed to her immediate surroundings, she might have been less shocked with the light of morning—and the sight of the bizarre sea around her.

It was when the red haze of dawn first illuminated the surface and filtered gradually down into the dusky waters below that she finally beheld the rabble of misshapen creatures surrounding her. Everywhere in sight were swarms of GillFin unlike any she had ever seen in her life. Their heads were far too big for their bodies, while their jaws—which spanned as high as their giant heads—were narrow and filled with long spiny teeth. And clustered all about her were bits of broken plants that were as twisted and misshapen as the ugly angler fish gliding through the murky water.

Piper had barely a moment to ponder her odd surroundings before she picked up on the broadcast of something large...and not far behind in the gloom. At first she wondered if she was in a dreamy half-slumber, because what was registering in her head told her she had to either be dozing or crazed. Perhaps she had damaged her scanners in her flight from the pursuing pack, for what she now detected simply could not be! She had drawn an image of a creature nearly the size of a HunterKin—seemingly a Snag-Tooth of some queer sort. She scanned its high dorsal fin and the slow-moving beat of its tail brushing back and forth in a precise lateral pattern. But its face displayed a snout that was flat, like some sadistic force had crushed the thing's head and bent it that way on purpose. From its ends, two cold eyes peered out from a pair of bulging sockets. Never had anyone spoken of such a creature!

Piper felt the light streaks over her brow start to

throb. She twitched nervously. She did not like this mysterious dark sea and all the gruesome forms of life that filled it. A disturbing image rose up in her mind, and she trembled, trying to suppress it. But she could not. *Piper knew precisely where she was*. She forgot all about the HunterKin that still stalked her. She had to flee—fast!

Piper zoomed off, flukes thrashing wildly. She did not bother scanning the nearby hammerhead shark again—or any of the other bizarre lifeforms around her. She was a creamy streak slicing through the misty waters, fleeing an Evil she had feared her entire life.

Then she saw it.

The air-sacs inside her melon throbbed like jelly, warning her of the thing looming directly in the path of her flight. Blind panic washed away her sense of caution. Piper had never seen a Stinger so large! Even at Kwi Coast, the largest any jellyfish ever grew was no more than the size of a mackerel. But this—this pale monster's blob of a body was larger than her own! Its flimsy "arms" dangled so far down into the depths she could not tell where they stopped.

Several sleek silverjacks had tried slipping by the glowing white jellyfish, only to find themselves trapped in its sticky clutches. The white monster slowly curled in its draping, venomous tentacles, drawing the hapless entangled fish closer to its anxious maw.

Piper had seen enough. She knew what the small Stingers of Kwi Coast could do with their own poisonous grasp. There was no telling the strength of this horrid giant. If it was not Lord Arkitu himself, it was most certainly akin to him in some way.

Truly she was in the Black Waters!

The young dolphin squealed and fled, hoping to put a safe distance between herself and this evil being while it feasted. Her lungs groaned in protest, for she had been under far too long. But she did not want to alter her straightaway course. Distance was crucial now!

Far below, she saw flickering lights. She did not know what they were, though she had seen them before, at the start of her exile. Did Lord Arkitu command them? She shivered and swam on. Soon she would need to turn for the surface. So she veered toward the waves, twenty-five feet above. Piper cast one more downward glance at the tiny lights below—and beheld Death itself rising out of the ashen fog.

It was a Snag-Tooth…but unlike any she had ever seen in her life. Enormous and pure white, it emerged from the deep like a silent ghost. Its mouth was filled with glittering teeth, large and strong enough to crush a Whistler the size of Commodore RamStrong with a single snap! The face was pale and cold, its lower jaw slung back as though in a leer. This beast was astonishingly larger than the leader of the HunterKin pack. Again, Piper flashed back to the memory of the eerie giant that had tailed her months earlier. And she recalled SlugFlukes' tale of the White Giants of the Snag-Tooth race who had prowled the seas of long past. And this one here approached even the old GhostFin in size!

She squeaked in horror, and a single bubble flew out from her blowhole, betraying her alarm and causing her to panic. Piper tried breathing, but a rush of cold water slipped into her lungs, past the tiny valve of a muscle that was always pressed shut whenever she submerged. Everywhere now was a misty, sibilant whirling.

In a flurry of flippers and flukes, Piper struggled to the surface and heaved out a stream of the salty water she had inhaled. She gasped heartily for precious intakes of air. Her brain cleared as she expelled the plume of vapor and water. She dove again, wanting to stay submerged where she could mark the movements of the silent giant. It was only then she realized the entire region was now deserted. And as she probed with her scanners, the waxy nerves in her melon throbbing and amplifying every sound, she homed in on the bulk of the massive Snag-Tooth. It had not followed her to the surface, but was still lurking close enough…

Piper knew she needed to somehow outwit this monster. If she dove, she might confuse it the way she had fooled the band of HunterKin that had plagued her for so long. So she plunged into the depths…deeper that any dolphin should have dared go. She soared through the gray-greens of the sunlit zones, then the darker blues of the twilit regions, through the rubble of drifting plants and torn weeds like the macrocystis that grew at depths of hundreds of feet…and finally approached the abysmal regions and the darkest of waters where a near sightless void loomed up through a haze of eerie flickering lights.

A thousand feet beneath the surface, her sonar was attuned acutely to her surroundings in the blackest of ocean depths where her cetacean sight was useless. Piper paddled off in a direction she hoped would not lead her back toward the giant Snag-Tooth. She had lost her bearings during the daring dive, but to her relief the beast did not appear to be anywhere in range. Caution was crucial now. She would have to time her need for air exactly, zoom for the surface quickly enough to breach before her pressured lungs burst, take in several strong breaths, and then plunge back down again before the monster had time to home in on her.

Now, though, a strange wave of euphoria swept through her. All of a sudden it seemed a lovely world she had entered: dark and private. It was so quiet…so peaceful. Not even SlugFlukes had ever been so deep that he knew of the mysterious effects the sea's depths had on the mind of one unaccustomed to it. The longer Piper remained submerged, the more she would long to remain there.

Her dreamy thoughts were interrupted as the source of the flickering lights was finally revealed—terrible swarthy creatures that reminded her of eels, the Slithering Ones. Their narrow jaws were filled with spiny teeth, and their bodies wriggled and glowed in the dark like waxing moons. *Arkitu's minions!* What else could they be? Piper bolted away from the fearsome-looking dragonfish.

Then the thrumming began.

Her lower jaw shook, signaling the presence of something of great mass close by. Drunken curiosity drew her to within thirty feet, and she homed in on the bulk of the monstrous thing. Fear seized her.

She was in the Cold Lord's lair!

This was Arkitu! And he was just as the Commodore had always said—the long, coiled arms springing out from the crusty body of shells, the homely beaked face larger than she had ever imagined. Arkitu could have gobbled up the giant Stinger she had seen earlier, and could have done so in a single gulp. He was much bigger than the huge white Snag-Tooth that had frightened her down into these depths. Yes, now she saw it all too clearly: *the Snag-Tooth and the giant Stinger both served the Cold Lord.* And they had driven her down here into the waiting arms of their Master!

Even SlugFlukes could not have measured up to this Evil Lord of the sea.

Piper was frozen. Where was there to flee? Arkitu's denizens were everywhere. At any moment she expected one of the ten flailing arms to reach over and draw her into his gaping maw. She waited, unable to even move. But Arkitu did not seize her. Had he failed to detect her, so close by?

All at once, an inky spray gushed out from somewhere and cast a dark cloud around the Cold Lord! Then Piper felt a powerful surge of churning water, and she spun over and over in a wild swirl. It was the emergence of another being—one of tremendous bulk.

****

While the terrified young dolphin quaked in horror—a thousand feet beneath the waves—the great white shark, well above it, swam on silently, uninterested in the fleeing little Whistler or any of the other insignificant creatures it had frightened off. The giant Snag-Tooth had feasted earlier and had no need to eat again for a while. Still, it was pleased with the instant panic it had created, as always.

Lazily it swam on in the direction of the warmer waters it preferred. Its keen nervous system responded to the pressure waves which signaled the presence of a distant, prowling orca pack. That would not deter his course. He was cautious of the HunterKin, always, but brazen with the security that came with his size— knowing well that all who dwelled in the sea were leery of the madness possessed by his kind. Countless eons of survival had spawned such arrogance—that, and the simple wisdom which told even the mightiest of Snag-Tooth that there were no "Masters of the Seas," only survivors. Those who thought otherwise were doomed. He knew that. The Megalodon white shark swam on toward the warmer Southern Seas—and his favorite haunts—heedless of killer whales, dolphins...or even giant squid.

****

Drenched in the filthy spray that had spewed out from the giant squid, Piper struggled to break free of the icy fear that had gripped her. If she fled now, she might escape the Cold Lord and this other terrible Monster of the Deep that had suddenly burst out of the pelagic dark. At first she thought it might have been the giant Snag-Tooth returning to its Master's Lair. But this creature was even bigger than the massive Snag-Tooth!

Piper calmed herself long enough to scan the behemoth. It was shaped like a huge Floater. But how could a Floater move beneath the waves? It took the young Whistler another instant to realize that this was a living being—and that it had attacked Arkitu! The Evil Lord Arkitu, Master of the dreadful Black Waters, was fighting desperately for his life, trying to escape the clutches of some monstrous being bulkier and even more powerful than he!

Piper sent out a series of echoes and zeroed in on a dark, scarred hulk which appeared as a great mass of moving rock. For a fleeting moment, she thought it might have been SlugFlukes. But this creature—though it bore some resemblance to the old GhostFin—was so much larger. And it had teeth, huge teeth that lined its long underjaw. Piper was amazed as she scoped further and discovered a single blowhole off to one side of the sperm whale's massive head. Why, this magnificent being might have routed the entire HunterKin pack! Here was one so powerful it could invade the Lair of the Cold Lord and even overpower him. For there was Arkitu, thrashing in desperation with his terrible arms, while the giant BigFin hauled the squirming Cold Lord toward the surface. Did Arkitu weaken when taken from his lair?

By now, Piper's lungs ached desperately for air. She was doomed if she remained under any longer. She had to fly swiftly for the surface. She found renewed energy as she sped upward, aware how fortunate she had been to have survived the terror of the Black Waters. Truly it was the Master Of All Seas who had saved her!

She would return to Kwi Coast. It was her destiny to save them all. And Piper knew she would win their hearts with a wonderful tale, one that would last forever in the Lore of the WhistlingFin.

Chapter Eighteen
The Way Back

Piper recalled little of her flight from the Black Waters, only the memory of the terrible Cold Lord and the incredible struggle she had witnessed. She did not know how the battle had turned out, but when she had left, Arkitu was still trapped in the clam-like grip of the great Sea Lord's jaws. Perhaps this was what SlugFlukes had meant when he'd said he knew things about the mysterious depths she would not be able to understand.

Ever since Piper left the Black Waters—her sophisticated cetacean mind charting a course away from the cold Northern Seas and back toward Kwi Coast—she'd reflected on her journey, which now took her farther and farther into strange, unknown waters. She passed over sunken valleys and sloping mountain ranges and the wreckage of more broken Floaters. And always she beheld scores of Snag-Tooth (of so many different breeds) gathering near the rubble and preying upon the smaller creatures that dwelled there. Piper scanned those ghostly scenes—always from a safe distance upcurrent—witnessing the quarrels and scuffles that often erupted among the sharks. Were these the diabolical denizens of the Deep that sought to rule the sea?

Piper saw that it was wise to avoid contact with

them, for they seemed as ill-tempered and vicious toward one another as they were toward their own prey. But she could not conceive of them organizing themselves into any kind of mass attack on others...though the brief flare-ups she had witnessed did give hint of what a full Fury seizure might well be. No, it would not be wise to bait them into any sort of war, but prudent indeed to know how to defend against them.

She thought of such things as she rode the friendly currents of the ocean toward her home waters at Kwi Coast. The worst was most certainly over, she felt, unaware how close she had really come to death at the jaws of the hungry orcas.

****

The big bull leader had been furious with the young Whistler's coy ruse. The little pest that had meddled with their kill and then caused the death of one of their prowling Pod had earned their wrath. They'd had a good deal of difficulty in tailing her through the pounding sea, but they had followed her relentlessly. The HunterKin band had managed to come within a half-mile of their scurrying prey—when a veritable giant of a White Snag-Tooth had emerged from out of the pelagic gloom.

Normally, four strong orcas were more than enough to make any shark flee, but this ghostly monster was over twice the size of any in their group. The Megalodon's frosty glare showed its contempt for the Humunz-like "Half-Gills" that often plagued his own race—these cocky HunterKin who often acted as though they ruled the seas. The Megalodon did not come across them often, for it was rare—other than to feed—that he ever emerged from the oceanic depths where few cared to venture. And when he did, it gave him a primal pleasure, which he only vaguely understood, to remind such cocky Hunters of an ancient breed that they and so many others had long forgotten.

HunterKin never liked to yield. But the big bull leader sensed in the glare of this ancient white giant something he was too young to fully comprehend. The creature had clearly seen many more seasons than he or any of the other three. Something of menace rumbled within this eerie visitor from the Deep…something that caused the young bull and the other three to part from the Megalodon's course.

The giant survivor of over two centuries glided by the orcas with a low hiss of triumph.

The lead bull withheld a rasp of rage, reaffirming the debt to be paid the vile little Whistler that had caused all this. He and his small band of Hunters sped off, humbled by their encounter with the massive white predator from the ocean's depths. They had traveled barely a mile more when all four fairly froze.

A bristling, gargantuan shark nearly sixty feet long and apparently straight out of the sea's legendary Lore was enough to make the HunterKin respectful and cautious. But an Odon—a sperm whale of a good seventy-five feet and as many tons—was enough to invoke a bit more. The enormous toothy predator, having just feasted, was feeling brazen in its recent conquest. And the Odon now bristled at the presence of its smaller marauding cousins, the prowling band before him apparently on the hunt. The mighty leviathan thrashed its huge flukes in a gesture of warning and menace. The four HunterKin, finally recognizing the consequences of chasing an enigmatic little Whistler through a seemingly malefic sea, abandoned their hunt and departed for waters more familiar and welcoming of their needs.

Piper swam on, coasting with the eastward currents and feeding on lantern fish, mackerel, and other small GillFins. She was unaware of the obscure alliance she had made with two monarchs of the seas—neither having been at all interested in the hysterical little dolphin they had both inadvertently saved.

At times her journey home was wrought with the same loneliness Piper had known at the start of her exile. But the purpose of her return and the struggles of the past three and a half months had lent her a greater strength than she had ever known. And so she pressed on.

Once she came across a large pod of Whistlers—saddlebacks. They were a smaller breed than her own, and handsome with their patchy brown-and-white markings. It was the first time she had actually spoken with her own kind since her exile from Kwi Coast. The sensation of being with Whistlers once again had sent waves of excitement through her. They had asked her to join them, and the lonely young bottlenose was sorely tempted. But Piper knew her purpose and had declined, telling them she had been separated from her own Pod while fleeing the HunterKin. And just the mention of their larger, predatory Kin made the highstrung saddlebacks uneasy and eager to be on to safer waters. These were *natural* Whistlers, thought Piper. They roamed the Open Sea and were familiar with its dangers. She had warned them of the Killer Imps too, and the saddlebacks had grown anxious. Unlike the carefree Jumpers, or those of her own reclusive Clan, these Whistlers went many places and listened to others carefully. They were familiar with the legends of the mighty GhostFins—and with the obscure rumors that spoke of strange doings in the Western Seas. The saddlebacks had thanked Piper and moved on. She was heartened to learn that all the WhistlingFin were not playful simpletons or thick-brained fools. She felt there was hope now. Perhaps her Pod would indeed listen to her—and to what the wiser ones of the sea had passed on to her. She wished again that SlugFlukes had come back with her...or that she could have persuaded a few of the saddlebacks to come to Kwi Coast. Then there would be no doubts. But she was on her own... And the sea stunned her with yet another peril impeding her journey home.

It came upon her as she soared her way through strangely murky waters that shifted in temperature most queerly. Piper found herself pondering whether she'd somehow drifted north of her destination...and then possibly south, for just when the sea had felt warm upon her smooth cetacean skin, a chilling frost would creep over her that sent streams of discomfort through her body. Not wanting to tarry in the polluted seas, she hustled on, but hunger had seized her once more, and she scanned a silted watery plain below that was not especially deep. The image that bounced back to her was one of perhaps a small squid or some edible diatom...soft crustaceans she might easily ingest to quell her building hunger.

What Piper found flapping gently between two sandy stones was a seemingly sticky and loose creature she did not bother to examine and fairly inhaled it, till it caught horribly in her throat, causing her to gasp and heave horribly, nearly choking the life out of her till she finally expelled it! Not wanting to probe the essence of this latest peril she had encountered in these tainted waters, Piper fled as though Hunterkin were pursuing her once more—leaving behind the balloon labeled "Happy Birthday."

Chapter Nineteen
Return

Buffer gamboled about in the waves. It was a bright afternoon, and occasionally he would stop to sun himself in the warm rays that beamed down to the sea. Months earlier, such frivolous behavior in him would have been deemed odd, but now it was just another hint of changes that had come over him—changes that perturbed Commodore RamStrong. *Piper*, the old dolphin would muse sourly. Buffer reminded him so much of her, of late. Even in Exile she was a nuisance. The Commodore recalled how, at the end, Piper had managed to make him appear so cold and harsh when she had voiced her love for the Pod. And not long after she'd been banished, it had come back to haunt the entire Clan.

Piper, in truth, had never really been disliked by any of the Pod Whistlers, not even RamStrong. It was difficult for any of them to see her as an actual traitor. Once everyone's anger had subsided in the wake of her exile, talk had begun that Piper's violation of the Code may have been due more to a brief spell of madness: "We all knew how eccentric and frail she was; she wasn't as strong of heart as her brother; the death of her parents surely affected her more severely than any of us realized. Perhaps a less harsh punishment may have been in order."

RamStrong had listened uneasily to all of it. At Clan Gatherings he would remind the Pod that he, Thane SilverFlukes, and the Elders had to enforce the Code lest their very survival be at stake. "Yes, it is tragic that some should suffer greatly for their deviant behavior, but it is far better than becoming an undisciplined lot who might then fall easy prey to the Snag-Tooth!"

That had always assured everyone that the High Clan had acted rightly and knew what was best. After a while the grumbling had died down and eventually faded away.

All but one was satisfied.

Buffer had never accepted it. Often, great spans of time would pass when none saw him. Some mornings the rest of the Pod would waken only to find that Buffer had gone off again on a private hunt. Other times, no one knew where he had gone. But still he was always on time for the Drills and practiced with a greater diligence than ever, though he now appeared less interested in old RamStrong's praise than in the past. A silent passion seemed to drive him instead. And at times he even displayed what appeared to some as a restrained contempt harbored quietly toward the old Commodore.

RamStrong had found it all disconcerting but chose not to act on it just yet. Buffer was still a valuable Squad member and nearly as worthy a battler as QuickFin. Together the two were as superb and efficient a fighting duo as any of the veteran pairs. As long as Buffer still knew his place, he would be tolerated. Tolerated in spite of those troubling times when the young bull would return from his solitary outings looking ragged and bruised. The Commodore had no idea where he had gone, or why he usually returned in such condition. But a day would come when he would secretly follow and scan Buffer's covert excursions. Then he would know precisely what to do about his brash young charge.

****

Buffer poked his head out through the shining surf. He was watching for Floaters when he heard the call— first a familiar piping…then the very distinct flutter of a small pair of flukes, perhaps out near the rocky caverns of the Slithering Ones. A familiar whistle sang out over the waterways.

Buffer was alert instantly. He watched eagerly as— out from the haze of the early morning sea—came a familiar sight: the sloping leaps of a sleek gray-and-white Whistler, spinning and twirling through the green swells. There was a moment of bewilderment as Buffer blinked and looked again, unsure of his own senses.

The careening beauty was—*Piper*!

For the first time in his life, Buffer failed to restrain the youngling in himself as the morning sun beamed down bright upon the coastal sea…and two joyous dolphins came together in the surf and gently touched beaks.

Chapter Twenty
A Futile Forecast

For Commodore RamStrong, Piper's return was like the faraway rumble of a gathering storm. With guarded wonder he regarded her miraculous survival. He now held a begrudging respect for the youngster, which he was loath to disclose. Both the Commodore and the Council of Elders saw the signs: the blackest of threats to dissenting Clanists had been dealt a telling blow—all due to the resourcefulness and strength of one they had all gravely underestimated.

Even Thane SilverFlukes seemed enraptured by Piper's triumph. He looked back on the chain of events that had led to her banishment—the killing of the huge black Snag-Tooth, the grim trial, and those final touching moments he had spent with her. For a fleeting instant back then, SilverFlukes had wanted to violate the harsh Code himself and override its judgment. But, as with the Commodore, it was the Thane's sworn function to uphold the Code and to punish violators. The actions he'd taken had been necessary. He knew that. But now the scrappy youngster had done what no living Whistler had even thought possible. For the first time, SilverFlukes would hear from someone other than the Commodore and the Elders about the World Beyond their Boundaries. There was much to be learned from one who had journeyed the seas as young

Piper had done.

And there was no greater joy than that felt by QuickFin. Though he had believed, reluctantly, that Piper's punishment was just, he had been overwhelmed with grief at the thought of her all alone in the treacherous Open Sea. QuickFin had kept up his role as a Squad Leader, but his heartiness during the Drills had diminished notably. A cloud often surrounded him as he went about his duties, and he was strangely hesitant to speak or associate with the others. Guilt had plagued him constantly. But with Piper's return to Kwi Coast came the return of the old QuickFin as well. He marveled at it—having never realized, before, what strength she truly possessed.

And though it had been Piper's intent to wait until the Clan Gathering to tell of her journey, she had not been able to resist sharing with her brother her courageous rescue of the GhostFin. QuickFin had swelled with pride as she related the astonishing tale to him.

She found the Pod less receptive.

For two hours the Clan listened and debated fiercely at the Council Cliff. Though it was a mild day—the waters jade and calm, the bright kelp forest that encircled the crags blossoming in a rich brown—the discussion taking place marred its beauty.

"And you expect us to believe, now, that these terrible Humunz you call Killer Imps are our greatest menace, eh?" snorted RamStrong cynically.

"That's what the GhostFin called them...because Humunz are all tiny compared to our larger Kin like him," answered Piper sullenly. She was not at all pleased with the way everything was going.

"Ah, of course," snickered RamStrong. "The, uh, GhostFin? Yes. And these…Killer Imps…they might just come all the way over here—across the entire Open Sea—from this western land of theirs, and snatch us all up in nets like so many GillFin?" The Commodore's glossy eyes twinkled in hard merriment. Wherever Piper had come up with such nonsense was a mystery to him, but he was not sorry for it. Already, Pod members were gaping in disbelief at what all seemed farfetched, fatuous notions.

"Those were the Killer Imps of the faraway Western Seas," she pleaded softly, trying hard to make them understand the terror she had witnessed in the cove where the Japanese fishermen, armed with clubs and spears, had brutally slaughtered the spinner dolphins. She could not afford to let the Commodore unnerve her, not this time. "They slew all the Jumpers…"

"Of course," quipped RamStrong.

"…in the shallows of a *cove*!" Piper pressed on steadily. "I saw them! And so did SlugFlukes. He has seen it many times!"

"Your friend the mighty GhostFin, whom you courageously rescued from the HunterKin," said the Commodore in mock awe.

"Yes—my friend that I saved, Commodore," Piper retorted icily. She did not want to show how much that last quip hurt. Piper had secretly yearned that old RamStrong would be proud when he'd heard of the valor she'd displayed. She had even looked forward to especially telling him about it. Now he mocked her instead. "SlugFlukes' whole Clan was slain by Killer Imps," she continued. "And he has seen them slaughter many WhistlingFin who live near land masses…and in the Open Seas too."

"How do they slay them, Piper?" Thane SilverFlukes asked politely. For all the peculiarity of the youngster's tale, he did not appreciate the way RamStrong was handling it. A survivor of the sea's greatest perils deserved better treatment.

"They come in their Floaters," she began softly, trying to sound even and self-assured. "Sometimes they even sneak across the sea to where very few know about them. And some of their Floaters look just like the ones here. That way they might fool us into thinking they are harmless GillFin hunters, and not a threat to us."

"I see," said RamStrong sardonically.

"They go where the great schools of GillFin gather, and they wait there," Piper continued, trying to ignore the Commodore's little jibes.

"And how would they go about, eh…catching *us*?" inquired one of the decrepit Elders. "Do they simply reach over and snatch a Whistler right up out of the water?"

Laughter.

It hurt Piper. She looked pleadingly to SilverFlukes. The Thane clicked sharply, his turquoise eyes glowering. The outburst ceased instantly.

They broke for air silently and then reassembled. SilverFlukes wondered how much longer he should allow this to go on. It certainly wasn't doing Piper's newly attained status any good. And so much of it sounded farfetched even to him.

"The Killer Imps have very strong nets, which are so thin we cannot even scan them. Whistlers get caught in those nets when they go after the GillFins, and both are swept up in them," said Piper.

"But you haven't seen this for yourself," mused another Elder.

"*I watched those horrible creatures butcher a whole pod!*" cried Piper, fed up at last. She was tired of the constant ridicule and all the deliberate taunts in their questions. "Do you think the murder of an entire Clan amusing?" she demanded, first of the High Clan, then of the entire Gathering. Her beak wagged furiously at them, and her tail flapped savagely, sending a parade of ripples through the water.

"Do you think the Snag-Tooth a laughing matter?" countered RamStrong. Or have you forsaken *all* of our Lore? Are we to abandon our defense against our worst enemy because of your mad forecasts?"

A clamor arose again. RamStrong had timed it all so well. The moment had now come for the crucial confrontation. Piper had finally been drawn out and all was in an uproar.

Two Pod members had remained entirely silent during the Gathering. Buffer, seemingly detached and expressionless, gave no indication of what he was thinking, and QuickFin stared back and forth from his sister to his Commodore, lost in a muddle of thoughts that flew at him like opponents' beaks in a Drill session.

SilverFlukes ended the clamor again. When all was still, Piper continued in a softer, more measured tone. She knew it was the only way if they were to take her seriously...

"Every moment you spend here at Kwi Coast, wasting time with your Fury Squad, you are in great peril. You cannot destroy the Snag-Tooth. They will always be here. I have seen them all over the sea and in numbers you cannot imagine. And this 'madness' of theirs is nothing more than a sickness that comes over them. They do not wish us any more harm than the other fierce hunters of the seas. It is the Killer Imps we must fear."

Piper heard the inevitable grumbling she knew would erupt and pressed on—a bit too hastily. "So we must abandon our folly here and flee this Cove before those evil Humunz come for *us*."

"Hear! Hear!" bellowed RamStrong. Piper had finally trod her way into the treacherous waters he had been awaiting. "Now we must abandon our *home* as well as our ways...forsake our beautiful Coast where our Clan has dwelled for over twenty-five seasons. And give up our Fury Squad, which protects us from the evilest creatures in the seas!"

RamStrong's outburst was echoed by the Elders and by many of his partisan Clanists, who were all growing more and more leery of the now mysterious Piper who had come back to them from the unknown. "Ah, but the Snag-Tooth 'mean us no harm,' " cried several Elders in mock echo of Piper.

RamStrong had won, and he knew it.

"Is it a lust for power that makes you try to frighten us all into believing such gibber?" he pressed on relentlessly. "Is that why you have returned with all these lurid tales? 'Evil Humunz.' Why, the Land Dwellers have always been our friends. Have we not seen them slay the Snag-Tooth many times?" The Commodore's face looked like a worn fishing net as he hefted himself up onto the lip of the Council Cliff, wagging his beak in small circles. "Is it not enough that Thane SilverFlukes has been generous enough to uphold the very Clan Code you disobeyed and allowed you back here?" said RamStrong, eying Piper hard. "But no…you continue mocking our sacred Code, even after the Thane treats you with honor. You fill us with this Waif's chatter of your wonderful heroics and your grim tales of horror. Is it Commodore you now wish to be? Or even *Thane*?" His rictus seemed to curl into a mocking sneer.

"Not anyone can thwart a pack of HunterKin!" chimed in the she-Elder. Again the cruel sneers at the exploits that had brought her to her beloved SlugFlukes. Piper's heart sank. She paddled listlessly to the surface as Thane SilverFlukes mercifully signaled another air break.

Above the waves she caught a glimpse of QuickFin. He looked grieved—lost in the bleakness of her situation. He slipped over and nuzzled his sister softly on the neck. He made to speak, but SilverFlukes signaled an immediate return.

It was obvious the Thane was not pleased with any of this and wanted an end to it. Piper could not blame him. Everything had come out wrong. She wished that, just this once, SilverFlukes could forget his own past in the Commodore's Fury Squad and assert his bloodline authority over the blustering fool. Why couldn't he just govern as he saw fit? Did he always have to let the Commodore have his way?

Calm was restored. The cackling Elders had resumed their usual posture and RamStrong had settled himself back pompously on his crusty flukes. Piper turned so she could address the High Clan and the rest of the Pod as well.

"I only know," she began quietly," that none of you has any idea what lurks out in the Open Sea, or what lies far to the west." She hesitated, weighing whether to pursue what she knew would stir them. *"But I have lived through it*—and well past your feared Hundred Dawns. I have passed through the Black Waters and lived! Who here can say as much?"

Piper paused again, studying their stunned, dubious faces. She had challenged the sacred Code once already and survived the consequences. What did it matter now? "Come now," she snickered in coy mimicry of RamStrong, "do we not all agree that a Whistler in Exile will surely perish when at the mercy of the Black Waters? Is there anyone here who disagrees that Lord Arkitu, coiled before his minions, is the most terrible fate one can suffer? How is it, then, that I am here now, eh?" Her voice rose in pitch, and she wondered if it might be wiser to tone it down a bit, lest her superstitious Pod think her some secret emissary for the Cold Lord.

The Commodore had remained silent during it all, suddenly unable to bandy words with her.

Piper, meanwhile, reveled in the momentum she had gained. No, she would give old RamStrong a taste of some stinging words for a change. "Tell me," she persisted with her scathing invective, "why return to a Clan that banished me, when it was clear I no longer needed you to survive? Answer me, Commodore!" Piper cried defiantly, surprising herself and everyone else too.

RamStrong still said nothing. He glowered at her from behind the scars of his melon, annoyed by the return glare of the smooth-skinned youngster. No…this was not the same Whistler they had banished. Gone was that defeated little scamp who was cast out so long ago. This was a sea-worn scrapper that had returned, as worthy an adversary as he'd ever known. For an instant he was reminded of a bitter young Whistler who had just seen his entire Pod sheared to bits. He wavered as he locked glares with Piper—and for that moment, something flickered in his eye that only Piper saw. It was but a moment.

Then Thane SilverFlukes spoke, and all eyes turned to him.

"It may well be that Piper *has* seen such a menace, for she has also spoken of wonders and of perils known to us too. We have long heard of the legendary GhostFins and…and of the HunterKin."

The last words dribbled out, barely audible. SilverFlukes did not consider mention of their predatory cousins a light matter. He dreaded the thought of them—as though speaking their name aloud would bring a band of the notorious black-and-white marauders bursting out from the kelp jungle.

"And it is true that the mighty GhostFins did once flourish over all the seas, for we have heard those stories too. Has Piper not explained to us *why* the GhostFins have been named so? I have yet to hear a better reason." The Thane paused, clearly weighing his own thoughts. "So…perhaps we are not as informed about the Land Dwellers as we would like to believe— though I admit, I too find all this talk of Killer Imps somewhat strange. Still, it is wrong to belittle her for it. Our own Code declares: 'Of one who returns from the Hundred Dawns, all past offense is absolved.' We will hear no more of Piper's offense. For who among you believed she would ever return? Who would have thought it possible?"

QuickFin raised his beak at that but said nothing. Inwardly the young squadron leader thanked the Thane for restoring his sister's dignity as the Clan fell silent. It was rare that SilverFlukes imposed his own regal grace in such matters, but when he did it was with the majesty and grace of a seaward dawn. Even RamStrong knew the extent of his own influence over the Thane…and also knew where it ended. Silently, the Commodore cursed from behind his beak, while the three Elders reluctantly nodded their heads in acquiescence.

For the first time since the Gathering had got underway, Piper felt comforted. This was why she had always admired Thane SilverFlukes.

"Very well," said RamStrong, "it cannot be denied what a marvelous feat young Piper here has accomplished. Surviving the Hundred Dawns and, eh, returning to warn us all of this…peril…is most admirable indeed." The Commodore's tone was strained, and it was obvious to Piper he was leading up to something. "But *how*, good Piper," the Commodore was careful to be extremely polite, "how did you escape the Black Waters? You have not yet told us of your encounter with the Cold Lord."

And at his mentioning the fell Dark Sea and its vulgar lord, another hush enveloped the Pod.

Piper had not expected it. With the intervention of SilverFlukes, she had felt sure the Gathering would now be dismissed—and matters of GhostFins and Killer Imps and HunterKin left to be mulled over. She would gladly have settled for that. At least then there would have been time for everyone to think further on all they had heard here. There would have been discussion in the days to come. She could have aired her views less formally, perhaps even swaying more support toward what she had told them.

RamStrong, however, could not simply let it go just yet. He had again managed to clog the matter. Piper had wanted to save her harrowing adventure in the Black Waters for last. The way this Gathering had gone thus far, she was leery of how the Pod might react, here and now, to what had happened there.

Fortunately, it was time for an air-break. As they soared toward the surface, she studied SilverFlukes. He appeared puzzled. Was he going to halt further discussion and adjourn in favor of another time? Piper dearly hoped so.

The water had faded to a misty gray, adding to everyone's discomfort and strife. So they refreshed quickly and gathered again before the craggy Council Cliff. Piper waited anxiously for SilverFlukes to intervene. When he nodded for her to proceed, her stomach rolled into a knot. She began in a hollow voice that did not sound like her own—as though it came from deep inside some cold, dark sea cavern, where she pictured a frail, gray-and-white Whistler held fast to the stony floor by swarms of Slithering Ones, all with distorted faces resembling members of her own Pod.

"I...I was chased into the Black Waters by the HunterKin," she said, barely audible. She paused. How was she ever going to explain this to them?

"Yes," rumbled RamStrong, "and how did you come upon the Cold Lord Arkitu?"

Piper could not believe how loosely the

Commodore had spit out Arkitu's name. The very mention of it brought back terrible notions of flailing spiked coils and two long arms clutching hungrily for her. He would not have been be so flippant about it if he'd been through the ordeals she had endured.

"Come, good Piper...for, with all due respect, I myself have difficulty trying to imagine how any Whistler might evade the grasp of Lord Arkitu and his legions." RamStrong affected the sweetest tone of courtesy, and Piper found it increasingly annoying. "Do explain, please..."

"I didn't realize where I was till morning, because the HunterKin had chased me all night," she began, trying to keep her voice steady. She was doing her best to make the unbelievable sound true. Piper understood their fears. She knew what she had been through was well beyond any of them. "I didn't want to use my scanners to see where I had fled, for fear of drawing that pack of Hunters onto me. So I paid attention only to what was right around me, just enough to avoid bumping into anything." She took another moment to see how the Pod was responding, and it seemed they were rapt with genuine intrigue.

"By morning, I could see...and there were the most horrid-looking little creatures all around me. They all had long fangs, like the Slithering Ones."

A pair of flukes ruffled nervously from somewhere within the cluster of Clanists.

"Then I saw something truly terrible," said Piper. "It was a huge white Stinger. Its body was a bubbling mush—as big as a Whistler's—and its poisoned arms hung down so far I couldn't see where they ended. I thought it might be Lord Arkitu himself, so I fled. I don't know how far I had gone when I began to notice flashing little lights below me."

"Little lights?" asked RamStrong with badly disguised sarcasm.

"Yes, *little lights*," she replied firmly, giving the Commodore a defiant look. "I thought I might have been followed by the giant Stinger that had already gobbled up several GillFins…and that maybe those strange lights were helping it find me." Piper paused, not sure how to present the next part of her story.

"I…I was about to rise for air when I saw…the largest Snag-Tooth in the sea charging up at me! Pure white it was, and bigger than any of the HunterKin who had chased me. I don't think there is a one of our killing Kin in the entire sea who could match up to it. It was so huge and savage-looking that I panicked. I dove…and since SlugFlukes had taught me to stay down longer, I went so deep the water all around me was no longer gray and gloomy but as black as a night when there are no lights above the sea, like when the Shining White Glow above is nowhere in sight."

"Did it seem this giant Snag-Tooth was going to attack you, Piper?" asked Thane SilverFlukes."

"I don't know," said Piper. "I never saw it again after that. But I was sure it had to be one of Lord Arkitu's evil servants coming for me. I just wanted to get away. You have to understand—*this was a Snag-Tooth unlike any you have ever seen*. It could have swallowed the largest of Whistlers whole! SlugFlukes had told me of the White Giants of the Snag-Tooth who grow as large as HunterKin—even larger—and they roam the Open Seas. And he said that long ago they even grew to be the size of BigFins!"

As soon as she'd said that, Piper wished she hadn't. She had been doing well, up to that point, even with mentioning the White Giant, which had sent a chill through every Pod member. But she would have inhaled back those last few words if she could have. It wasn't necessary to mention the old Snag-Tooth legends. It was asking them to accept too much at once.

"I think we should break for air now," said SilverFlukes, Piper didn't like his tone. It forecast an abrupt, brewing skepticism. And when they returned, RamStrong begged an audience.

"I must say, Piper, you have certainly seen things the rest of us have never beheld. I know I have never experienced such wonders in all *my* seasons," the Commodore said glibly.

Piper felt members of the Pod suppressing the urge to giggle. The Elders themselves sat back on their flukes, snickering as RamStrong rolled his jowly head up and around in the usual fashion when he wanted everyone to know he was right.

"This, eh, great Snag-Tooth of yours," the Commodore began, "why did you think it was a servant of Lord Arkitu's, if you yourself do not believe the Snag-Tooth to be an evil breed?"

A hush fell over the Gathering. RamStrong had struck home. Even Thane SilverFlukes nodded.

"I said it was *unlike* the Snag-Tooth any of us have ever known," said Piper. "And I did not say that all Snag-Tooth are harmless, either...Commodore." She glowered at him defiantly.

"Yes, of course," said RamStrong, ignoring her impertinence. "Do you suppose it, eh, has any old kin—perhaps even bigger than itself—swimming around a bit farther down in the Black Waters?"

"I don't know!" snapped Piper. He was deliberately leading her nowhere, and she knew it.

"Well, let's leave your big Snag-Tooth for another time, shall we? What of the Cold Lord, then? When did you see him? Or did you? Are you sure you weren't just looking at, ah…more giant Stingers? You know, we Whistlers really don't have such good sight down there—not even those who can dive so deep. We are a little better off using our scanners…that is, when the HunterKin aren't chasing us all about the seas."

RamStrong had turned and directed his final jibe toward the Pod, taking full advantage of the Thane's momentary bewilderment with Piper's story. "Please go on, Piper. Tell us of the Cold Lord," RamStrong said smoothly.

"I didn't *see* Lord Arkitu, Commodore," said Piper frostily. "I scanned his shape. One does not *see* in the pits of the Black Waters. Remember?"

RamStrong made to retort, but Piper pushed on. She was not going to let such idiocies rattle her any further. She would bandy words with this bully of a Clan leader as long as he insisted. She no longer feared doing so and knew how much that troubled him now.

"Arkitu is all we have ever feared," said Piper, addressing the entire Clan once again. "You see, I have not come back here to say that everything we've ever believed is not true—as some of you want to think." She shot another hard look at Commodore RamStrong and at the Elders, then continued. "The Cold Lord is more frightening to behold than any of you can imagine." She had their serious attention again and meant to keep it. "His *writhing and hissing* is the most terrifying thing I have ever known."

"Then how did you escape him?" RamStrong asked sardonically. He was certain now that she had to be making most of this up.

Piper hesitated, knowing this moment had been coming. "I...did not escape Arkitu all on my own," she said, recalling the image of the Great Lord of the Sea. As she spoke, she tried picturing for them an image of her magnificent savior. Then, feeling all the wonderment she herself had felt at that moment, she said with a glowing conviction, "I was saved by a magnificent creature—a giant of a BigFin—an enormous Toothed One. It rushed right into Arkitu's lair and *overpowered* the Evil One!"

Lost now in all the flowery mystique of her rescue, Piper shifted her sleek, light-skinned body so she might better address the whole Clan. "I believe that grand being was the *Lord and Master of All Seas.*"

There was a moment of prolonged grave silence.

"She is *mad*," uttered RamStrong.

Mad. The word crept over them all, slithering out from the flaky kelp jungle and crawling into the minds of every Pod member. "She is *mad*." The murmuring spread amongst them.

"Good Thane SilverFlukes, I was so wrong to condemn...to mock!" cried the Commodore. "For here before us is the true terror of Exile—this most dreaded of diseases. Oh, good Clanists, I wish never again to have cause to banish any of you. See what it has done to this poor creature!"

"*No!*" shrieked Piper. "No...please listen to me!" But the Pod had caught the fever. Whether that had been the Commodore's intent could not be said. Piper did not know, nor did she care. Everything she had told them of her valiant struggle for survival in the Open Sea had just been branded the ramblings of an insane creature—a sad lunatic to be pitied. Her mind was aghast with what that meant.

"She is *mad*! She is *mad*!" chanted the Pod members in unison. And above the clamor, Piper heard the husky voice of her brother quarreling vigorously with someone else.

"She shall never be cast out again!" RamStrong bellowed piously. "We shall care for her as the sick should be cared for—protect her, nurture her…guide her away from this *madness*, for which surely the Snag-Tooth and all their Evil are responsible!"

Commodore RamStrong was sincerely shocked at what Piper had just told them. Yes, the poor youngster had lost her senses. He also knew that it had won the day for him, too.

A chorus of shrieking dolphins cut the water with their piercing cries: "Yes, it is the Snag-Tooth who cause such misery. Avenge Piper!" They scurried everywhere, fairly howling as they whizzed up through the waves in hissing gray blurs.

SilverFlukes simply shook his regal head in sad agreement. Glumly he dismissed the Gathering.

After paddling back down in the gloomy Council Waters, Buffer gazed over at the crying, struggling Piper as she was escorted away by several Fury Guards. A few others tried restraining QuickFin, who had lost all control during Piper's outburst.

Then Buffer turned and glared at the preening hulk of Commodore RamStrong and the three Elders chatting smugly at the lip of the Cliff. Had any of them caught—through the gray haze—the chill in Buffer's frigid glare, they might well have shuddered.

PART IV
INVASION

Nicholas Checker

Chapter Twenty-One
Brooding

The days that followed were arduous for Piper. Between horrid flashbacks she was having of Killer Imps massacring the Whistlers in that cove in faraway Japan, and frequent visits from Pod members expressing concern over her "condition," she was ready to flee Kwi Coast and never return. Every day, several of the Clan would come to console her and to reassure her that "all was well."

"Yes, of course we all believed your tale—and we're taking every precaution to be sure we are *not* surprised by these 'Killer Imps.' Don't worry, Piper…just rest. You're very tired from all your journeys. No one meant to doubt you at the Gathering. We simply did not understand. But you just rest, and we shall all keep a good watch out for those impish rascals."

And Commodore RamStrong himself spoke grandly of "Piper's admirable courage" in again braving the perils of the sea just to return to her beloved Pod. And he called her a "a true hero and a worthy member of the Fury Squad," which of course they would have to build up even stronger if they were to deal with those evil scoundrels Piper called "Killer Imps." How unselfish of her to come back and warn everyone about them.

179

Piper sulked and fretted during all of it. She heard the underlying murmurs and whispers that lurked beneath the "praises" being sung of her recent exploits: "The Mad Whistler...Do not upset her. Thane SilverFlukes will be furious if there's another outburst like at the Gathering. She might even harm herself! Why else would Piper now be under constant watch?"

Already, Commodore RamStrong had named it the Great Madness: the worst fate that could befall a Whistler in Exile. "Pity is all we can feel for one so brave, yet so unfortunate!" the Commodore had proclaimed, his thick face mopped in sorrow.

And while Piper spent those days wallowing in misery and dread, the Pod went on with its usual ways. But whenever the Mad Whistler was about, they would all remark how the Commodore was busy organizing expeditions into the OutZones to search for signs of "those Evil Imps."

Piper wasn't fooled. She knew Commodore RamStrong had taken full advantage of the situation. The old dolphin's point about the horrors of Exile had been proven in the eyes of the Pod. No longer would his word on such matters be questioned in the least by anyone, not even by Thane SilverFlukes. And now the Commodore had finally obtained the Thane's permission to take Fury Squad members past the OutZones and into the Open Sea—to boldly attack and drive off the larger, more ferocious Snag-Tooth that roamed there. It also meant battling the dangerous blue sharks—sleek fighting machines that were not the least bit leery of a good spat!

As far as Piper was concerned, the true madness lay with the Commodore, for the more the Pod baited the scrappy Blues, the more chance there would be of drawing hordes of Snag-Tooth to Kwi Coast, possibly even a giant prowling White! Then what?

Far worse was the danger of splashing about so noisily near the OutZones and then returning to the cove each night. Soon, that would draw the attention of another sly predator.

What hurt Piper most, though, was that her own brother had finally given in to the notion that she had indeed gone mad. For days after the Gathering, QuickFin had isolated himself from all the others. He was sullen and moody, as he had been after her exile. This caused Commodore RamStrong a great deal of concern. So he had spoken with his valiant protégé, telling QuickFin that Piper's sickness was something that would soon pass, and that given time she might be weaned from her illness…but only through the loving care of her Clan.

"This is why the Thane instructed us to treat her so delicately," RamStrong had told QuickFin. "So she *will* be cured. It was wrong of everyone to ridicule Piper as we did at the Gathering," admitted the Commodore with all the sincerity he could muster. "But remember, we were all so terrified at the horrible effects of her exile—a good reason never to violate the Code, lest it happen to any of us. Now, if we are careful and gentle with her, we might someday have back that snappy young scamp we all loved so much."

RamStrong had seemed very solemn and truly concerned when he'd said that. "Ah, but it will take the help of everyone—especially you, QuickFin. So come now," the Commodore had added heartily, "let us see no more of this sullen pup here. We need a bright, robust QuickFin if we are to help our gallant Piper and see her back in the Squad as healthy as ever!'"

For a split instant, QuickFin thought he saw, in that crafty old face of RamStrong's, the need for an eager young squadron leader again. But it was only for a moment. He was sure the Commodore was right, as always. If anyone could help Piper, it was certainly her own brother. He would do as asked.

Yet, something else troubled QuickFin. Piper had been spending more and more time with Buffer. Exactly why, her brother did not know, but for whatever reason, QuickFin was not pleased by it. He was further annoyed to learn how Buffer had no qualms about bumping away the guard-Whistlers assigned to stay with Piper, so the two of them might slip away and speak privately. Even though he and Buffer had been getting along better than in the past, QuickFin felt a bit rankled, even hurt, that his sister was likely confiding in someone else. And he could not help feeling suspicious of the way Buffer would also go off on solitary excursions at times—often after talking with Piper.

One day, QuickFin finally asked her about it.

"Oh, I don't know, brother," Piper had answered smugly, some of her old spunk seeming to return. "I think Buffer's probably off scouting for the Killer Imps, like the Commodore claims he and his Fury Squad are doing."

QuickFin had remained silent at that.

"So please do not humor me, brother," Piper said icily. "I get enough of it from everyone else."

"But we only want you to get better," pleaded QuickFin. He knew it would insult her if he tried to carry the façade any further. She would put up with others doing that, but not her own brother.

"You weren't so ready to think me mad at the Gathering…were you? Was it the Thane or your precious Commodore who convinced you otherwise?"

QuickFin was embarrassed. Everything Piper had said was the truth. And he was confused. He didn't know what to think. The Commodore said one thing and it sounded right; then Piper would say something else, and that sounded right. Lost in the muddle of conflicting thoughts, he swam off.

****

Weeks went by, and little changed. Piper continued responding absently to the constant well-wishes of her fellow Pod members, who always spoke delicately to her. She had even managed to tolerate RamStrong's occasional visits. The old dolphin had made sure it was seen by everyone that he was genuinely interested in Piper's well-being. And always she would stifle a quake of discomfort whenever RamStrong would conclude his visits with a rough nuzzle from his scratchy beak.

Now and then, Thane SilverFlukes would seek her out. Piper had never lost the deep feelings she'd long held for the gallant Clan leader. It bothered her more than ever now to see him giving way to the Commodore's whims. Fury Squad attacks on the Snag-Tooth had increased, and she had tried warning him of the terrible danger it would bring…that such actions might well force the Snag-Tooth into banding together just to protect themselves, and how the sounds of such scuffling near the OutZones could draw hordes of more Snag-Tooth down upon Kwi Coast. Piper implored SilverFlukes that it wasn't necessary to bother any sharks at all unless they were roaming right along the Kwi Coast boundaries. But the Thane always disagreed.

"Yes, Piper, but let us not forget that the Commodore is still the only one ever to see the full might of the Furies. And if he says we're safer this way, then I really must agree," SilverFlukes sought to reassure her. "Remember, Piper, Commodore RamStrong has lived long and has kept us alive here for many seasons. Now, if the Snag-Tooth can bring on such terror, then we are best served by keeping them as far from our boundaries as possible."

Piper disagreed, but she knew she could not scold this grand lord of a Whistler the way she had scolded her brother. So she reminded SilverFlukes of all the dangers *she* had seen—which even the Commodore had never experienced. And the Thane would always listen patiently, sometimes with the intense air she often saw in Buffer, but all too often with the perplexity and skepticism she too often noticed in QuickFin's eye. Whenever Thane SilverFlukes swam off, Piper never had any clear idea of what he truly thought. But at least he had listened. Only time would tell.

The only true joy Piper had in those days was when she headed off with Buffer on her old, offbeat practice of playing in the waves or when they went on early morning hunts. At first, she thought the Commodore might attempt to prevent them from doing so, but he instead proclaimed it as a sign she was "truly recovering and their gentle treatment of her was the reason for such promising signs."

The Pod did feel it was indeed kind and understanding of the Commodore not to object to Piper's reverting to her old ways, and not to punish or even chide Buffer for batting away her watch-guards whenever he visited her.

"Anything that will help Piper recover shall not be denied her!" the Commodore often bellowed magnanimously.

Buffer never said much when they were together. He'd simply swim alongside her, patiently listening to all she told him. And before leaving, he would always vow to "keep a watch out for them." He would glance about first and scan the region, then remark to Piper very softly, "If you do think the Harbor Waifs will be the first to know of strange Floaters here, I'll look for this LoFin and her band."

Piper never felt that Buffer secretly humored her as did her fellow Clanists. His spunk, though at times overbearing, always perked her up. She was astounded that of all the Whistlers at Kwi Coast, it would be Buffer who believed her. It seemed a far cry from the day they had quarreled over the Basker killing. But then came a day of misery for Piper.

RamStrong had secretly followed and scanned one of Buffer's private ventures. They found that he had done a good deal more than sneaking off to the BreakWaters, or to the farthest of the boundaries...as the Commodore had thought. Buffer had gone well past the OutZones—*into the Open Sea*—where they had spied upon him as he battled with a young Blue Snag-Tooth.

The Commodore was furious! No one had given him leave to do that alone. Not even RamStrong himself had the authority to go beyond the OutZones without the Thane's consent. What had possessed Buffer into thinking he had such privileges? And why was he out there fighting the Snag-Tooth all on his own? Yet the old dolphin could not help admiring the deft manner in which his young charge had battered and rammed the nine-foot-long blue shark around, as though it were nothing more than a bundle of scraps tossed over the side of a boat. Not even QuickFin had been permitted to engage a Snag-Tooth all by himself. Quietly, RamStrong had been impressed, though that did not absolve the young stalwart of his irresponsible behavior.

"I knew you were following me, Commodore," Buffer told him smugly. I *wanted* you to see."

That had puzzled RamStrong. He could not decide if he was angry with the brash young brawler, or pleased. Very much unlike himself, the old dolphin maintained a silence as he and two husky sentries escorted Buffer away from the dark Open Sea and back to the familiar green of the Coastal Zone. This matter would have to be settled in front of the entire Fury Squad, himself, and Thane SilverFlukes.

****

"I went past the OutZones alone so I could fight the Snag-Tooth," Buffer proclaimed coolly to the Squad. "I am no pup who needs help chasing them off."

Piper was shocked as she listened to Buffer's testimony. She had been dreadfully worried about what would happen to him when the Commodore interrogated him...and how he might explain it all. But now what was he saying? Had he really wanted the Commodore to catch him? Why? Was that the real reason he'd been out there...just to impress Commodore RamStrong? Perhaps he hadn't really changed. Had his kindly treatment of her only been a ruse to gain favor—for "future pleasures?" Her lean face dipped in sorrow as a feeling crept over her that it might not have been wise to put so much faith in Buffer.

Other than Piper, QuickFin too had seethed as he watched and listened. His jealousy of Buffer's rapidly growing rapport with his sister had changed to a silent loathing. Buffer was a fool. He hoped she could see that for herself now.

Commodore RamStrong, meanwhile, wagged his bulky head, perplexed by Buffer's response. "For what purpose did you violate our Boundary Law? I fail to see your reasoning, Buffer."

"It was the only way you'd know how worthy a battler I truly am, Commodore," said Buffer. "You would never have allowed me to fight a Snag-Tooth alone if I had asked."

"I see," said the Commodore. "And what did you expect to gain from all this?"

"Your favor," Commodore," answered Buffer flatly. "Who is your best Fury Fighter now? Who but yourself has ever done what I have?"

RamStrong was stunned. All along he'd thought Buffer had been slipping away from him, that the youngster's jealousy of QuickFin was turning him into another Piper. Yet here he was, still seeking approval and favor. RamStrong knew he could not let on that he was secretly pleased, even flattered by it. But there was one nagging thought still bothering the Commodore.

"That is all very well, Buffer," continued the Commodore hoarsely, rolling his head round haughtily so he could appear more officious. "I must point out that I am not flattered by your intentions. There is no excuse for acting irresponsibly. There could have been several more Snag-Tooth around at the time, and then you would have been in a tidy fix, eh? You were very reckless!" pronounced the Commodore, sounding as harsh as possible. "But unless the Thane objects—and since this offense is lessened by its tie to our Fury Squad—I am willing to let it pass with an apology to the entire Squad. That is, with the understanding that a repeat action of this nature will warrant more severe consequences before the entire Pod and the High Clan!"

RamStrong turned grandly toward Thane SilverFlukes, seated at the Council Cliff all alone, and then to the Fury Squad, not unlike a slick trial attorney daring the judge and jury to find flaw with his smooth tacking on all angles. SilverFlukes nodded in agreement, assessing that the Commodore simply did not want to denounce too strongly a valuable but overly zealous Squad member. Perhaps this might even help Buffer mature, thought SilverFlukes.

The Squad, too, nodded in agreement with RamStrong's decision.

"However!" barked RamStrong suddenly. "There is still one small matter we have yet to discuss before we settle on this." He turned to SilverFlukes. "Thane...?"

SilverFlukes signaled a break, for they had been under a very long time, and a number of the Whistlers felt their lungs squeaking in protest. As they surfaced, Piper turned questioningly to Buffer, but he avoided her gaze. And Buffer did not fail to notice the ugly glare he got from QuickFin, who would have been content to ram him in the ribs on command.

When they regrouped, RamStrong gathered himself

up onto his heavy flukes and asked sternly: "Buffer, whether you are aware of it or not, my sentries have heard Piper pleading with you to 'keep a watch for the Killer Imps.' "

"Yes, she's done that with nearly everyone, Commodore," said Buffer.

"Ah, yes, my young scrapper," said RamStrong, surprisingly snide all of a sudden, "but what of your promise to Piper that you will also keep a watch out for her 'friends'—the Harbor Waifs?"

A chorus of clicks and squeaks and exclamations of astonishment followed. Piper went pale. She had not thought anyone heard their talks. What had become of the Clan's respect for privacy? Didn't the Code guarantee it?

"That was all said in private!" she cried.

"We are more concerned here with the safety and security of our Clan," exclaimed RamStrong, overriding her. "This may be one for the entire High Clan after all. Well…Buffer?"

Buffer eyed the Commodore coolly. "I was…simply humoring the Mad Whistler, as I should have," he answered, giving the Commodore a look that said, *As you and the Thane and the Elders ordered.*

Piper's heart sank into the pit of her stomach. Buffer too? She felt suddenly cold all over, and lost.

"That was cruel, Buffer," said the Commodore, much to the surprise of all. He truly meant it, too, for one look at Piper told RamStrong that she'd been devastated by Buffer's callous reply.

A commotion ensued, and it took several strong Fury Fighters to force QuickFin away as he flew out from the throng of gray bodies in a violent thrust at

Buffer, who barely avoided the lethal charge.

"Filthy thing of Arkitu!" QuickFin cried. "I will tear you to bits and feed you to the Snag-Tooth!" After several moments of struggle, and the firm voices of SilverFlukes and RamStrong, he calmed. When the clamor had subsided—QuickFin settled now inside a circle of Fury Fighters—Buffer spoke.

"If the Thane and the Commodore and my fellow Squad members all accept this explanation…" He paused, and they all nodded—well, all but two—wanting to get it over with. "…then I apologize to all of you for the misery I have caused any members of this Squad. For that, I am truly sorry."

Buffer stared straight at Piper when he'd said it, but she only glared back at him coldly.

And he knew she hated him.

Chapter Twenty-Two
The Humming

Two months passed. Piper saw nothing of Buffer. The young bull spent a good deal of time off by himself, although within the proper limits now. Except for Drill sessions, which had become very spirited between him and QuickFin, few of the Pod cared to associate with him. But there were a number of the younger fighters, particularly some of the females, who had been impressed with his notorious daring. Often they sought him out when he went for romps in the waves, and they would ask to hear tales of his exploits. That made Commodore RamStrong leery. He did not want his younger Squad members trying to emulate Buffer's reckless daring. They were naïve and impressionable. Such zeal had to be contained. The time of the Great Invasion would soon be upon them. RamStrong felt sure of it.

His Fury Squad had already tasted the exultation of battle and conquest in a number of open-sea skirmishes with the Blue Snag-Tooth. And they longed more and more for the all-out war they once had dreaded. If they were to prevail, and set a course for other clans to follow, it had to be done through discipline, not foolhardy heroics.

****

Then came the day when Piper heard it. She had

been bounding through the waves out near the BreakWaters, as far as her two watch-guards had allowed, when she heard a steady *hum* from far off.

It was a Floater, and a fair-sized one, at that. She scanned its locale—the beams inside the melon of her forehead shooting out, finding their mark, and seeping back in through the tissues of her lower jaw. They formed a picture in her mind of the craft's bulk as it stealthily approached the OutZones. It was not far from where the Basker had been slain so long ago. Piper did not know why, but this Floater's low rumble filled her with foreboding. It was not an exceptionally large craft—much smaller than the ones that gave off the strong bow waves she used to enjoy tumbling in until LoFin had cautioned her against it.

Then suddenly she became aware of another sound—one she had failed to notice at first. Piper ignored the ominous purr now of the approaching vessel and picked up on the fluttering and splashing of many GillFins instead. Hordes of them. "And many times the Killer Imps come in their Hunter-Floaters, following the great swarms of GillFins, knowing the WhistlingFin will soon come for a rich feast. Then they strike!" She fearfully recalled SlugFlukes' cautioning. Piper saw again his mottled old face, heard the coarse rumble of his voice once more as she remembered his tale of the evil Humunz' sly tactics.

She gave out a cry of horror! "It's them...it's them!" Piper wailed to her two watch-guards as she streaked over to where the pair eyed each other, puzzled at this seeming abrupt return of her *madness*. They both froze as she banged into them recklessly, shouting all the time—"Send for the Thane! It's the Doom...*our*

Doom!"

The watch-guard Whistlers both shook, narrow faces wagging sideways in discomfort. Then one of them, Prowler, took command. "Stay here!" barked Prowler to the other, SlickFin. "Try to calm her. I'll go and get the Thane."

Prowler thrashed her flukes several urgent strokes and was off, leaving a nervous SlickFin behind with Piper. And Piper rambled on as SlickFin nodded and softly agreed with the wide-eyed youngster, whose panicky chatter had been reduced to an eerie babble the watch-guard could not at all comprehend.

****

Thane SilverFlukes came immediately. He was grieved at the apparent reemergence of Piper's madness. But she calmed upon his arrival. Acting on her urgent pleas, SilverFlukes agreed to order the entire Pod to avoid the Floater that had just trudged into the OutZones. This caused some annoyance, because the wild splashing there told of superb hunting awaiting them. Abandoning so fine a delicacy seemed a great waste. But they would humor Piper and wait…hoping that these tasty GillFins gathered so close by would remain there until the Pod could finally feast on them. They would wait, though. Not even Commodore RamStrong cared to witness another of Piper's insane outbursts.

****

Piper and Thane SilverFlukes were alone at the Council Cliff. She had been very emphatic in insisting that the Commodore and the Elders *not* be included in their talk.

"Do you think I am mad, Thane SilverFlukes?"

asked Piper candidly.

SilverFlukes was not prepared for that. The rolling silver muscles of his back and tail slapped the water, swooping gracefully up and down. Piper looked soft and petite near the hulking Clan leader. She had not grown beyond her six-foot-long two hundred pounds of compact muscle, but the Thane could see the strength that lurked inside that small frame. She was a beautiful creature…and had she been a little older, he knew he would have viewed her in much the same way he eyed some of the ripened vixens of the Clan. He did not want to lie to her.

"I think…the Open Sea and some of its unknowns have affected you, yes," he answered evenly. "But do understand this, Piper. Not everything you've said has been dismissed by me. I only wanted to wait for you to regain…that is, before pressing you any further on what you first said at the Gathering."

Piper was pleased yet saddened that Thane SilverFlukes thought she had been so "affected" by her time in Exile. But at least he had been honest with her. She would just have to be careful in what she said here, and how she presented it to him. Anything that might sound far-fetched would have to be left out entirely. She decided there would be no further mention of the Black Waters or the Great Sea Lord again. Too much was at stake here. They were closer to their Doom than any might have imagined.

"Thane SilverFlukes, do you believe what I said about the Killer Imps? And do you accept my tale of the GhostFin…that he and I did watch the slaughter of the Jumping Whistlers?" Piper rolled her body coyly as she spoke. She knew how she appealed to the males of the Pod—and SilverFlukes was a male like any other, regardless how regal. He wasn't born *that* differently. Piper was prepared to do anything to convince him of the terrible danger now stalking them.

"It doesn't mean that I did not believe you before, Piper," he said awkwardly as they broke the surface for a breath. They stayed above the waves, taking in the cool mist of the gray afternoon. "I just found the tale you told us *difficult* to accept...not unbelievable. I really could not question if it happened the way you had said, because you've never struck me as one who would deliberately lie. You certainly sounded as though you believed all you said. Eh, that is..."

Oh, yes, the 'Mad Whistler,' Piper thought, annoyed.

SilverFlukes' head tilted to one side; but unlike Commodore RamStrong, who always looked ragged and cross when his head tilted in that way, the Thane appeared very majestic and wise.

"Piper," he began quietly, "for myself, it is more a matter of trying to decide exactly what you told us that I find most believable."

"Thane SilverFlukes, doubt most of what I said at that Gathering, if you must—*but believe me about the Killer Imps*," she implored. Piper rubbed up against the Thane the way she used to stroke Buffer. She understood exactly what she was doing...though she also knew this magnificent Whistler would have to decide what he ultimately felt was best for the Pod. So many times in the past, SilverFlukes had given way to the Commodore's wishes. But it was he who was Thane, not RamStrong. And she would do all she could to remind him of that.

"I know you want to believe me, Thane," Piper said soothingly.

"Well, there you are right, Piper," said SilverFlukes, again awkward in his tone. "To be truthful, I have thought more on this matter of Killer Imps than you might realize," he admitted. "And your tales of the HunterKin were not unlike those that have been told in our own Lore. And yes, the Land Dwellers are indeed a mysterious lot; they take GillFins and Snag-Tooth from the sea and rarely put anything back. I have often wondered why that is so."

The Thane paused, the cross marks of his regal brow knitting pensively. "Who is to say now there is not some evil breed of Humunz that might do the same with the WhistlingFin? And for what purpose? Why would this SlugFlukes have told you that they murdered his clan?"

SilverFlukes regarded Piper warmly, his coin gray face radiating in the faint glow of the sun as it emerged from behind a mountain of clouds for a sneak peek at the sea. "I do not believe you could have made up such a tale as the old GhostFin told you."

Piper felt her heart jump!

"That is why you are Thane," she chimed. And despite herself, Piper nuzzled him softly with her beak. She did not fail to notice the bristle of pleasure that rippled through SilverFlukes.

"And now, good Piper," said the Thane, hefting himself up, somewhat embarrassed by the sensation he'd just felt, "let us go have a look at this Floater."

Chapter Twenty-Three
The Floater

Like a swarm of tiny gunboats surrounding an invading battleship, a squadron of RamStrong's finest circled the Floater. It rested quietly in the gray sea, tilting and rolling subtly with the steady lap of the waves. The boat was a fair-sized one: seventy feet in length, made of durable hardwood and, based on the network of deep scratches all over its hull, and the gobs of lime-green algae that stained its wood, the vessel had seen more than its share of days.

The bow and the stern were both fenced in by a makeshift railing made up of a series of evenly spaced wooden poles, all joined together by several strands of thick horsehair rope. The section between the bow and stern was open. The deck dropped down about three feet below the sides of the boat—a good rock in the midst of stormy waves might easily heave a man overboard if he were not careful.

Just where the elevated deck of the bow dropped off, a huge mast soared skyward—a stream of strong lines flying out in all directions, each finding a roost somewhere on the wide deck. The boom shot over the open middle deck at a thirty-degree angle, its end hovering just above the roof of a small cabin near the stern. Behind the cabin, a few feet from the stern, was a smaller mast which poked skyward about ten feet.

It was definitely a fishing vessel, for lines had been cast overboard, as well as a number of thick, gangly nets that were already hauling in heaps of fluttering, snapping mackerel. Men garbed in long, heavy fishing coats and slick hoods pulled past their foreheads to shield them from a driving rain that had come on abruptly, strained at the nets. Nothing appeared unusual.

Waiting some thirty yards away, the small band of dolphins stared hungrily at the sight of the sputtering mackerel all going to the Humunz. Disgruntled, the dolphins still maintained their distance.

"Can't you feel the Evil here?" Piper asked SilverFlukes. Another feeling of deep foreboding had crept over her, reminding her dreadfully of when SlugFlukes had led her to the Cove of Death.

"To be honest, Piper, the only feeling I have right now is our Pod's growing discontent with my command to stave off a hearty feeding here," he said, shaking his beak under the heavy downpour. "I see nothing more than a harmless Catch-Floater seeking to take advantage of a fine hunt; as should we."

Piper was hurt. Had the Thane only been humoring her again?

As though sensing her very thoughts, SilverFlukes answered: "Piper, I do believe your story about those Killer Imps in the Western Sea. I mean it. He stared at her hard, neither of his turquoise eyes giving hint of a lie. "And I do think it was wise to be cautious today," he continued. "I thank you for it…as will the rest of the Clan."

A murmur passed through the ranks, but a cross glance from the Thane quelled it.

"Because of your concern for our Pod's safety, and your firm reasons for caution," said SilverFlukes, "I will issue a command to relieve your watch-guards of their duties. You are free to once more roam about without escort. And any who insist that the Madness is still upon you shall answer to *me*."

RamStrong, who had been hovering nearby and listening intently, turned his head away.

"However," SilverFlukes followed up, "as I see no apparent danger here—"

"But the nets!" interrupted Piper. "What of…"

"As far as I or anyone else here can tell," SilverFlukes pressed on, ignoring her blunder of cutting him off, "the only nets anywhere are those that might easily be avoided."

"But…"

"Yes, I know, Piper…the thin nets even our scanners cannot detect. All right, we will wait the rest of this day out. But if still there is no sign of any ill intent by the Humunz on board that Floater, then tomorrow we will take advantage of this fine hunt before it passes on to other waters. Now let us hear no more about this, Piper," concluded SilverFlukes. "I have the entire Pod's wishes to consider."

And I have the entire Pod's survival to consider, good Thane. Piper knew she had done all she could. But she was still convinced the Humunz on this dirty Floater were not in these waters simply for the GillFins. Even now she noticed how they all were eying the small band of Whistlers around them. They were likely baffled over why this band here had not come in at the bait and got themselves snagged; or perhaps the Imps were saving their thinner nets for when the Pod was foolish enough to swim in closer.

Piper wished they could all flee Kwi Coast until this sinister Floater filled with its hunched Humunz left. What of SlugFlukes' tale of the fire-sticks—and of the screaming death that exploded right in the water? Would these Imps try that if they saw her Pod would not venture in closer?

Piper was aware of one thing the others either did not recognize or simply refused to admit: *Humunz were by far the most cunning hunters in all the sea.* And the presence of this eerie Floater, with its killing breed on board, made her realize she would rather face a pack of HunterKin than these creatures.

Her brooding thoughts were interrupted by the Commodore's voice.

"Thane SilverFlukes, we've detected a small band of Snag-Tooth cruising this way from the south. May we have permission to drive them off?" RamStrong's big glossy eyes stared heavily into the Thane's. "They may be after the GillFins. Isn't it best we at least be rid of them?" And he added smugly, shooting a glance toward Piper, "After all, we are already losing prey to one hunter," he said, indicating the Floater with a wave of his beak. "Why surrender a well-deserved catch to yet another?"

SilverFlukes did not care for the Commodore's abrasive manner, though he understood the older dolphin's rising frustration. Others of the Pod shared those same feelings.

"Very well, Commodore," said SilverFlukes. "Do as you must—but only to drive them away and nothing more!"

The Thane knew how zealous RamStrong and his

Fury Squad had been of late, due to their vaunted attacks on bands of other roaming Snag-Tooth. But he also knew he did not want an entire horde of fierce-fighting Blues swarming down upon the Clan. Not all of Piper's forecasts had been in vain. More and more, SilverFlukes had recognized the increased fervor with which the Commodore and his Squad had been going after the Snag-Tooth. He wondered how much of that zeal he'd overlooked in the past. It was time to assert himself more as Thane. It was *he* who led the Clan, not RamStrong.

****

It was a scattered group of perhaps some twenty or so burly bull sharks and sleek sand tigers that had swarmed upon the scene haphazardly. They were not very big, the largest being only seven feet long, but off in the distance, the dolphins detected evidence of a few more roaming by that had also picked up the scent and clatter of the fluttering mackerel.

The Squad attacked instantly.

It was more of a struggle than any had anticipated. The sharks had nearly frenzied—the immediate scent of blood almost touching off their renowned Furies. If so, it might have been more costly for the Kwi Coast WhistlingFin. But the charge of the fierce-fighting dolphins had been well-timed. They had the advantage of these sharks that were banded together by accident and seeking a rich harvest in which they might partake heartily. Instead, the sharks found themselves locked suddenly in combat with a potent enemy. The dolphins were primed and rallied, the sharks startled and confused, sadly outclassed by the speed and power of the larger, swifter cetaceans.

After several minutes of futile struggle, the band of bull sharks and sand tigers vanished, but not before giving a fair account of themselves, as might have been expected. Two Fury Squad members were cut and bleeding, while another needed help getting to the surface, due to ugly rips in his flukes.

The mackerel had all fled during the skirmish.

Piper had stayed out of the fighting, as had SilverFlukes, who had remained by her side. Both had studied the Floater while the other twelve battled the Snag-Tooth. The Floater had never moved...though Piper did notice the Humunz on board all pausing in their work to watch the clash between WhistlingFin and Snag-Tooth. And they had done so—it seemed to her—with more than mere curiosity.

Confusion reigned as the small band of Whistlers returned to their coastal cove, leaving the fishing vessel alone on the darkening sea. A bristle of disquiet seeped through Piper, for she knew every eye on that Floater had followed them as they swam off.

Chapter Twenty-Four
Grim Findings

It was well into the evening when the excitement and confusion of the day finally subsided. Only then was it known that Buffer and three others were missing. When the four young Fury Fighters failed to answer the Gathering call again, the Clan was ordered to disperse and find them.

Someone suggested they scoot out to the far boundaries and do a "distance probe," but SilverFlukes quelled that. The Snag-Tooth were always out in greater numbers for their nightly hunts, and would have the advantage of the dark, which the superstitious Whistler Clan feared.

So scannings went up from the sanctuary of the Cove. Still there was no sign of Buffer or the other young bull, LongFlukes, or either of the two females— LightFin and Squeaker. Finally, a small unit of elite scouts led by SlickFin were sent out by Commodore RamStrong to scan as close to the nightly boundaries as they dared.

Meanwhile, the Clan assembled to determine the next day's activities. SilverFlukes kept his word to Piper by opening the Gathering with a formal proclamation that it had been in the best interest of the Pod to pay heed to her warnings.

"Despite the loss of prey, it was wise to be

cautious. There will be other hunts," he assured them. Then SilverFlukes went on to formally decree that Piper was "again fit as any other Pod member, having fully recovered from the strains of her arduous journey."

Piper was mildly consoled, though she noticed there was still some quiet grumbling over missing out on a hearty feast. She did not care. At least now they were safe. It mattered little what they thought of her. Perhaps now the Floater and its brooding presence would be gone, and she could continue working on Thane SilverFlukes. Once he was convinced, the Pod might then depart this dangerous Coastal Zone.

Shortly after, the four from the scanner patrol returned. For one frozen moment, no one spoke. They all simply stared at the four trembling gray Whistlers trying to steady themselves in the dusky water. The silence of the misty world was broken by SlickFin. His voice wavered as though he were a newborn calf.

"We...scanned the remains of...Whistlers, sir," said SlickFin to the Commodore. The words barely choked out from his blowhole. SlickFin was their finest scout. He had scanned the Open Sea often from the Coastal Boundaries and was not one prone to fear. Something had shaken him and the others badly.

"Remains!" burst out RamStrong from behind his knotted melon. "What do you mean *remains* of Whistlers? What happened to them?"

SlickFin tried composing himself as he faced his Commodore. "We think it was Snag-Tooth, Commodore...Thane SilverFlukes...good Elders," fumbled SlickFin, trying to address the entire High Clan at once. The other scouts nodded in perturbed unison.

"Snag-Tooth?" snorted RamStrong.

"It was far away, sir," added SlickFin to no one in particular, "but we did pick up traces of…of teeth stuck in their flesh. It was horrible," he whimpered.

"Are you saying that Buffer and the other three have been slain by the Snag-Tooth?" asked SilverFlukes, resuming command.

"The bodies were very badly torn, Thane," said Whipper, another one of the patrol. SlickFin was overcome and unable to continue. "But there were enough, uh…remains to tell it was several Whistlers. It's the most terrible thing I've ever come across, sir. They'd been that way for some time. I…I couldn't scan it again," Whipper added sickly. She looked pale.

A deathly hush fell over the Pod, but only for an instant. A clamor then arose, first a squeaky whisper, then swelling to a deafening rising of many high-pitched cetacean voices.

"Death to the Snag-Tooth! Slay them all! Death to their Furies! They have slaughtered our Kin!"

It took a good while for the High Clan to calm the Pod. Even the Commodore lost control for several moments. The Elders, too, joined in, adding their own feeble squeals to the chorus of oaths. Thane SilverFlukes called loudly for an air-break, and the Pod responded, settling down as they rose for the surface. They returned quietly.

"Buffer was off on his own again," grumbled RamStrong. "Leading his little band of eager followers off on a hunt for more heroics…the fool!" He shook his mottled head, angered at the young bull's foolhardiness and grieved by the loss. Not even the Commodore wanted anyone to learn a lesson so harshly.

"Yes," said SilverFlukes. "They must have followed the Snag-Tooth in all the confusion while we were on our way back. The Snag-Tooth probably turned on them when they realized there were only four. What a terrible death it must have been."

"It wasn't the Snag-Tooth," a small voice uttered with conviction. It was Piper. Her eyes were wide and filled terror. "It was the Killer Imps who killed Buffer and the other three. Then they threw what was left over to the Snag-Tooth. SlugFlukes told me how they do that."

"Bah!" wheezed RamStrong. "I am sick to heart of all this gibber of Killer Imps!" The scars and wrinkles on his face throbbed as he rambled on. "We have spent the whole day cowering from a harmless Floater, from Humunz who are probably convinced what an easy place this is to catch GillFins because the Whistlers here do not compete for their prey. If not for my command, the Snag-Tooth would have got the same notion." He hefted himself high up onto his flukes, rising up over everyone else on the lip of the Council Cliff. "I say let us seek out these murderous Snag-Tooth and teach them what happens when they attack and slay any of our WhistlingKin!"

"Let us not be rash!" barked SilverFlukes. The clamor subsided. "It is folly to pursue the Snag-Tooth into the Open Sea. You yourself know that, Commodore."

RamStrong settled back in his perch on the Cliff lip, ruffled by the unexpected rebuke by the Thane.

"However, you are not completely in the wrong," said SilverFlukes.

Piper's heart sank. She had thought SilverFlukes

was going to consider that it might truly be the Killer Imps who were responsible for the slaughter. Something was not right here. Buffer wasn't that foolish. She regretted ever having cursed him now. Yet she couldn't argue it any further. Buffer had been killed. He was gone for good. She felt sick and weak…defeated.

"Tomorrow, we shall go to the OutZones," said SilverFlukes. "And if these Snag-Tooth return…" There was a long pause as the Thane drew his entire ten-foot, six-hundred-pound frame up high, his silvery colors still glowing in the darkened sea, glowing with the regal radiance that was his. "If these Snag-Tooth return, then *we shall not leave a single one of them alive!*" he proclaimed solemnly.

There was a queer silence, a shock at hearing such militancy from the Thane.

"But we shall attack only on my command!" SilverFlukes added emphatically, eying the Commodore especially.

RamStrong nodded in acquiescence. Yes, my Thane, he thought to himself. And we all know that *I* shall be the one to lead that assault. "Death to the Snag-Tooth!" bellowed the Commodore defiantly. And the Pod took up the cry once more as the Gathering broke up.

Piper paddled off quietly, too grieved by the loss of Buffer, who, despite what he had done to her, was one she had still cared for deeply. Now he was gone.

She heard QuickFin's voice along with all the rest, shrieking for vengeance. And she made up her mind that if her Pod was going to fall victim to the sly, predatory Humunz on that sinister Floater, there was absolutely nothing she could do to save them. Oh, if only SlugFlukes had come back with her. But she would save her brother—even if she had to fight him to stop him from going to his death.

She swore that, as she fluttered toward the surface. Soon she drifted off into a half-slumber and would coast on that way until dawn rustled her fully awake.

Chapter Twenty-Five
Dolphin Doom

At dawn, the Kwi Coast Pod gathered near the far boundaries. The Floater had remained through the night, anchored about a quarter mile away. Early scannings revealed that some of the roaming mackerel were back and were being hauled in by the fishermen onboard. There was no trace of the ravaged Whistler carcasses. The tide had evidently whisked them out to sea—or perhaps Snag-Tooth scavengers had returned to finish off the remains of their victims.

Piper thought it suspicious that the Floater had not gone off elsewhere. As she recalled from her spying days, Floaters rarely stayed in one place that long. But she ruled out the idea of bringing it up to the Pod. Their minds were made up. Yet there was one she would still mention it to. QuickFin. Piper was intent on saving his life…and save it she would.

As expected, her brother thought she was making much more of it than she should have. "Piper, we all know you're better now," he crooned diplomatically, "but don't you think there's a chance you might have frightened yourself so badly with these Killer Imps that you are jumping at the opportunity to blame them? I mean, I'm as grieved at the loss of Buffer and the others as anyone else—more than you may realize. But we still have to think clearly when there's a crisis like this," he said as the two of them swayed in the cool morning current. They were lingering at the tail end of the Squad. No formal command had been given to assemble into battle ranks while the Scan Patrol scouted for Snag-Tooth, and so QuickFin was at leisure to break from his own formation and join his sister temporarily.

"Do not get yourself fouled up in our little herald's cries of deadly Killer Imps," RamStrong had cautioned QuickFin previously.

Don't start crying, then, when those evil Humunz turn you into scraps for the Snag-Tooth, you old bone-face, Piper thought when her brother told her what the Commodore had said. Yet QuickFin also made Piper think twice about her own feelings. What if he was right? Was it possible she was indeed overreacting to the presence of this mysterious Floater? Was she now given to the same fears that had driven the Commodore wild with his dread of the Snag-Tooth? It made her understand him a bit more. Did she and Commodore RamStrong not share a common experience? And wasn't his a worse one, having witnessed his entire family being slaughtered?

But that could happen again if they weren't careful. Because now, both the Killer Imps and the Snag-Tooth might bring on the Clan's doom, even if she was wrong about the Floater and RamStrong was right. How could a Pod of some seventy Whistlers hope to deal with the hordes of blood-lusting Snag-Tooth that would surely be drawn to the sounds and scent of so fierce a battle? Didn't the Commodore realize how hopelessly outnumbered they would be once the Mad-Eating struck their foes?

True, Buffer was dead. But there was no way the

Pod could avenge him and the others against such impossible odds. It would take much more than their vaunted Initial Thrust to chase off so many Snag-Tooth. If all the Whistlers left now, those four would not have died in vain. But if they stayed, they would be making the same mistake Buffer and his small band had made. But how could she convince the Pod of that?

As far as RamStrong was concerned, the sea was not going to be safe until every Snag-Tooth in it was dead. But did she not see Humunz in much the same way now? How different was she herself from the Commodore, all due to a terror she alone among them had witnessed? The more she thought about it, the more confused she became. But one thing was clear. She would save her dear brother, at least.

"QuickFin, listen," she began, "why don—" Piper was cut off by sudden shrill cries.

"The Furies! The Furies! They are upon us!"

The cry rose from the gray sea, cutting through the misty salt air. The Scan Patrol had returned, reporting they had detected a mass swarming of Snag-Tooth out by the Floater. Instantly, every scanner was tuned sharply to the faint sounds of snapping jaws and throaty growls. It was a noise only RamStrong had ever heard—the frightening call of a great Snag-Tooth pack. A pallor washed over the Commodore's normally dauntless face. This was *not* a drill, or a boundary skirmish, or a small group of wandering predators seeking to raid the coastal waters. This was the alarming report of a massive horde swarming to the fight in all the malevolent grace of their snaggle-toothed breed.

Hysteria swept the Pod, hysteria born of secret

fears and dark superstitions—and pure inbred hatred. So shaken were they all that none homed in a sonic picture of the massing invaders they'd all heard. The Scan Patrol had not bothered, for the frightening report of the approaching sharks had sent the small band of dolphins scurrying back to Thane SilverFlukes and Commodore RamStrong. *Hearing* the snapping and thrashing of the advancing pack had been enough.

RamStrong and SilverFlukes and the Elders instantly barked out commands to assemble for battle. QuickFin gave a smug twirl of his beak to Piper and swerved to dart back to the front ranks.

Then the truth hit Piper.

It slammed into her so hard she nearly spun over backward into a somersault. She squealed in alarm at QuickFin, so wrought with terror that she accidentally popped open her blowhole. She felt the grotesque sensation of cold salty water gushing into her lungs, as she had while in the Black Waters. A large single bubble flew out from her blowhole, Piper streaked for the surface, expelling the salty spray as she broke through the waves, choking and gasping.

"*No!*" she screamed, startling him as though she'd read his very thoughts. Piper caught the look of disbelief in his eye. "SlugFlukes said the Killer Imps sometimes catch Whistlers by luring them to their Floaters with sounds they make themselves. He said he doesn't know how they do it—but that they put *something* in the water, and it makes noises like the GillFin. *But the GillFin aren't really there*. It just sounds like they are!" she cried, wagging her beak in small circles.

QuickFin just stared at her, his handsome face a

mask of bewilderment. What was his sister saying?

"Don't you remember that I said the Humunz stopped their own hunt when you were all fighting with the Snag-Tooth—and they were all watching us?"

QuickFin recalled that. He nodded his beak slowly.

"The Humunz couldn't understand why we wouldn't come in for an easy catch of GillFin—but they saw that we would attack the Snag-Tooth!" Piper felt dizzy. A raging sea storm was bursting through her head. Great swells were rising and crashing against the inner walls of her mind. "Brother—*there is no Snag-Tooth pack out near that Floater!* Just a few GillFins…and the noises the Killer Imps are mak— QuickFin, why are those GillFins still there if so many Snag-Tooth are close by?" she cried chillingly.

QuickFin felt his innards freeze. Certainly the school of little GillFins would have fled already at the sight of so many hungry Snag-Tooth.

"Please!" shrieked Piper, her delicate features contorting practically into a mask of something that seemed more like a thing of Arkitu's. "Do not think me *mad*! It is death out there. *Death!*" she shrieked.

Whoever's voice had come from the twisted form of his once-delicate sister, QuickFin did not know; but it shook him terribly. He heard the Fury Squad roaring away, probably not even noticing his absence in all their fervor. The proud squadron leader felt the pull. They needed his beak, the blinding charge which he knew that few Snag-Tooth could withstand. But Piper actually made sense now. In all her hysteria—she was making sense!

And something else tugged at him, too. If he went with the Pod now, whether Piper was right or not about these Killer Imps—or whatever it was out there—she would indeed go mad. And in the end, his love for his sister won out. QuickFin stayed behind with her.

They both waited. The boundary region was now deserted. Except for two mothers and their calves that had remained back in the Cove, every other Whistler had gone for the call to alarm. Even the Elders took part—as battle marshals who helped direct the movements of the squadrons. Weaker Pod members also went along to help tend to the wounded, as did the older Whistlers, and even some of the younger ones who were not yet ready to join the fray.

RamStrong's long-rehearsed plan was not without ingenuity. But he had made a great error in taking nearly every Pod dolphin with him.

Piper and QuickFin waited, and soon they heard the cries.

Chapter Twenty-Six
The Slaughter

Their first impulse was to flee. The cries that pierced the morning fog and spread over the waterways informed all in range of the local dolphin pod's plight. Piper tried shutting out the pitiful squeals, but it seemed they were everywhere. The cries followed her beneath the waves, then back to the surface when she breached. And she knew it was the Killer Imps and not the Snag-Tooth who were slaughtering her Clan. For those were the screams of bewildered dolphins, trapped hopelessly in wire-strong netting, as rough hands hauled them on board a filthy old vessel—hands that belonged to wicked Humunz who would then brutally club the hapless Whistlers to death,

The cries tugged horribly at her. QuickFin had followed her back to the surface and, for the first time ever, Piper beheld absolute terror in her brother's face. She knew it made sense to flee now. There was nothing the two of them could do anymore to save their stubborn Pod. They had all brought this Doom upon themselves. They had ridiculed her, banished her, vilified her, deemed her *mad*, scoffed at everything she had learned and held precious. They were all sheltered little Cove dwellers that had never been anywhere, yet had dared snicker at her hard-earned wisdom. She had tried so hard to help them see the truth. It was fitting then that they die this way due to their own stubborn ignorance. How much pomp and glory was there now for the old Commodore?

That thought stopped her.

She suddenly forgot thinking of them as "the Pod" and thought of them once more as Whistlers she had known her entire life: SlickFin, Whipper, Thane SliverFlukes, and…Buffer, all victims of the Killer Imps.

A rage rose up inside her.

Piper looked to QuickFin, who was thrashing alongside her in the misty sea. The regal bearing he'd always sought to maintain was gone. His sleek ripple of steel-gray muscle was now tight and shriveled, like wet knotty rope. In place of the once-proud warrior now fluttered a frightened pup of the sea who had just learned how tiny his own world truly was. It was not so much his fears of the vicious Humunz pack but more the frightening realization that if not for his sister's frantic pleas, his own voice would be among those now crying out in anguish.

"Let us be off, Sister," he said, hearing the quake in his own voice.

Piper's round, ashy eyes stared woefully into the cloudy gray of her brother's. "They are *our own*, Brother," she piped hoarsely. "Can we leave them like this?"

"But they cast you out, they mocked you!" QuickFin was confused. He couldn't think straight; his head hurt. What was his sister saying? Go out there? He wagged his beak incredulously. "Piper, you yourself said all we can do is flee."

Piper paused. Her horror and her misery were

slowly changing form. She wanted to have at these foul Land Dwellers who thought they could just sail across the seas and destroy her Clan. No, SlugFlukes may have had to watch his Clan perish, but she was not going to see it happen to hers!

"QuickFin, all I've learned from my exile will have been for nothing if I flee now." Her eyes flashed mischievously. "Come…let's teach these filthy beasts that they can't go about slaying the WhistlingFin as they please."

QuickFin snapped out of his daze. "We two? Alone?" He could not believe what he was hearing. "Piper, how are the two of us going to teach a Floater filled with Killer Imps that— Please, let us be off!"

"Ah… Is this the brave and mighty QuickFin I hear now? Bold leader of the Sea-Flash Squadron? Afraid now to follow little Piper against the bent creatures that tricked and ambushed his own Pod?"

Piper's face was afire with contempt. Not for her brother's lack of zeal for facing the Killer Imps, but for anything that ever attacked a Whistler. For an instant, QuickFin wondered if she might even be possessed by the Commodore now, for she certainly sounded like him. And the look in her eye was a familiar one the young squadron leader had seen during many a spirited Fury lecture. Was this snarling, wild-eyed creature— who had been to Arkitu's lair and back—truly his sister?

"Well, Brother?" She beckoned.

QuickFin shivered. Piper meant it. She was going back out to that terrible OutZone where who knew what kind of horrors she would find! But just as he would not desert her earlier, he knew he could not do so now.

Frightened as he was, QuickFin would never let his sister go off alone again.

"Very well, dear Sister," he said, trying to sound poised and cool but knowing he was neither. "Let's go and have at them," he said resolutely.

"Don't worry, QuickFin," Piper said shrewdly. "I know a way to do this."

"Oh? And what's that?"

"Now that those Imps have trapped everyone, we'll know exactly where all the nets are."

QuickFin did not follow her line of thought. "So…?"

"So while they're pulling them all out of the water, *we'll chew through the nets*," she said.

"Piper, that…that might work!" exclaimed QuickFin.

"If it's not too late," said Piper. "We must hurry!"

And they soared through the foggy sea at a blistering pace, images of the sinister Floater and the Killer Imps aboard it urging them on.

****

Piper hoped it was not too late; but as she and QuickFin sped through the choppy water, she was hesitant to home in on the ghastly scene they both dreaded. How many of the Pod were already butchered and stretched out on the deck of the Floater?

The screams grew louder. Above the din of the wailing dolphins, Piper and QuickFin also heard another cry—the shouts of the Imps celebrating their wretched harvest. The two sped on, cruising the surface but reluctant to use their sonar. What they were soon to see would be enough. They were in no hurry for visual images of this massacre. The sounds that carried over the waterways were vivid enough.

When they were finally within sight of the Floater, both felt as if they might heave out their stomachs. Piper and QuickFin stopped some fifty yards short of the fishing boat. It was far worse than they could have imagined. Piper felt like she was back in the Cove of Death with SlugFlukes.

A swarm of hustling, bent forms scuttled about the deck of the dark Floater, like crabs crawling over the carcass of some long-dead animal they would never have dared approach were it alive. The men wielded heavy sticks and clubs which they swung up and down at things lying prone at their feet. Others were hunched over the sides of the boat, hauling in large black nets, so fine in texture that only the thrashing, befuddled dolphins trapped inside them made it possible to see the dark lining.

Underwater those nets were virtually invisible.

The dolphins tangled in the netting struggled momentarily, then quieted to a stilled shock, helpless in their terror. Piper and QuickFin submerged. Beneath the waves, the pathetic shrieks and cries of the WhistlingFin—mixing with the throaty calls of shark recordings—made both dolphins tremble. The underwater speakers gave a perfect rendition of a shark pack caught up in a vile feeding frenzy. Piper did not understand how these foul Humunz did it, but it certainly worked well enough.

SlugFlukes had been right.

The two dolphins drew closer and rose to the surface. Both writhed as they realized what the Imps were pounding at with their clubs, thick clubs that rose and fell with gruesome precision. There was a dull *thwack* every time wood connected with flesh. Then, amidst the noise of the beatings, Piper heard the high-pitched wail of a single Whistler.

Her stomach curdled as she recognized the voice of Thane SilverFlukes.

"*No!*" she shrieked, her eyes wide with horror. Piper reared up and charged toward the Floater, paying no heed to QuickFin's cries for her to wait and think out the rescue. He was just behind her as she came abreast of the Floater. QuickFin watched her leap clear out of the water—at least ten-feet into the air—startling the baffled Norwegian and Russian whalers aboard the old vessel. She glared at them from eye level for the split second she was suspended in midair, her smooth gray-and-white body twisted grotesquely out of shape. My, but these Imps are an ugly lot, she thought as she barked viciously at the startled poachers.

Then Piper tumbled back into the water. She rose up again, just beyond the nets filled with the tangled dolphins. Savagely she gnawed at the fine strands of netting, ripping through it like a buzzsaw slicing through wood. QuickFin watched for a moment, then followed her example in earnest. Both dolphins chewed frantically with their teeth at the thin black ropes that held their comrades imprisoned.

Two trapped dolphins wriggled free as one of the nets parted, their shock broken once they tumbled back into the sea. Still the two frenzied cetacean rescuers ripped fiercely at the nets.

Several portly-looking men yanked hard on one of the nets, straining to haul in another trapped dolphin before the fiercely nibbling pair freed another. Suddenly Piper leaped out of the water, right to the edge of the middle deck—and bit down hard on the calloused hand of one of the poachers. The man yowled in agony, letting go of the net as he beheld his severed pinky finger gushing blood like a small geyser. Piper dropped beneath the waves once more, spitting out the tiny bit of finger that had been stuck in her teeth. She rose to tear at another net…and found that she suddenly could not maneuver.

She was trapped!

Piper had fallen into the wiry strands of an open net. She squirmed violently, cursing and screaming in rage as she was hauled up. She sensed the presence of QuickFin as he leaped up beneath her, attempting to save her from the ghastly fate that awaited her on the Floater's deck.

Piper grew dizzy and confused inside the tangle of the net. Then she felt a bone-crunching force that made her skull seem like it had just split! Tremors swept her entire body. The last thing she knew was a sense of aimless drift.

Chapter Twenty-Seven
The Shame of the Killer Imps

For several minutes, Piper lost all contact with her surroundings. The impact of the club had shattered some of the bones in her forehead, and soon she felt the coarse tickle of tight rope strands slicing into her smooth flesh. She floated through a foggy world, mindless of the activity around her. She was never altogether unconscious or she would have stopped breathing and suffocated. Finally she began to regain a semblance of her senses.

Instinctively the first thing she tried to do was paddle away as quickly as possible, but her flippers and flukes beat impotently at the air. She was stretched out on her stomach on the surface of the middle deck. The late fall sun had finally poked its way through the barricade of clouds and now beat down viciously, burning the young dolphin all over. And since she was out of the water, her flesh sweltered under the sun's stabbing rays. All about her were the limp forms of Pod members beaten and scorched beyond recognition.

Piped glanced around furtively and caught a fleeting glimpse of the scurrying shapes of the Killer Imps. One passed right by her, and Piper shivered at the sight of the hard face that surveyed the heap of dying Whistlers. She was aghast at the man's cool, casual manner as he strode passionlessly past the whimpering, suffering creatures on the deck—ignoring their repeated pleas for an end to their misery. Two others joined the first. Both were tall, burly, and heavily bearded, their flesh as pale as the foam in the BreakWaters. Different, Piper thought, from the sallow-skinned Imps who had slaughtered the Jumper pod in the faraway cove. Yet not so different, she mused.

A grunt from her right interrupted her thoughts, the sound of a dying creature trying desperately to cough out its last words. Piper twisted and rolled her aching body, awkward now that she was out of water. The sleek frame that had once sped through the sea with such grace and ease was now cumbersome and clumsy on the deck of the ship.

Piper finally succeeded in twisting round to one side—and peered straight into the crushed, bleeding face of Commodore RamStrong. "So you came back to try and save us anyhow," croaked the old voice, so much older than it had ever sounded. The words wrestled feebly out through his partially clogged blowhole. "You beautiful little fool…after all we did to you." He fell silent, pained from the strain of speaking. Everything all over the Commodore hurt—and Piper cried inwardly for him.

"Yes," she said softly from behind a pair of sorrowful eyes. "You…you are my Pod, sir."

The old dolphin tried vainly to maneuver himself so he could see her better, but his once majestic old body was now a battered hunk of bleeding flesh. "We were not worthy of one so gallant as you, my fine young scamp," he croaked affectionately. The Commodore's voice had faded to a low whine, and Piper had trouble making out what he was saying. "Had we paid heed to your wise forecasts, and had I not been so driven by the Snag-Tooth… Ah, but that does not matter now, does it?" he gasped. The old eyes were closing under blood-clotted lids. "You should not have tried to rescue us…you would be free now. Ah, but then, that would not have been like you—would it, my brave Piper?"

Piper remained silent. She felt pity for the old Commodore. She shuddered as she tried to picture how horrified he and all the others must have been when they'd found themselves charging into the wide spread of nets—and no Snag-Tooth anywhere.

"I've been waiting to tell you—hoping you were still alive so I could tell you—please believe me, good Piper," gasped RamStrong, heaving the words out painfully, "I truly wanted only to be a good Commodore. *I did love my Pod!*"

And then the old Commodore died.

Piper felt hollow. She was numb to her pain for a moment, saddened as she watched the demise of a Clan giant whom she now knew she had never truly disliked.

Then the pain came back, and she was aware, once more, of the carnage of wounded and slain Whistlers all around her. She was repulsed by the ways of these vile Land Dwellers. Piper could not understand what reason there could be for such cruelty. The WhistlingFin never harmed them. Why did Humunz do this? Knowing that she and her Kin would be ground into pet food and fertilizer would have sickened her all the more…and that such fishermen saw their own actions as securing greater catches of fish for themselves, along with the added treat of dolphin delicacies they might also peddle for profit.

Neither Piper nor the rest of her cetacean cousins were aware of how rapacious Humunz thrived on the slaughter of her kind—usually for food or for trinkets and souvenirs. So she cried in her ignorance of human cruelty and shame. She glanced around the filthy old fishing boat, eyeing the tall masts and the thick strands of rope running everywhere. She did not know what any of it was—or its purpose. Nor did she understand the function of the men on the upper deck, hacking away with long, sharp tools at the rows of already dead dolphins. By the time the poacher vessel rendezvoused with the factory ship, most of its catch would be already sheared and readied for processing.

Piper turned her head away, sickened by everything around her. Her gaze shifted toward the bow of the ship, not far from where she lay, and what she saw there made her heart stop. Stretched across the deck was the limp form of QuickFin! He had been caught in his attempt to rescue Piper from the grip of the nets and got himself snagged too. A sour taste welled up in her mouth.

It was her fault, she thought.

If not for her hasty attack on the nets, they might have freed more Whistlers and then fled safely away. Now she had led her brother and herself to a cruel death. She hated herself.

A wild racket distracted Piper. It was the sound of a Whistler squealing in agony and terror. She recognized the voice. She didn't want to turn and look. Piper knew what she would see—and she did not want to believe it was truly happening, but she forced herself. She gasped and groaned as she twisted her body, and through the cracked lids of her eyes she beheld the

225

wriggling, battered form of Thane SilverFlukes—struggling frantically as he was borne in the arms of a large cluster of cursing men.

They were carrying him toward the upper deck!

SilverFlukes' proud physique no longer shone brightly with the hue of South Sea Coral. Now, ugly welts from the repeated pounding of sticks and clubs—along with gory sun blisters—festered all over him. And he writhed and screamed in a way that Piper could never have imagined of one so regal.

She was aghast, mortified that this cluster of Imps, and the two bearded ones who directed the procession, prepared to hack to bits the once elegant Thane—as they had done with a number of the other Whistlers. Piper mounted the last of her ebbing strength and thrashed madly, squirming her way toward the filthy bearers of her beloved Thane. She hoped she might be able to distract them, perhaps annoy them enough so they might take her instead of SilverFlukes.

The feisty Thane was not going willingly, either. He snapped and twisted like a snake caught in a trap, lashing out everywhere with his sharp teeth. He managed to raze one of his bearers. Then his long tail swiped loose and caught another of them clean in the chest, sending the man sprawling across the bloodstained deck. One of the bearded poachers grabbed a heavy club and brought it down angrily upon SilverFlukes' head—and the royal Thane of Kwi Coast was no more.

The two bearded ones spoke with one of the older men who acted as though he were in charge. Then the rest of the crewmen muttered curses as they hefted the limp carcass of the big dolphin back up again. They headed for the upper deck once more.

It took a dozen of them to finally haul SilverFlukes' body up to the higher level of the rear deck, where the butchering crew waited. They had just started hacking at the ten-foot-long cetacean carcass when Piper came flapping and twisting toward them along the lower middle deck, like a flatfish that had just flopped out of a fisherman's bucket and was trying vainly to reach the safety of the water.

She screamed at them: "No! No! You cannot... He is our *Thane*! Please cast him back to the sea!" But to the Norwegian and Russian poachers, it was nothing more than the senseless chatter of a stricken, half-dead dolphin which looked ridiculous as it tried to tumble over to them; clumsy and stupid. Some of the men stepped toward her, clubs raised high. They wanted to silence this screeching pest and get back to their work. Enough time had already been wasted with the bigger dolphin.

Piper rolled under the spindly legs of two of the crewmen as they climbed down to the middle deck. They both toppled over, and Piper sank her teeth viciously into one of the men's legs. He wailed in pain.

Now the whalers lost all patience. Their grim faces contorted and were ablaze with fury. The two bearded ones and the short, older leader cursed and hollered commands at everyone else. And in all that commotion, the six-hundred-pound body of SilverFlukes tumbled off the rear deck. It fell hard onto one of the men who had tripped over Piper. There was a squishing noise as the sheer weight of the Thane's limp body nearly crushed the life out of the wiry little man. Then came another loud crunch as a hard stick fell upon Piper's skull.

Piper's head rocked. She stared up through a red haze and saw the pale-skinned Killer Imps slicing away at the once regal body of Thane SilverFlukes. She watched helplessly, barely conscious as they once again went about their gruesome task. The haze in Piper's brain thickened as she witnessed the defilement of her Thane. The heat scorched her already dried-out skin as she struggled to retain consciousness, but her mind slipped into a fog.

The world around her dimmed and grew gradually darker. It was no longer hot, but cool, then cold...very cold. Everything on the deck of the Floater had chilled abruptly and blackened.

Something was wrong.

A low hissing began, rising in pitch until it filled the air all around her. The sea itself rose higher and water soon spilled over the sides of the deck in small black streams. Then the waves came, rolling and crashing down upon them. And out of that inky gloom, Piper beheld a frighteningly familiar coil, dotted with row upon row of curled teeth. More coils appeared and hovered over the deck, groping about like fingers in the dark. And the sea, which by now had risen above the level of the middle deck, was filled suddenly, as if by magic, with hordes of ugly misshapen monsters of all sizes that chanted and sang in a grotesque cacophony of discordant voices.

And Piper saw it. Just as the Floater began slipping softly beneath the blackened waves, she caught sight of the beaked face and its gaping maw.

Lord Arkitu had come to claim them all.

A loud *boom* filled the air...and Piper was jolted

out of the gray oblivion she had passed into…back onto the scorched deck of the old fishing vessel. Another thunderous *crash!* This time the Floater pitched and heaved violently. It was no hallucination. The Killer Imps scuttled about the deck in panic. Piper heard the coarse voices of the two bearded leaders of the poachers—now bellowing in alarm. Another booming *crash* and the morbid contents of the rear deck spilled down onto the middle section. A gush of sea poured in over the sides, and all the Humunz cried out in terror.

The Floater was sinking!

Chapter Twenty-Eight
A Vengeful Ghost

Piper shook in horror. Had she truly seen a vision of the Black Waters and its Cold Lord? Had Arkitu escaped the grasp of the Great Sea Lord and come here to claim the victim he had been cheated of in his own lair? Was it now to be that she and her Clan and even the Killer Imps were fated to wind up as feed for the Cold Lord?

Piper wondered which was worse, falling victim to predatory Land Dwellers—or being claimed by the Cold Lord. At least Arkitu belonged to the sea, she thought. What right did these Land Dwellers have to wreak such terror in the domain of the sea?

Suddenly an explosive crash rocked the air, and the fishing vessel split! Then the raging sea was everywhere. Men tumbled overboard, screeching in fright, while the dead and semi-dead dolphins also plummeted over the sides. The Floater pitched sideways as a sizzling roll of foamy water washed Piper into the sea. The cool water that filtered onto her parched skin was refreshing. It lent her aid in regaining her wrecked senses. The pounding she'd first heard had not let up. It sounded like a monstrous clap of thunder over a stormy sky.

The Floater slipped quickly beneath the waves, and Piper fought hard to orient herself. In the gloom, she made out shimmering images of drowning men and the mass of dolphins that had tumbled overboard. All were being sucked in by the vortex created by the sinking vessel. And through the swirl of thrashing bodies, Piper made out something else—something dark and gray and *massive*, ramming the Floater repeatedly. The monster attacked the sinking vessel with a might and a rage unlike anything she had ever beheld.

In a matter of moments she understood. *SlugFlukes* had come to finally claim his vengeance on the Killer Imps. And in these fateful moments, he had rekindled the terror the Hunter-Humunz once held of the mighty GhostFins—the legend which had struck fear into the hearts of the staunchest whalers. SlugFlukes, who had sworn he would one day repay Piper for saving his life. The grand old giant of the sea had not forgotten or abandoned his little friend from the east, nor the oath he had sworn to her.

Now, not ten miles out from San Pablo Bay, SlugFlukes did as his ancestors had done well over a century past. Piper was mesmerized by the majesty of his rage. Never could she have imagined the old GhostFin this way. Even his daring defiance of the HunterKin pack did not measure up to the power he now displayed. And so caught up was she in his rampage, she forgot about the vortex drawing in both dolphin and man indiscriminately. Too late, she tried paddling away, but she was weak and unable to resist its powerful pull.

Piper was badly in need of air now as the vortex sucked her in ever closer. She fell into the whirl that would eventually shrink into a smaller circle until she was completely absorbed. SlugFlukes could not help her. He was far too obsessed in his destruction of the Floater. Was *this* how it would all now end?

Suddenly she felt the impact of something fleshy and tough as it bumped her to one side. Then a familiar voice: "Must we Waifs do everything for you, my sweet Whistler?"

Piper's heart throbbed, her mind in disbelief. She recognized the chubby black-and-white form and the stubby flukes, but she could not believe it. *LoFin?* Was she dreaming? Was that snippy little Rover really here—right by her side? Or was it another hallucination…one brought on by the brutal beatings and her desperate desire to survive?

Her thoughts were interrupted by a *thump* on her other side. Piper shifted an eye—and what she saw there convinced her it had to be a hallucination. She must already have drowned and gone to some dream world, perhaps one they all passed through before oblivion. It had to be so. For she knew she could not possibly be looking at…*Buffer*.

Was she still on the Floater imagining all of this? The cool water seeping into her pores and soaking her previously parched flesh told her it was indeed real and happening right now!

She could still hear SlugFlukes ramming the battered Floater and thrashing at it with his flukes, while LoFin and Buffer bumped and brushed her gingerly toward the surface. Above the din of SlugFlukes' rampage—and LoFin's complaints that the "oafish Whistler trying to assist knew nothing of gentle rescue"—Piper detected the whimpers and cries of more lamed Pod members being similarly rescued. She weakly scanned the images of more Rovers and

Whistlers—were they Buffer's followers?—scouring the tainted waters for survivors and then bumping them away from the deadly whirlpool.

Soon, another sound filled the surrounding waters, one that Piper fearfully recognized. It was dangerously close...and real this time. And it carried the grim promise of death.

The Snag-Tooth were coming. Their most ancient of hunting calls had summoned them: the thrashing of creatures in distress. And it was the Killer Imps that had drawn the attention of the sharks, luring them on with their immediate panic when their vessel was bashed to bits by an enraged monster of a gray whale. Though Piper's sonar was badly damaged from the beatings she had suffered, she still managed to pick up the rhythm of sleek bodies approaching steadily, beating through the murk with rapid swipes of their bristly tails. The nerves inside her forehead quivered at the report of the silent hordes that were now massing almost magically. Every second came the signal of one after another—appearing spontaneously as when an artist wrings a wet paint brush all over a clean sheet of paper, filling it with hundreds of dots in a second.

Piper gasped hungrily for air as she and her two rescuers rose above the foggy sea. She started to speak but they both cautioned her against it.

"We must not tarry here long, my spunky friend," said LoFin grimly, fear in her eyes. "The Snag-Tooth are here for their gruesome feeding."

"Piper, come," Buffer urged gently but firmly. "Death as you've never imagined is on its way. And," he added, "there's much I have to explain once we're away from here."

Piper's brain was as much a whirlpool as the one created by the sinking Floater. It was all happening faster than she could think. She nodded in agreement, but she knew there was something she had to see before she fled.

"A moment, please!" she gasped urgently. Still vigilant, Buffer and LoFin slid gently away from her, accommodating the desperation in her plea. Piper ducked under a few feet so she could scan the scene of the wreck. What she saw through her sonic eye made her understand, finally, what had long ago filled Commodore RamStrong with such fervor. Now she truly forgave him.

It was monstrous. Everything the old Whistler had said about the Furies, she now beheld. It was a scene that would remain with her the rest of her life. Nearly every breed of the Snag-Tooth had come. Their eyes gleamed with senseless hunger, while their lower jaws were slung back, showing row upon row of glistening fangs. Darting out from all directions, they descended like aquatic demons—roaring down upon the writhing men and the stricken dolphins. And now, Piper could make out more clearly the hazy shapes of Buffer's and LoFin's small pack of rescuers, still gallantly trying to save the surviving Whistlers from the slashing jaws of death.

Piper turned to say something to Buffer and LoFin, but only Buffer was there now, his eyes pleading for her to depart. Above the noise she could hear LoFin's shrill voice. The glib little Waif certainly wasn't without courage, she thought, as the porpoise had zoomed off—outside the mass of frenzied sharks—and was trying to call off SlugFlukes before it was too late.

LoFin cried frantically for the GhostFin to break off the attack and flee the blood-filled waters. But the old whale was now as crazed as the slashing sharks that tore away at the drowning men. The gray giant continued goring the broken hulk of the Floater.

Poor old RamStrong, thought Piper. So this was what drove him so *mad* that it tormented him his entire life. By now, the Furies had grown into so savage a welter that some of the Snag-Tooth turned their attacks upon themselves. Piper felt sick as she watched them chewing out their own entrails and then trying to eat the shreds, only to have them spill back out again in bloody hunks. Occasionally a clutter of red-stained arms and legs would fly loose. Other times a frenzied shark would rip out select chunks of flesh from one of the wriggling human bodies. The more frantic the Humunz became, the more excited the Snag-Tooth grew, capricious in the fury of their hunger.

Soon, the panicky floundering of the drowning men drew the main body of sharks away from the injured dolphins, allowing the small rescue band of porpoises and dolphins to save a few more. But they had to flee soon—and flee fast—before the unpredictable Snag-Tooth shifted their pattern again. Somewhere in that unholy midst, Piper knew the lifeless body of Commodore RamStrong had come to the grisly end he had long feared. And that made her think of Thane SilverFlukes, also out there in so many different pieces. She wondered what had happened to QuickFin. Was he alive, dead, half-eaten, or…had he possibly been rescued? She hoped…

Buffer nudged her, interrupting her thoughts once more. Piper's beak tingled as she drew in the sonic image of a burly man, half-devoured, staring senselessly at his own innards spilling out in a scarlet heap. And she knew it was the big one that had dealt SilverFlukes his death blow. The man screamed hysterically as his lungs burst from the rush of water pouring in.

Piper felt no pity for him, or for the others. Nor did she scorn the savagery of the Snag-Tooth as they darted wildly through the bloodied OutZone like wispy shadows of a bizarre justice.

****

LoFin finally managed to signal SlugFlukes away from the demolished poacher vessel, which now lay in splinters on the sandy bottom. What an enemy this old one makes when aroused, thought LoFin. The chunky porpoise marveled as she watched SlugFlukes swipe away several lolling sharks that had foolishly tried assaulting him. One blow of his roaring flukes was all it took for him to bat the four dolphin-sized sharks into oblivion.

Once the old GhostFin was sure Piper had been saved, SlugFlukes drew himself away from the wreckage. All debts were settled, and he rumbled off in triumph, bellowing a song of victory that filled all of Kwi Coast, a chant that spoke of an aged giant who had finally taken his long-awaited vengeance.

As the tiny band of Whistlers and Rovers fled the nightmarish waters, followed by the GhostFin, the tormented cries of those dying echoed throughout the waters like a dirge—reminding all who could hear that not even the powerful Land Dwellers could claim to be masters of the sea.

Chapter Twenty-Nine
Kwi Coast…and the Sea

A month passed. One quiet morning, with the sun golden and bright overhead, Piper rose for her usual hunt. The sea was pale and green, perfect for her early activities. The rest of Kwi Coast was still asleep, as it was too early for them to be up and about.

She did not frolic these days. Once she caught her morning meal, she spent the next couple of hours cruising the old boundaries, ever in hope for signs of her brother. QuickFin had not turned up in the rescue, and Piper was grief-stricken by it. She hoped he had been dead before he hit the water and was therefore spared the agony of the Snag-Tooth's jaws. But deep inside she also wanted to believe that somehow he'd survived it all, though she knew it wasn't likely. So she brooded often.

Permanent scars had been left on her—the ghastly slaughter of over half her Clan, the humiliating demise of Thane SilverFlukes, and the tragic lamentations of old RamStrong at the end. But comfort had also come…in the form of knowing Buffer had sought out the Harbor Waifs, day after day, all that time the Commodore had wondered where he'd been spending his time.

"I believed you from the time you came back, Piper," the burly youngster had admitted, days after the

Massacre. "Anyone who survived the Hundred Dawns deserved more respect than you were given."

"Was that all of it?" Piper had asked with a flutter of her fins.

"Well, perhaps not," he added, twirling his beak slightly. "And you know I've always been sort of miffed about how the Commodore never used to give me the kind of praise, well...that he gave to...um, others," he said awkwardly, knowing Piper politely ignored his blunder. Then he added quietly, "You see, not being in the old Commodore's favor gave me a chance to drift back a little and see what was really going on, Piper. I didn't care anymore if I broke his rules."

Buffer urged her to the surface for an air break and then continued. "But when you returned, he saw you as a threat to everything he'd ever believed in, Piper. You lived through what no Whistler had ever survived. The Commodore just couldn't accept that. I'm not saying he deliberately always tried to make you look bad. He was just, well...scared. And he didn't know what to do about it because it had never happened before. Then you came up with an even worse danger than the Snag-Tooth! You know, sometimes I think Commodore RamStrong may have even secretly wondered if you were right."

Piper had pondered that, knowing such a notion had never entered her own thoughts.

"Still, after seeing what the Furies are really like, can you blame him for being the way he was? Old RamStrong was so tormented by his own past that everything happening to him—everything in the entire sea—was affected by it. Your return and your story about the Killer Imps shook him so much, Piper, that in his own haunted mind he probably felt the Pod was doomed as long as you were around to bump us all off course."

"I know that now, Buffer," she had cried softly. "Oh, you should have seen him at the end."

"I'm glad I didn't, Piper."

Buffer had been uncomfortable and feeling quite awkward that day as he'd explained to her his reasoning for the ruse that had duped everyone in the Clan. The two of them were cruising the afternoon sea near the BreakWaters, blowing out plumes of gray vapor as they "porpoised" gently in the rolling surf, he helping her carefully along. It had been only a few days after the Killer Imp Tragedy, and Piper was still feeling weak.

"You do realize, Piper, I had no choice but to say what I did when the Commodore caught me fighting that Snag-Tooth. It could not have been helped. You see, he wasn't entirely wrong about them, and if I'd told Thane SilverFlukes and him that I was out there waiting for a Harbor Waif to let me know if she'd found your friend the GhostFin, you can imagine what they both would have done."

"Oh, Buffer, you beautiful oaf," Piper had said affectionately. "Of course I realize that. SlugFlukes and LoFin told me all about it. And I'm very proud of you." She nuzzled him gently with her beak. "Why, if you'd not believed me in the first place, we'd all be dead now."

Piper thought back to those moments with Buffer. More and more she had come to admire him. He was the one member of the Pod she always looked forward to seeing now. He was so changed, so…grown. So poised. Buffer had never seemed poised before. Of course his swagger was still there, and he was as haughty as ever. Then again, it wouldn't be Buffer if he were any other way. Some things never change, she thought, and maybe that was just as well.

****

Buffer had come upon LoFin during one of his unauthorized excursions into the Open Sea. The gregarious porpoise band had at first been leery of the bristling young bull—until they realized he was a friend of the white female who had been banished. Buffer had conversed with the chatty LoFin longer than expected. He'd marveled at the Waif's ability to talk, and from her he learned of a great GhostFin slowly plodding its way across the Open Sea toward the Northeast Waters. And knowing also that he was likely in danger of having been followed by RamStrong's sentries, Buffer hurriedly told the astonished porpoises all that had happened at Kwi Coast since their hasty flight from there over five months earlier.

Buffer and LoFin had then agreed to remain in contact with one another, the Rovers promising they would seek out the GhostFin and tell him of Piper's safe return home—and of all that happened after it.

For over a week, Buffer had scouted the OutZones and the Open Sea as often as he'd dared. At times he'd had to ward off the advances of curious sharks that had attacked sporadically. And always he had waited to detect sonic messages from LoFin.

It was shortly after Buffer's covert excursions had been discovered by the Pod that LoFin began seeking him out. The porpoises had finally made contact with the GhostFin who was now sloughing his way steadily toward the gray whale southern breeding waters. And the porpoises bore tidings of a dark Floater bearing down on Kwi Coast, which SlugFlukes had recognized as soon as they'd described it. But Buffer, under the constant watch of Pod sentries, had not dared venture anywhere near the OutZones till the fervor over his lone skirmishes died down. And not hearing at all from Buffer, all that SlugFlukes and LoFin could hope for was that time would not run out on them.

Unfortunately, SlugFlukes was every bit as slow as his name indicated, and the small band of Rovers did not dare approach the hostile Whistler Clan on their own. So they hurried SlugFlukes along as fast as they could…but it was too late.

The unexpected school of mackerel, though, had been a stroke of fortune, even if it did give the Killer Imps a chance to bait their trap. For the scavenging sharks that had happened by and drawn an attack from the excitable Pod had given Buffer and his small band a chance to break away. His followers, of course, had had no idea of their leader's intent. As far as they knew, they were off to rout more of the Snag-Tooth. And though Buffer did not know exactly how he was going to explain to them that they were really enroute to rendezvous with a pack of Harbor Waifs, he never did have to explain it. What they saw after the Pod headed back to Kwi Coast had spared him the need for it.

A few sharks had lagged behind, and Buffer had commanded his group to scatter them off. It was the break he'd needed. He knew the three trained Fighters could handle the young Sanders easily enough, and it would also give him a chance to slip away and search for LoFin. Then he might return later and say he had merely been chasing a lone straggler. But just as he'd prepared to sneak away, Buffer noticed, as Piper had earlier, that the Humunz aboard the Floater had been watching carefully all that the Whistlers had been doing during their fight with the Snag-Tooth.

Buffer waited. There had been something bizarre—something of *menace*—about these Land Dwellers, and it had made him leery. He had hoped Piper might indeed have been overreacting, but now he was no longer sure. Meanwhile, LightFin, Squeaker, and LongFlukes easily drove off the struggling sand tigers and then rejoined their leader as he spied on the Floater.

What they saw next had sickened them.

A few more Snag-Tooth had strayed by the Floater, despite the presence of Buffer and his Fighters. And the poachers onboard were tossing out bloody chunks of flesh to the sharks. All four dolphins were aghast at what was being cast overboard: *severed strips of dead Whistlers*.

If there had ever been need of proof that the garbed figures aboard the Floater were indeed Evil Hunters who preyed on the WhistlingFin, Buffer and his band of followers had found it then and there. Worse, it seemed as if these sly Humunz had somehow also befriended the Snag-Tooth!

It wasn't until days after the Slaughter—after hearing Piper's full account of what had taken place—that Buffer concluded how the Killer Imps had cunningly tossed the torn Whistler carcasses into the sea…so the Snag-Tooth would gnaw at them and be blamed for what would appear to be "Fury killings."

Witnessing the dolphins' attack on the sharks had given the poachers the idea of luring the strange pod into a trap—using the recorded sounds of an approaching shark-frenzy as bait. And when Buffer and the other three had sped off in a frantic search for LoFin, they had never supposed the Pod would mistake the bloody Whistler carcasses for the four of them, else they might not have gone.

Still, Buffer knew that neither the Thane nor the Commodore would have believed him anyway. The only real proof had been in the hope that LoFin was nearby and had found the wise old GhostFin. That most surely would have eliminated all doubts.

The tiny group of dolphins had finally picked up the report of the porpoise pod—and the gruff cry of the old whale. The eerie sight of the gray giant had at first frightened Buffer and the other three. Seeing the GhostFin for the very first time, Buffer had been awestruck by its sheer size and had marveled once again at Piper's courage.

SlugFlukes, meanwhile, had worried himself fitfully. And after hearing about the Imps' Floater, he had scorned himself. "Ah, what a decrepit old fool am I! I should have known," he told LoFin sourly. "Let a billion toothy barnacles infest my skin if any harm comes to that gentle creature," he'd moaned.

It was as if a cold harpoon had struck him, for his worst fears had come to pass. SlugFlukes knew he would never forgive himself if Piper died because her Pod had refused to heed her tale. Here was this wonderful little SongFin who had saved him from being a feast for the HunterKin, and all he had done in return was frighten her with a grotesque display by the Killer Imps. He could have listened to her pleas to go back with her and help warn her beloved Pod of the danger that stalked them. He knew she was not the sort of creature to leave them all to such an ugly fate, in spite of what they had done to her. Yes, he had known this was the way of those who refused to listen to truths they did not want to believe.

But there was still time, he had thought, for here was the bold and brash Buffer she'd spoken of so fondly. SlugFlukes had seen right away what Piper liked about the young bull. His courage was very much like hers. And so the guilt-ridden old giant had hoped there was yet time enough to avert disaster.

It had been near dawn when they'd all finally met. The odd party of dolphins, porpoises, and gray whale had hurried as best they could—allowing for the GhostFin's plodding pace—and when finally they drew within range of Kwi Coast, the air and sea carried the sad cries of the stricken Pod members. They also heard the high-pitched yipping of the triumphant Killer Imps—and that had turned the approaching rescue party's horror to rage.

A plan had been laid out. SlugFlukes would unleash his might upon the Floater, while Buffer and LoFin commanded the rest in an elaborate rescue of the living Whistlers as they spilled over the sides of the sinking wreck. SlugFlukes had guaranteed the Floater would sink, and that once the Killer Imps on it tumbled overboard—with no other Floaters in sight—they would panic. And he emphasized the need for haste in the rescue, for he had also guaranteed the emergence of the Snag-Tooth, en masse.

The old whale, as usual, had been right.

****

Piper was relieved that SlugFlukes had remained at

Kwi Coast following the tragic events. Like Buffer, the gray elder had brought her moments of comfort, often scolding her whenever she tried pushing her injured limbs beyond their limits. And always she looked forward to chatting with LoFin, who, at times, managed to cheer the young Whistler with her usual Waif humor and wit, and her endless banter about anything and everything. What a dear friend the Pod had missed out on in LoFin…and in her fellow Rovers, thought Piper. So much they seemed like the WhistlingFin…

Most of the time, though, it was Buffer's company that Piper sought. The cocky young bull had grown in both size and stature, and she made no secret now of the strong attraction she felt for him. In time, he would reach the size of the late Thane. But that was not all. Piper had noticed a more *gentle* air about Buffer, a tenderness that had gone unnoticed before. She thought it made him more appealing.

What was left of the Pod, as well, had developed a new respect for Buffer. The wisdom he displayed in plotting their rescue had been the salvation of the Clan. Against everyone's doubts, Buffer was the only one who had never questioned Piper's sanity. He had indeed believed her from the start. Had he not, all that LoFin and SlugFlukes would have found would have been the remains of whatever the Snag-Tooth left, every bit as gruesome as SlugFlukes and Piper had both witnessed in that dark cove along the coast of Japan.

For now, though, Buffer cared only about being with Piper. He felt obligated to nurture her back to health, and to protect her. And unless she assured him that she was off to visit either SlugFlukes or LoFin, he stayed right by her side. It took a good deal to convince him that he could leave her alone during her early morning hunts, but with SlugFlukes' persuasion, Buffer was convinced of Piper's need for solitude, realizing finally it would be almost impossible for him to understand all that she had been through, or why there were times when she simply chose to avoid everyone else.

Despite the warm company of her friends, and the intimacies she shared with Buffer, Piper's life was a void at times. Too many memories haunted her. Not a single veteran of the old Clan had survived the Imp Massacre. The oldest member of the Pod now was twelve seasons of age. She wondered what that would bring, and often she beset SlugFlukes with questions about it, over and over.

"If I had explained it differently, could I have saved the whole Pod, SlugFlukes? Wouldn't my brother still be alive today?" Piper had asked so many times, but the old GhostFin remained ever patient.

Always, SlugFlukes would reply, as though having heard it for the first time, "Nothing would have changed their thinking, my little SongFin, as I've told you before. They were too set in their ways. Be thankful you saved as many as you did—and that you managed to convince at least your young friend Buffer. Things might have gone *much* worse if not for that." Those words from the wise old GhostFin always comforted Piper, until the next time—and then they would go through it all again.

****

It was a bright morning, and Piper was on her way to the OutZone to visit with SlugFlukes again. The Pod was still in slumber, but when she cruised out there, she found the great gray whale also dozing. So she journeyed off to the BreakWaters instead, passing through the region where she had first met LoFin. She thought how tragically things might have gone had she never met the merry wayfarer that day so long ago. As she streaked through the green sea and toward the BreakWaters, Piper was careful not to soar in too close to the foaming swirl. Her strength was not completely back to normal, and she was not anxious to test it against the powerful tug of the thunderous surf.

The choppy zone was more at ease this calm morning, and Piper was able to zip in a bit farther than she had expected. Ever since that first meeting with LoFin, Piper had felt mesmerized by the wild swells she enjoyed riding—in place of the ones caused by the Floaters—on days when it was not so treacherous. She was sorely tempted to do so now but thought better of it. She knew if she were unable to break away at the last instant, she could fall prey to its tremendous grip and wind up either dashed to death on the nearby rocks or stranded somewhere on the sandy beach. So Piper resisted the urge to romp. Instead, she scanned the region for the porpoise band. It seemed they had already wakened and gone off on the hunt, for there was no sign of the Rovers anywhere.

Suddenly Piper picked up on the faint tremors of an odd rhythm, different from the pattern of the white breakers. It was a sort of *flutter* coming from farther away, somewhere in the OutZone. The sound had been blanked out earlier by the heavy roll of the BreakWater swells, but as she drifted away it came on much stronger, arousing her curiosity. The two light streaks on her brow pulsed fiercely as she echoed for the source of the noise. She beat her light flukes swiftly, zooming through the pale green that turned gradually to a deeper shade of blue as she came out near the Caverns of the Slithering Ones.

Soon it came in clearer.

The tiny distance scanners in the melon of her forehead reported the erratic thrashings of some creature, larger than herself, making its way toward Kwi Coast. The sounds of the neighboring BreakWaters still interfered, though, and Piper had difficulty homing in for an accurate sonic picture. All she made out was a rough notion of its size and that it was having difficulty swimming.

Then another signal came to her, strong and clear. There was no mistaking this one. Piper increased her pace, speeding toward the Open Sea until she came to within a hundred feet of a jutting mass of mossy rock fairly smothered in kelp. Many ominous-looking holes peppered the sides of the huge cliff, where vicious predatory eels lurked, including the dangerous morays. Near it, Piper discerned the shadowy form of the wounded creature she had first detected. It struggled toward her in a crippled flight from another creature that was barely fifty feet away.

Piper did not have time to draw a precise image of the wounded animal, for she recognized now its pursuer—a husky young bull shark streaking silently through the icy blue. At first the shark was only curious of the wounded creature, merely circling the lame animal and probing through the fine electrical impulses that lay beneath its toothy hide. Then abruptly the Snag-Tooth shook all over, sending its intended prey into a futile panicky flight. The shark broke from its circling pattern and roared down upon its victim, grazing the stricken creature with "tasters" that would inform it if its prey was edible. A gash appeared on the wounded animal's soft hide—and the scent of blood, seeping into the burly shark's nostrils, drew it instantly into a frenzied state.

With a throaty rasp, the Snag-Tooth curled back its lower jaw and attacked!

All happened in the few seconds in which Piper first spotted the young bull shark. But she had not bothered scanning and identifying its helpless victim—*it was the Snag-Tooth she wanted.*

For here was the cause of her Pod's misery. Was it not the queer *madness* of these silent killers that had driven the Commodore so insane with hatred? Weren't they the reason Thane SilverFlukes and QuickFin and all the others were now dead? Did they have to kill everything they found in the sea?

Yes! she thought in all her rage. The Snag-Tooth were to blame for it all—they were Evil, like the Killer Imps! "Go for the gills!" They would not stop until every living being in the sea fell before their Furies. "Go for the gills!" She hated them. She always had, she could see that now. "Go for the gills!" she heard the old Commodore's voice commanding her—as though he had returned from the dead and now cried out for justice.

Piper heard a squeak of pain…and terror. It had come from the wounded creature. Now she knew this Snag-Tooth had to die. She attacked. And the Commodore's gruff commands bellowed and echoed through her head as she charged: "The gills…it cannot swim or breathe once you strike it there…it will drown!" Piper drove in like a six-foot-long torpedo, startling the snarling bull shark that was at least a foot longer than she was. She forgot about her own wounds, which were not completely healed. She forgot her fears. Piper bore down on the dark Snag-Tooth with a charge that would have made old RamStrong bellow with pride. It was as strong a gill-thrust as he could have asked.

Too late, the Snag-Tooth wheeled around to meet her attack. In its frenzied state, the shark had not noticed Piper lurking nearby. Now, instead of an easy kill, the young bull shark was confronted by the assault of a fierce, white-finned Whistler that had roared down upon it with the ferocity of one of the HunterKin! A violent wave of tremors shook the Snag-Tooth's body, as though it had been scooped up from the water in a net and rattled back and forth.

Piper felt the telling impact of her thrust. And for that split instant she reveled in the damage she knew she had wrought. She shrieked an eerie cry of triumph as she felt the Snag-Tooth's innards crumble under the force of her blow. It was the first time in her life she had ever driven her beak into another living being—and the destructive force of its impact caused her to shudder.

The cluster of tiny remora fish and pilot fish that accompanied the Snag-Tooth—feeding on the always-available parasites and scraps on its thick hide—scuttled away upon the impact, unaccustomed to their master's defeat. And the shark itself had had enough. It felt sick and now sought only to escape. Feebly it tried paddling away.

Meanwhile, the wounded animal Piper rescued had

managed to struggle its way to the surface. It was badly in need of air and, not sure of its rescuer, did not want to remain about if it was merely going to wind up as a morsel for some other predator.

Piper, however, took no notice of that. She was spinning around in a cloud of foam, readying herself for another charge. This one would finish off her enemy. Then she beheld the lame shark struggling to steal away in its crippled flight—broken of its Fury and stripped of its pride, a beaten warrior, deserted even by its own jackal-like worshippers, the pilots and the remoras. For some reason it reminded her of the broken husk of Commodore RamStrong, so demeaned on board the Floater.

Abruptly, the angry voice in her head softened.

Piper saw the Snag-Tooth, once again, as nothing more than mysterious creatures that simply had their own ways…like any other sea dwellers. She let the shark go.

A feeble whimper from above the waves reminded Piper of the Snag-Tooth's intended victim. She soared toward the surface to see what kind of creature she'd saved from death. And when she broke the waves, her heart nearly leaped out of her mouth with joy—and disbelief…

It was QuickFin.

Chapter Thirty
A Strange Ordeal

It was two weeks before QuickFin had healed enough from his wounds and could speak of his ordeal. His first recollection was that of nearly succumbing to the dry heat on the deck of the Floater. SlugFlukes' timely rescue had spared him that.

"When the Imps' Floater sank, I had no idea what was going on. All I knew was that I was grateful," QuickFin told his four companions. He gazed fondly at the massive form of SlugFlukes, who, along with Buffer, Piper, and LoFin, listened with intrigue and wonder. "A few more moments and I'm sure I would have boiled to death. That cool water drenching my poor burnt skin was a relief beyond what I can explain here."

"I think I understand," quipped Piper in dour memory of her own suffering on the Floater's deck. She and Buffer were guiding QuickFin around the OutZone, while SlugFlukes and LoFin swam behind them. QuickFin was telling his story in bursts and spurts, often tiring and needing to pause for breaths.

"I was cast very far from the Floater when it pitched over. In fact, I was flung high, right through the air, and when I splashed down into the water, I was far enough away to be free of that sucking force you told me about, Piper. And the sinking Floater made big waves that pushed me away from it. I was too weak to swim away—and I knew if those horrible Humunz hadn't made such a fuss when they fell in, too, I'd now be in the belly of some Snag-Tooth. I felt a lot of them sliding by me silently and going right over to the struggling Humunz. I was lucky, I know, but I still wish I'd been healthy enough to have at some of those Snag-Tooth myself."

"That's the Commodore in you speaking, my friend," said Buffer, wagging his beak. "The Snag-Tooth are a queer lot indeed, and I've had my fill of them too. But there's far more to them than we know. I think Piper can tell you the same."

Piper nodded in quiet agreement, still not believing what she had done only two weeks earlier.

"I suppose you're right, Buffer," said QuickFin, his now lean body shrugging softly. "I just like to believe the Commodore wasn't all wrong."

"He wasn't," said Buffer. "And more on that I'll explain later." He and Piper exchanged knowing looks. Both knew what old RamStrong had meant to QuickFin, regardless of what the Commodore had become near the end. The death of the old Whistler, Thane SilverFlukes, and the three Elders had shaken QuickFin badly when he had first been told. But the heroics of his sister, and the truth about Buffer—and how he had helped rescue the Pod—had warmed the proud youngster. He had grown closer to Buffer during his healing period, and a mutual respect had evolved between the two…to Piper's delight.

"But go on, QuickFin," urged SlugFlukes. Both he and LoFin, who had remained unusually silent during the tale, were intrigued by the young Whistler's odyssey.

"Well, I was soon carried so far from that dreadful place in the OutZone that I took a chance and tried quietly monitoring my movements. I recalled what Piper had said about seeing the Snag-Tooth Madness, and from what I'd seen for myself, I didn't want to go squirming about too much. Often I drifted with the tides, and most of the time it was toward the land mass. I tried avoiding it as much as I could, but my bones felt like they were crushed. I couldn't muster enough strength to resist the fierce currents unless I really wanted to strain…and that would have meant thrashing hard and the risk of drawing the attention of stray Snag-Tooth."

"But how were you able to stay alive for so long?" asked Buffer curiously. "You've said nothing of food."

"I…" QuickFin glanced sheepishly at LoFin. "I…fed off scraps the Land Dwellers in passing Floaters were throwing out into the water."

"Ahhh," the porpoise said sweetly.

All three dolphins looked embarrassed, and SlugFlukes withheld a quiet chortle.

"It…it was the only way," said QuickFin, ruffling his battered fins.

"I suppose it's what any of us would have done," said Piper, glancing over at LoFin, who cocked her stubby head smugly.

"It seems the Humunz catch many more GillFin than they can eat themselves, and so they throw the small ones back, even though most of them are dead by then," QuickFin mused, somewhat perplexed.

"And it seems they also make sure there are fewer WhistlingFin, Rovers, and BigFin in the sea to eat the

GillFins they want all for themselves," SlugFlukes grumbled cryptically.

The others regarded him curiously, but the whale said nothing more on the matter, though LoFin nodded subtly to herself, catching a knowing look from one of the GhostFin's baleful eyes.

"Do go on with your tale, good QuickFin," SlugFlukes urged softly.

"I tried to paddle my way back to Kwi Coast, but it was hopeless. Then one day, I got caught in the current and drifted so close to the BreakWaters that the powerful white waves picked me up and carried me all the way in to the sandy shore. I was stranded there. I couldn't move. Fortunately, though, it was early, and the heat wasn't so bad there. I tried flopping back to the water, but it seemed to move farther away with each new wave. So I lay there like that—in terrible pain from trying to roll back to the sea—for a long time. Then the strangest thing of all happened.

"A group of young Humunz came down onto the beach. But I was barely aware of them because it had become almost impossible for me to move or even breathe. The Orange Glow in the sky had grown much larger during the time I'd been lying in the sand; it cracked my skin, like when I was on the Floater. I was so scared those little Land Dwellers were going to beat me. These Humunz…there's so many of them, and they're everywhere, it seems…and I'd learned how cruel they could be."

"Yes, indeed," the old GhostFin muttered to himself, but loud enough to be heard.

"But these young ones didn't try to harm me. Instead, they all gathered around me and started talking very fast to each other in their high voices. They sounded almost like Whistlers—they were so excited. Then, the next thing I knew, they were pouring and splashing water all over me. At first, I couldn't see how they were doing it, but when I was refreshed enough, I saw they were scurrying down to the waves with little round things they were carrying, which they used for scooping up the water. I was still miserable and in a lot of pain, but I felt good knowing that these little Humunz were trying to help me. I…I'm confused by it, though."

"I've known of such things happening, rare as it's been," said SlugFlukes, as though struggling with the admission. "Not all Land Dwellers are bad. It's just hard to find the good ones."

"Those were their younglings, who probably had not yet learned the crueler ways of their elders," LoFin added cynically. SlugFlukes gave a whale's frown and seemed about to reply, but QuickFin had resumed his tale again.

"Oh, yes, that brings me to the next part…when the bigger, older ones came down there," he began. "The sea had risen back onto the beach, much closer to me now, and when I saw all those older Humunz coming— and speaking in their much deeper voices—I grew frightened and began thrashing and flopping back toward the water. The waves came close enough again so I could reach it, and they were strong enough to tug me out to where I could swim a little. I was afraid those bigger Humunz would try to come after me, but instead, they stayed by the edge of the sea, calling softly to me. It was very…soothing."

SlugFlukes shot LoFin a smug glance through one

eye, and the chubby porpoise cocked her head obstinately in response.

"I knew I couldn't stay there, though, because I still wasn't strong enough to keep from being thrown back up onto the sand again. So I started to swim along the shoreline, away from the rocky region on the other side, until finally I got to where the surf wasn't as strong. If the Humunz came after me there, I would at least have been able to swim away because the current didn't pull so hard. But I was curious now. The young Humunz and the bigger ones kept following me and always calling softly. At any time they could have jumped into the water and tried to come after me, but they didn't.

"After a while, some of them left. When they returned, they had dead GillFins with them and threw some of them out to me. I was starving, so I ate it—they tasted horrible. Then I stayed there, swimming around just enough to keep from being pulled back in to shore. I didn't want to go back out to sea just yet, because I wasn't sure if I could make it through the roll of the heavier waves…and there was still the danger of roving Snag-Tooth."

QuickFin paused a moment, tiring from not only the telling of his ordeal, but the reliving of it, too.

"The next day, more Land Dwellers arrived with more food. They didn't do much more than toss more dead GillFins out to me and call out funny things that sounded strangely friendly. Then later in the day, a large pack of them appeared all over the sand, just like the Snag-Tooth did when the Floater sank. They were everywhere! It seemed they had all suddenly begun to quarrel, and then some of them started to come into the water. I became frightened again. I didn't know what they wanted, and after the Killer Imps, I didn't want to find out—so I fled! It hurt everything inside me to force my way through the BreakWaters...but I was far enough away from the main roll of waves to make it. I was exhausted and bruised from fighting the current, and when I finally made it to the OutZone, I rested, hoping to regain my strength. The next morning I felt a little better, but I was very weak from lack of food. I hadn't been able to hunt at all because I was so tired from my flight through the BreakWaters. No Floaters went by, so there weren't any scraps to pounce on. And when I finally did try to catch a small black GillFin, I failed. But I made such a racket chasing it that I drew the attention of that Snag-Tooth. That's when I tried to paddle toward home, hoping someone would hear me. Fortunately, you were close by, Piper."

All four cetaceans stared at QuickFin in wonder. The sleepy roll of muscle he had once flaunted was gone, and much time would pass before he looked that way again. But a new strength had taken hold—inside him—one that made the others marvel as they all swam quietly and slowly back to Kwi Coast.

Chapter Thirty-One
Aftermath

A day came when Buffer called the entire surviving Clan to a Gathering at the Council Cliff. It was seven weeks after the Killer Imp Massacre. Nine months earlier, in the shadow of that very Cliff, Piper had been deemed a traitor and banished from the Clan that would one day proclaim her its savior.

Buffer and QuickFin—also heralded now as Heroes of the Pod—were settled back on their flukes. Buffer was in Thane SilverFlukes' former groove; QuickFin, recently chosen by Buffer to be the new Commodore, was settled beside him.

It had come as a surprise to QuickFin that the role of Commodore was even to be continued, and that the honor had been bestowed upon him. No one disputed that the desire to survive had been instilled in them all by old RamStrong. Buffer felt it fitting that QuickFin be the one who continued in that service.

A form of the Fury Squad was also to be continued, though differently than in the past. Buffer had reaffirmed that the Commodore had not been entirely wrong about the need for a Pod's defense. And it was up to QuickFin, and those who served on the Fury Squad, to see that defensive measures were not carried too far.

Though the Elders had all perished in the Imp

Massacre, it was still felt there was a need to maintain a full High Clan—where no single Whistler could dominate. LightFin, SlickFin and Piper were therefore appointed as the High Council. Two of them were now seated on the lip of the Cliff.

Piper had not yet arrived.

Nearby, on the outskirts of the kelp forest that surrounded the cluster of young Whistlers, was the Kin Clan—the local Rovers. Piper was with them.

"They may not be ready for this yet, Piper," said LoFin with a wag of her head.

"I know that, but we really cannot wait. The longer we put this off, the less chance there is they'll feel right about it," said Piper.

"Change is not easily accepted here," answered LoFin acutely.

"Who knows that better than I?" said Piper.

"All right," said LoFin with a wave of her blunt snout. "I just hope you know what you're doing. I would wait. But then we Waifs have never been as earnest as you, my sweet friend."

Piper eyed her.

"I wish you success, all the same. We'll try to help," said LoFin resolutely.

"Thank you, my merry scrap-eater," teased Piper. Then in all seriousness she added, "I owe much to you."

"Of course you do," quipped LoFin. "Now be off about your business!"

Piper turned and scooted off to the Cliff. It was strange to see Buffer and QuickFin in place of Thane SilverFlukes and Commodore RamStrong. Would she ever get used to it? And would the Pod?

Both large males glowed regally in the morning

gleam. QuickFin was showing early signs of his old physique, and Buffer carried himself so differently now. Piper was proud of them both. She felt good when she coasted up onto the lip of the Council Cliff and settled herself between LightFin and SlickFin.

Then Buffer called the Gathering to order—all that was left of the Kwi Coast Clan: seven males, five females, two younglings, and the new High Clan. Once they had numbered over seventy. Now there were only nineteen.

"We're going to help you as best we can," Buffer said to Piper. "But we must let them decide for themselves, you understand."

"I understand," said Piper with a nod of her beak.

"I wish you well," LightFin said softly. The company of another female in the High Clan gave Piper added comfort.

"Thank you, LightFin," said Piper. "I'll show you some fine hunting when this is over."

"Fellow Clan members…" Buffer bellowed grandly, "and you of the Kin Clan!" He nodded toward the porpoises. A chorus of merry whistles came down from the surface, where LoFin and her band hovered, breaking through the waves at frequent intervals for breaths of air. Someday, thought Piper, she would show them all what SlugFlukes had taught her about staying under longer.

A loud crunching and crackling of kelp stalks, followed by a snort and a raspy bellow, informed the Pod that SlugFlukes was in hearing range, having imbedded himself somewhere nearby. He did not dare come too close for fear of splattering the entire Council Zone into splinters with his cumbersome bulk.

"Today," said Buffer from his perch, "we have gathered to make a difficult decision." There was a row of chatter through the small group. Buffer hefted himself above the cliff's lip, puffing out the gray-white of his burly chest. "We have known grim times of late. And were it not for the one this Clan once called a traitor and a fool—those times would have been far worse. *We would all be dead!*"

The Clan fell silent. Piper fluttered her flukes awkwardly.

"It is Piper, then, who will offer her wisdom this day," added Buffer. "We of the New High Clan have met already on what she has to say...and we agree with her. But the final decision will rest with the entire Pod. So when we return from the break, you will all hear her out and then decide."

With an upward swing of his beak, Buffer signaled the break. The Clan clicked obediently, excitedly, wondering what this great choice was that had to be made, and they were amazed the final decision was, in fact, *theirs*.

The break was quick, a score of vaporous clouds spewing high from every blowhole. Then they plunged back into Council order, and Piper gathered herself before them amidst a chorus of whistles and squeaks. The fair-skinned female looked sleek and prominent before the Clan, no longer the snippy rebel they had all once known. Now she was the very image of cetacean grace.

"Brothers and Sisters of Kwi Coast—when you hear what I have to say, you might not cheer so heartily. But please hear me before you judge."

A hush fell over the Clan.

"For as long as any of us can remember, we have dwelled in these coastal waters—in a Cove—hiding, plotting, waiting...waiting for an enemy we never had to truly fear. And it cost us the death of nearly all our Clan. But we feared the Snag-Tooth, just as we feared the Open Sea...and the HunterKin...and the Cold Lord. We hid from them all. And because we did, we also hid from the truth."

A murmur swept the Clan. Piper followed up quickly. "We massed for the Snag-Tooth. We thought only of how to protect ourselves from them. And we were very nearly destroyed by the Killer Imps...those we knew nothing about."

"Are you saying, Piper, that we should desert our home?" exclaimed one of the Clanists suddenly.

"Not desert," she answered softly, her black eyes fluttering as she answered the interruption. "We can always return whenever we want to. But we need to *explore*—to discover what else there is in the sea. Our Kin Clan has done that, and they are still alive and content," added Piper, waving toward the porpoises with her beak.

LoFin nodded approvingly. Piper was doing well for herself.

"But to stay here forever, friends, is to stay ignorant of what lies out there. And it is a wondrous world which I myself have learned so much about."

Piper paused a moment.

Then Snapper, a former battler of the Fury Squad, and one of the oldest to survive, spoke up. "Yes, the wondrous world that also nearly killed you, Piper!" he said, sounding just like old RamStrong.

"Why, we will be cast upon the Open Sea—

alone—and without friends!" cried another fearfully.

"Not quite alone," rumbled a husky voice. For the first time during the Gathering, SlugFlukes had spoken. "Hmph! You could do worse than win the friendship of my likes." By now he had rambled through the outskirts of the kelp jungle, crunching and parting the giant kelp strands like so many twigs before his gargantuan frame. "Do not be rash in your judgment of the Open Sea. It is not as perilous as waiting for Hunter-Humunz to come by and slaughter you! Suppose little Piper here had never returned with the tidings you all scoffed at? Where would you all be then, eh, my fine SongFins?" grumbled SlugFlukes, lifting his motley head as he spoke.

Piper hoped his cantankerous manner had not frightened them. She didn't want the Clan to be intimidated into the decision. Commodore RamStrong and the Elders had done that often enough.

"You'd all be chopped into tiny bits on that foul Floater if she hadn't come back, sweet Whistlers!" snipped LoFin.

"Not everyone scoffed," grumbled Buffer. "But the Rover is right. This Pod would have been destroyed, make no mistake about that!"

"There is also the Great Lord of the Sea," reminded Piper. "Does anyone doubt me now about the magnificent Lord who saved me from Arkitu?"

The Pod agreed quietly. No one doubted any of Piper's tales of the Deep anymore. But SlugFlukes winced at her mention of the mighty sea lord. He knew of the toothed BigFins—the Odons—and he knew also of the perpetual battles between sperm whales and giant squids that would go on till the end of time. Piper's

"Arkitu" was nothing more than one of the deadly Many-Arms. SlugFlukes knew them well, and he knew how dangerous they were. She had been fortunate that the Odon happened to be on the hunt and nearby at the time. He knew, too, that to convince any of this Pod, even Piper herself, that neither the Odon nor the Many-Arms were unworldly Lords of the Sea would be an impossible task. At least for now it would be. Perhaps some things were best left be...for a while, thought SlugFlukes.

The Clan had quieted gradually. Then QuickFin spoke. "This coast is all we have known...all *I* have known. And it's been a good home," he said softly. "And I, too, am scared of what might lie out there waiting for us. But who is to say now that more Hunter-Humunz will not come here? For all we know, those who attacked us might even live on these land masses nearby."

"That is so true!" chimed in LoFin, soaring down in front of the Clan. "Do you think those Imps of the West the GhostFin showed Piper are the only ones who prowl the sea on such ugly hunts? They are a cunning, treacherous lot—all of them!" she cried out in a rare burst of excitement.

Not all of them, thought SlugFlukes, but he would take that up with LoFin later.

It was time for another air break. Buffer and the rest of the new High Clan agreed that the Pod should now gather amongst themselves and decide. All that needed to be said had been spoken.

It was time.

The main body of the Pod went off on their own, while the New High Clan, SlugFlukes, and the Rovers returned to the Council Zone. LoFin and SlugFlukes entertained them with a spirited exchange on the nature of Land Dwellers. Piper could see they were all in for even more spirited times whenever the two of them were together.

Finally the Pod returned. It was the burly Fury Fighter, Snapper, who spoke for them.

"Our world here has been destroyed," he began, "and it may never be as it was before. Perhaps, if we had listened, things might have been different. But maybe it was meant to be this way." Snapper's voice broke a little. "Who knows? No one can say for sure. Can we find joy and comfort in the Open Sea—as our KinClan has done? Can we find peace there? No one has the answer, do they?" Snapper paused before adding, "We are ready to try, though. We will follow you there!"

Piper nodded quietly to Snapper. She felt very warm inside.

"You are the WhistlingFin—and SongFins are loved by many in the sea, for you are not a cruel or greedy lot," SlugFlukes rumbled with affection. "But know your enemies and learn to avoid them when you can. And do help your own Kindred when you see them in need. Warn as many as you can, and carefully, of those monstrous Imps who bring disgrace to decent Land Dwellers—and to the sea itself. *For it is a good sea.*"

The Pod clicked respectfully...and the small band of porpoises echoed their sentiments.

"And now, friend SlugFlukes?" asked Piper brightly.

"The sea is there for all of you, my little SongFin,"

he added softly. "Take heart," he added. "Sometimes the Sea's Strong Justice serves us as well as it teaches us."

A word from the author...

I am a previously published author with The Wild Rose Press—the first book being my historical fable, *The Saga of Marathon*, about the young Greek foot-courier who ran on a mission to save the future of the world's first democracy.

I also have two other novels, *Scratch* and *Druids*, published by Oak Tree Press, and have written many short stories that have appeared in the literary market.

I have written and directed a number of independent short films that have been featured in cinemas and film festivals across the country, and have written stage plays that were produced, including at the prestigious Eugene O'Neill Theater Center in Waterford, CT.

I also write freelance news features and teach creative writing to students, many of whom have gone on to attain publication.

Thank you for purchasing
this publication of The Wild Rose Press, Inc.

For questions or more information
contact us at
info@thewildrosepress.com.

The Wild Rose Press, Inc.

www.ingramcontent.com/pod-product-compliance
Lightning Source LLC
Chambersburg PA
CBHW051537260626
47170CB00003B/975